ISOBEL BRITE

Rosamunde Bott

Cover image:

Detail from *Girl with a Basket of Fruit* by Frederick Leighton

Detail from *Drury Lane Theatre* by Richard Phillips c.1804

Cover Design by Eliza Bott

PART I

1838-1840

.

Come give us a taste of your quality, come, a passionate speech

William Shakespeare, *Hamlet,* Act 2, Scene 2

1

CHAPTER ONE

Isobel held her breath.

An actor, dressed all in black, stood alone on the stage in shimmering gaslight. The restless, noisy audience grew hushed in the charisma of his presence, and the actor spoke.

'O that this too too sullied flesh would melt,
Thaw, and resolve itself into a dew;'

He continued, building up Hamlet's passionate conflict and holding the audience in wide-eyed awe.

Isobel, oblivious to the stench of rotten fruit, lamp oil and orange peel that had at first offended her nose when she came in to the little barn-like theatre on her uncle's arm, leaned forward on the wooden bench. Her eyes shone, and her hand gripped the handle of her fan, now still, despite the muggy heat of the August night. Her shawl slipped from her shoulders without her noticing. Never had she seen or heard anything that touched her so deeply in her very soul, not even the Sunday preacher whose dramatic proclamations and gestures seemed false, cold and hollow in comparison.

'Fie on't, ah, fie, 'tis an unweeded garden
That grows to seed...'

Here was a man who spoke of real emotion, real feeling. *Surely*, she thought, *this player knows real anguish, to be able to interpret those words with such power and meaning?* Her heart went out to him.

'Frailty, thy name is woman.'

Tears filled Isobel's eyes as Hamlet spoke of his mother's betrayal of his dead father and his own wounded feelings.

'It is not, nor it cannot come to good.
But break, my heart, for I must hold my tongue.'

The soliloquy ended, the other actors entered the stage, and Isobel sat back on the bench, slowly pulling her shawl around her shoulders once more, and cooling her flushed faced with her fan.

Henry Hartley, unbuttoning his Horatio costume as he came off the stage after the curtain call, eyed Frank Douglas, the company's new young leading actor, and thoughtfully nodded his head.

He's good, he thought, *very good. A good actor, and a very good voice too. But his character off the stage is a little wanting in modesty for my liking. There is nothing that spoils an actor so much as conceit in his own abilities. Yet, damn the boy, he has that arrogant, boyish charm that one cannot help liking, and sets women constantly at his feet. Now, look, there, indeed is my own wife singing his praises and I had better go and rescue her at once.*

'My dear Mrs Hartley,' Frank was saying as Henry came within earshot, 'your delightful praise would not be quite so appropriate were it not for the fact that one has such excellent fellow players such as your good self. Why, Hartley, my good fellow, I was just saying to your charming wife here how her portrayal of Gertrude is such strong support to a green actor such as myself. Do you not think so, my friend?'

'Indeed, Sir, though it would be pertinent to add that the part of Ophelia would be more suited to her years,' replied Henry, with a wink at his wife, 'it takes great acting ability to play the mother to someone of your, er, maturity.'

Caroline laughed in her good-natured way.

'Oh, Henry,' she said, taking his arm and patting his hand, 'Come now! Mr Douglas was being quite delightful and sweet, and I am sure I hardly deserve it. Eliza is far more suited to Ophelia. And anyway, the play belongs to him, after all; and you know that his Hamlet was compared to the great Kemble himself in the recent reviews.'

Frank gave a little mock-humble bow, and Henry raised

one eyebrow.

'Compared? Yes, indeed, that may be so, my love. But, you know, there are good comparisons, and then there are the other kind.' This was said with a grin and a twinkle in his eye.

'Oh, now, don't listen to him, Mr Douglas. I know full well that he admires your work just as much as I do. Why, only the other day I looked over his shoulder when he was writing to his brother and read his description of our new "quite brilliant" leading player, and that he felt no doubt that he would become one of the leading stars of London sooner or later. Is that not so Henry? Go on, you have to admit it!'

'Of course, my dear, there is absolutely nothing in that letter that I would wish to withdraw,' replied Henry, thinking of some other remarks about Frank in the same letter, such as 'conceited' and 'arrogant' that Caroline had tactfully left out, 'quite so. Now, Thomas has sent a note asking us to dine with him with George and Frances after the show, so hurry and get changed.'

Caroline playfully poked him in the stomach and ran off towards the cramped changing rooms behind the stage. She looked forward to dining with Thomas Gery, who was the theatre company's solicitor, and had become a close friend of her husband's.

Henry fondly watched her go and made towards his own dressing area. A strong arm across his shoulders waylaid him.

'I say, Hartley, a jolly good move of yours, marrying the manager's daughter, and a very fine woman too, if I may say so.'

Henry stiffened, irritated by the man's insulting implications.

'A love-match, I assure you, sir. Now, if you will excuse me, I have an appointment…'

'Just one moment, my friend. I wanted to ask you

something, as a man of the world.'

Henry's left eyebrow lifted for a moment and he turned, questioningly, to his colleague, forcing the other to take his arm away from his shoulders. Frank Douglas lowered his voice.

'This town of Daventry; you are obviously well in with the company solicitor, Thomas Gery? You must know something of the town. I wondered, being myself a stranger here, and you know how difficult it is to meet the right people in our line of business, whether you might know of some young… people, you could introduce me to? Particularly those of the feminine persuasion, if you understand me. A discreet arrangement, of course…'

'Mr Douglas,' Henry interrupted in a harsh whisper, 'Am I to take it that you are asking me to procure meetings with *women*?'

Frank chuckled a little.

'Oh, come now, Hartley; as your wife so sweetly said, "Don't be so stuffy". After all, our profession is not a naïve one; "rogues and vagabonds" don't they call us? Are we not all tarred by the same brush? Surely you must know of some suitable young ladies within the town?'

'Young ladies, yes, I know a few,' said Henry, staring him candidly in the eye, 'but "suitable" for your… requirements, I do not think so.'

With that he turned and stiffly walked on his way, through the creaking doors at the side of the stage to the little back room where he found George Partleton brushing off his hat. The rest of the cast had already gone.

'A good house tonight, Hartley,' said George, a younger actor who was married to another of Jackman's daughters, Frances, 'let's hope the weather holds for the rest of the week.'

Henry sat down and started to unlace his boots. He was still bristling from his conversation with Douglas, and muttered, 'yes, let us hope so.'

5

'Well, I will see you at Gery's, then,' said George and left Henry on his own.

What an impudent young man that Douglas was! Yet, as he pulled off the cramping stage boots and stretched his stockinged feet, curling his toes with relief, he could not help remembering that only a few years ago he himself was not dissimilar: a young actor, full of arrogance and self-importance, revelling in his own ability to impress and influence young women, purely because of the attractive 'glamour' and disreputable nature of his profession.

A 'rogue' and 'vagabond'? Well, it was still possible for actors to be flung into gaol on such a charge for playing without a licence. Henry frowned and sucked his teeth. In the eyes of some he was no more than a strolling player, a vagrant, of no fixed abode. That had not mattered to him when he was a young man of 20. In fact, he had rather enjoyed the feeling of rebellion; the sense of being different to the people he had grown up with, and the freedom it gave him from the rather restricted life he had previously led as the son of a respectable schoolmaster in Oxfordshire.

He still enjoyed the life. It was exciting and gave variety to one's day-to-day existence. But to a man approaching 30, playing the supporting role, or the clown, or singing a comic song, in what was usually no more than a fitted-up barn, many of them cold and draughty, walking miles from one theatre to another from week to week; playing to pits full of noisy and often not-too-fresh agricultural labourers; well, it was becoming a little tedious.

Oh, to find a place in a London theatre! So many times now had he thought of it. Proper, purpose-built theatres; warm because of their terraced positioning with other buildings; no need to travel cross-country; and a far, far better quality of audience, and real, brilliant actors to work with. He had tried so long now to find a manager to take him on, but there was always some excuse: they were taking on no new players; they had no funds; no need for a comic actor. *One day*, he thought, *one day… I must break in to London. That's the place to be, or else, or else…* Well, there would be no other alternative, for he knew he could not play the circuits for very much longer, and sooner or later he would have to make a decision.

As his wife came to meet him he had one other thought. If Frank was going to find a young lady to amuse himself with, at least it would divert his attentions away from Caroline's younger sister, Sophia, who, Henry was sure, had become rather infatuated with the new star actor.

Isobel stood in front of her mirror, holding the candle next to her face and watching how her eyes sparkled in the reflection. Slowly, noting every movement on her face, she widened her eyes, her lips parting, and her eyebrows lifting in an expression of fear and horror. She spoke in a whisper.

'*O! What a noble mind is here o'erthrown.*'

She clasped her throat.

'*O! Woe is me, to have seen what I have seen…*'

The door opened, and her sister, Cassandra, came in, dressed in her nightgown and also holding a candle.

'Izzie? Not undressed yet? Mama will…'

'Oh, Cassie, Cassie!' interrupted Isobel, grasping her younger sister by the arm and pulling her to sit next to her on the bed, 'I have had *such* an evening! How I wish you'd come! I've been *dying* to tell you! The theatre is wonderful, you can't imagine! There are lights, and moving boards that change the scene, so one minute you're in a royal palace, and the next minute outside, in a graveyard; and there was a ghost who came up through a hole in the stage, and a duel at the end, and, oh, Cassie, Hamlet himself, all in black, and such passion!'

'Izzie! You mustn't let Mama hear you talk like that!

You know she didn't want Uncle George to take you at all. If she hears you say such things, why, she'll think you've gone quite mad!'

'Oh yes!' sighed Isobel, lying back on the bed with the candle-holder perched on her stomach, 'perhaps I am mad, just like poor Ophelia!'

'You mustn't say such things!' whispered Cassandra, who had a horror of lunatic asylums ever since she had been taken to visit one as a special treat by another uncle.

'Oh, Cass. I can't bear it. Tomorrow will continue just as normal and go on for ever and ever; dull and boring, with nothing to do but help father make shoes, and even after marriage it would be just the same, except with the extra drudgery of raising a family and endless penny-pinching, and sewing and sewing and sewing...'

'Oh, Isobel, I wish you wouldn't talk like this. Why, anyone would think that you didn't want a husband and family!'

Isobel did not answer, but shut her eyes, thinking once more of the athletic young man in black, and the way he fought in the duel scene at the end; his untimely death... *Farewell, Sweet Prince...*

The door banged open and Isobel jumped; Cassie gave a little scream as the candle was nearly upset onto the bedclothes, but just managed to catch it in time, though tallow dripped onto the embroidered spread.

'Isobel Brite!' said her step-mother, standing framed in the doorway, her face illuminated from below by yellow, flickering flame, 'What do you think you are doing with that candle! You would have us all burnt to the ground one day, I am sure of it! There's the very devil in you, girl. No doubt about it. You'll end up in the workhouse and that's a fact. They must have known Isobel Brite lived here when they built that one on the London Road. It's there waiting for you. Just look at that bedspread! And you still in your best gown! Cassie, go down into the shop and see if you can find some turpentine.'

'Yes Mama,' said Cassie, scuttling away.

'Just what are you thinking of, not in bed yet, and playing with candles?'

'Mama, I wasn't…'

'Nineteen years old last month and still behaving like an infant. This is what comes of letting your father's brother take you to that dreadful place. Theatre indeed! I know I should never have allowed it. Oh, you'll be the death of me, and no mistake. Nothing but a den of sin and corruption. If Mrs Chapman knew I had allowed you inside that building with all those vagabonds…'

'But, Mama…'

'…it makes my heart sick to think how she would look down her nose at me. Well, never again, that's for sure. Your father persuaded me once; he's soft on you, and I'm softer still for listening to him. All that nonsense about education for girls. It won't happen again, you can be sure of that. Do you hear me, Isobel?'

Isobel's cheeks were burning red.

'Yes, Mama.'

'And take off that dress before you spoil it, and when you've cleaned the spread you'll have to hang it up by the window to dry.'

'Yes, Mama.'

Mrs Brite turned at the door, pausing before she left.

'No doubt you can't help the way you are. I suppose you get your character from your mother. Thank God she died before she could have such an influence on Cassandra. I pray for you every night, but it may do no good. I've done my best, and that's a fact, but the sooner someone takes you off my hands, the better, though I seriously doubt whether any decent young man would take you. If you don't pull yourself together, you'll end up in the workhouse, and that's the truth. The workhouse, Isobel.'

Shaking her head, she left the room.

Isobel stood for a while, digging her nails into the palms of her hand. She did not care what her step-mother said about her, but when she insulted her own dear, beautiful, red-haired mother she found it almost too much to bear. She thought now of her mother's soft voice, its lilting Irish accent and the way she used to sing her to sleep when she was a child. She could still remember the haunting melody of that old Irish lullaby, and she sometimes hummed it to herself when she couldn't sleep. Her mother had died of consumption when Isobel was six, and Cassandra but four years old, and her father had very quickly found another wife to take care of his two children.

Isobel held back hot tears and when Cassie returned with the turpentine and cloth, she had begun to undress, slowly unlacing the front of her bodice.

'What did Mama say?' asked Cassie, her eyes wide, as she scrubbed at the bedspread. Isobel wrinkled her nose at the pungent smell of turpentine.

'Oh, the usual sort of thing,' she said, nonchalantly, 'threatened me with the workhouse, as she has done since it was built last year.'

Cassie shuddered, 'Oh Izzie!'

Isobel's dress fell to the floor and she stepped out of it, then leaned on the bed pillar while Cassie unlaced her corset.

'Cassie,' she said, her head against the plain wood, 'Do you think I'm pretty?'

'Oh, Izzie, how can you ask such a thing? Of course, you are! Why, haven't I always envied you your green eyes and white skin and fine cheek-bones? And your hair is so thick! I've never been able to keep my hair in ringlets for more than two hours before they drop out; but look, yours are just as curled and bouncing as when they came out of the rags. And the colour! You have that beautiful auburn colour that lights up in the sun. Why, mine is just *brown*! Would you like me to brush it for you, Izzie?'

Isobel smiled, and watched in the mirror as Cassie brushed out her hair. What a shame it was to have her lovely thick hair that 'lights up in the sun', as Cassie had said, permanently tied up and hidden from view underneath a poke bonnet! Her eyes and hair were certainly her best features, and she knew she had a sweet smile. She must be a constant reminder to the second Mrs Brite of her beautiful predecessor; no wonder she was so jealous. Isobel smiled. A pity, though, that her father, so devastated at his wife's untimely death, had been so in need of a wife, and had married a young woman from a strict Methodist family, producing four more children.

Isobel stared at herself, fascinated. Her step-mother was wrong. She would have no difficulty finding a man, and the sooner the better. If she *had* to lead a life of drudgery, then better one where she would be mistress in her own home, rather than one where she was constantly treated like a naughty child.

I'll show them all, she thought, as she snuffed out the candle after she and Cassie were both in bed. *Then I can go to the theatre whenever I want, and I don't care how shocked they are. I'll do as I please, when I'm married...*

She slept, and dreamed that Hamlet was escorting her to a ball, speaking to her in beautiful sounding language that she could not quite understand, and when he offered her a glass of rum punch, it smelt distinctly of turpentine.

CHAPTER 2

Isobel yawned loudly as she made another stitch in the thick leather uppers. After the excitement of the previous evening her head felt dull and heavy, and although she had lived all her life with the stifling smell of leather and tanning, today it combined with the closeness of the humid August day to make her feel as though she could not breathe. The constant rumble of carriages, the clatter of horses' hooves and the occasional coaching horn as the regular Daventry traffic made its way up and down Sheaf Street seemed louder than ever, and there was always the bustle of travellers who stopped at Daventry for refreshments on their way to and from Liverpool and Ireland, London, Shrewsbury, Manchester, Birmingham, Oxford and Coventry. Her head had begun to ache. She yawned again.

Her father, laying out a skin on his large worktable, ready for the intricate process of cutting to a pattern, looked up over his small round spectacles and surveyed his eldest daughter. He had suffered a rather heated discussion with his wife the night before about the propriety of letting her out amongst the disreputable company of common theatregoers. Although he had argued that the young queen Victoria herself was an avid theatregoer, he had had to admit that perhaps, on hindsight, it was a foolish idea. The Daventry barn theatre, full of agricultural labourers and cowmen, was hardly to be compared with the West End, after all. But Izzie was so enthusiastic in her desires, and he had always felt a sharp fondness for her high spiritedness, even though this was the very element of her character that Mrs Brite saw as her weakest. He knew that Isobel had inherited these parts of her character from his first wife, whereas Cassie tended to take more after him. This was why he was more tempted to indulge Isobel. She reminded him of his beautiful, wild Kathleen with whom he had fallen passionately and foolishly in love. She it was who had chosen the names for her two girls, loving the romantic sound of Isobel and Cassandra. He sighed, remembering that heady time, twenty years ago, when he had somehow managed to win the heart of the most beautiful girl in the town.

His brother George (never a favourite of the second Mrs Brite) had convinced him that the outing to the theatre would be good for Isobel, working on the idea that to see a bit of the world would satisfy her cravings and inevitably calm her down. He watched her now, sullen looking, her eyelids drooping over her work, whilst her foot showed every sign of impatience in its continual tapping of the floor. Was this a calm Izzie? Or merely bored? Had he been right to teach his eldest daughter to read and write, or had this just led to her restlessness?

'Ow!' she suddenly squealed, wringing her hand and sucking a finger in turns, 'Oh, this wretched needle! That's the fourth time I have pricked myself this morning! I am sure this needle is bewitched!'

'Izzie,' said her father, 'I think perhaps you lack some attention in your work today. And Cassandra looks tired too. I suppose you kept her awake with tales of the theatre yesterday evening?'

Isobel and Cassandra looked sheepishly at each other. Isobel grinned because she knew her father bore her no grudge and merely said such things out of a sense of duty.

'Perhaps it would be better for us all, Izzie, if you and your sister took the rest of the morning off and took a little air…'

'Oh, Papa!' Isobel leapt up, throwing her work to one side and tugging Cassie's sleeve, 'You're the best father in the world! Come on, Cass, we'll go for a walk.'

'...but don't forget your outdoor shoes, and be back for luncheon. What your mother would say if she knew I had let you out…'

Isobel went over and kissed Mr Brite on his forehead, and scampered to the back of the shop, followed by a more sedate Cassandra.

'Thank you, Papa,' said Cassandra, 'are you sure you can manage?'

'Oh, go on, pet. An hour won't bring the world to an end; anyway, you'd better go and keep an eye on your sister. Make sure she doesn't get into any trouble!'

He returned to his work, shaking his head and chuckling softly to himself, whilst his youngest four children sighed with envy that their elder half-siblings should be given such freedom, and continued with their work.

'Oh, what a relief!' sighed Isobel as they walked across the grass on the far side of Cow Lane, 'I thought I would die of suffocation in the shop today.'

'Ye-es,' said Cassandra, thoughtfully, 'I do hope father can finish the shoes for Mr Hickson, though.'

'Oh, blow Mr Hickson!'

'Izzie! A man of God!'

'Well. I know. Still, I don't like the way he looks at me from the pulpit. He always seems to pick on me to look at when he says anything about the Devil or burning in Hell.'

'Oh, Izzie, I'm sure you just imagine it. What is it Izzie?'

Isobel had stopped and grabbed Cassandra's arm.

'Look! Look over there! You see those two men who have just appeared from behind the theatre? Cassie, that's the man who plays the part of Hamlet! The handsome one on the left. Oh, Cassie, what shall we do?'

'I don't know what you mean, Izzie. Why, what can we do? There is nothing to do about it. Izzie, where are you going? Izzie, you can't! Izzie! What would mother say?'

Isobel was dragging her sister along by her sleeve towards the two men who were walking down the side of the theatre towards the bend in Cow Lane where it turned down towards the town.

'Come on Cassie! If we can get to the Peacock Inn before they do - but we'll have to walk faster - Come *on*! And stop pulling back, you must look natural, as if we were just hurrying down to the market.'

'But Isobel, what are you going to do? You cannot surely mean to speak to him? If Mama knew you introduced yourself to a young man, well, I dread to think…'

'Oh, Cassie, do stop whining. I am perfectly capable of arranging a chance meeting, but you must leave it to me. Look, this is the inn where all the players stay. I'm sure that is where they are heading… yes, here they come! Now, give me your purse…'

'Goodness, Izzie! Whatever are you doing?' exclaimed Cassandra as Isobel spilled the contents of her purse over the roadside. Pennies and ha'pennies rolled chaotically into the middle of the road.

'Shhh!' hissed Isobel, pinching Cassandra's arm. In a loud voice she uttered, 'Oh, Cassandra, your purse! Haven't I told you and told you that you must mend that hole before you lose all your money! What are we going to do with it all in the road! We're bound to be run down if we try to pick it up!'

'May we be of assistance?' said a resonant voice behind them. The girls turned, and Isobel thought her heart would burst right through her stays when she found herself looking into the blue eyes of Hamlet.

Frank swept his top hat off his head and handed it to his companion. With one bound he leapt into the road and started to pick up the scattered pennies from the dust.

'Look out!' cried his companion, as a carriage and four clattered round the corner.

Frank hopped to the other side of the road to let it pass, and swiftly swooped back to pick up the remaining coins before an elegant barouche with its hood down came past, and he dodged back to the others, took back his hat, lifting it in salute to the party of onlookers watching him in amazement from the carriage. He turned back to the girls, holding out his hand to show a pile of dusty and gritty coins.

'I hope I have found them all.' he said, dusting them with a handkerchief and handing them to Cassandra, who bobbed a curtsey and replied a whispered 'Thank you.'

'Allow me to introduce ourselves. This is my colleague, Mr Partleton,' (the young man bowed and lifted his hat), 'and my name is Douglas, Mr Francis Douglas, actor, rogue and vagabond at your service,' and he again swept off his hat with a deep bow.

Isobel giggled, and then, clearing her throat, announced, 'Miss Isobel and Cassandra Brite at yours,' and dipped a curtsey, 'Indeed, Sir, I already know who you are, for I was at the theatre only yesterday evening, and, I must say,' she said, stammering and blushing only slightly, 'I was most enchanted with the play, and by the performance.'

'Is that really so?' said Frank, his eyes warming with interest to the pretty face before him, 'Why, that is gratifying! I was only saying to Mr Partleton here what a very friendly reception we have in Daventry, and what a fine theatre it is. And your family live in this fine town?'

'My father is a shoemaker on Sheaf Street, Sir, near the Wheatsheaf Inn. We have lived here all our lives.'

'Sheaf Street? Yes, I know it. A shoemaker you say? Well, you know, this is a happy meeting, for my walking boots are all but worn out and it is difficult to get a decent pair of boots fitted when one lives such an itinerant life. My problem of course is that we leave for Northampton at the end of the week, and…'

'Oh, do not worry,' said Isobel, 'my father will be quite happy to send them on, if you leave a forwarding address.' She blushed again.

'Is that even so? Well, Partleton, my friend, it seems that

my poor, blistering fcct havc bccn saved by this excellent young lady. What a happy meeting. Well, "Parting is such sweet sorrow," but we meet again, on the morrow, perhaps. Farewell, ladies.'

He again lifted his hat with a bow, and was gone, sweeping Mr Partleton along by the elbow (who had been constantly resisting the temptation to roll his eyes heavenwards; it was not the first time he had seen Douglas on the scent of an innocent female).

The two girls stood breathless on the street, each with differing emotions.

'Cassandra, did you notice the way he looked at me? Why, he could not take his eyes away!'

'Yes, Izzie. But I do not think…'

'Do you think he will come to the shop tomorrow? Oh! I don't think I can bear to wait!'

'But Izzie, do you really think Papa can…'

'Oh, what a charming man! And did you see how glad he was that I had been to the play? Oh, Cassie, I really think I might be in love!'

Cassandra looked at her sister with horror.

'But Izzie, a travelling actor! You cannot be serious!'

'Oh Cass, now you sound just like Mama! Can't you see? It's a wonderful life; never stuck in one place, audiences applauding and cheering every night. What is wrong with that? It cannot be any worse than being stuck here year in, year out, married to a boring old tradesman, raising babies and never seeing the world!'

Cassandra started to walk.

'I think we should go home now Izzie.'

Isobel took a final glance over her shoulder towards the Peacock Inn, but as she did so she saw the frightening sight of her step-mother appearing round the corner from the High Street with a grim look on her face.

'Mama!' she gasped.

Cassandra froze in her tracks and then turned back,

grasping Isobel's elbow for support.

'Oh dear,' she said.

Isobel stood firm, sticking her chin out defiantly. 'Isobel Brite! What have you been up to now? And what do you think you are doing out of the shop?'

'Father said we could, Mama…'

'Never mind that!' Mrs Brite grew another two inches as she pulled herself up to her most indignant and frightening posture, 'What is this I hear about you and Cassandra talking to two young men on the street! On the street, Izzie! Cassandra, you should be ashamed of yourself.'

Cassandra looked at the ground and moved closer to her sister.

'And not only that, but one of the young men actually capering around in the street like a madman! What are you thinking of girl, to be associating yourself with such people, and unescorted too!'

'Mama, they were helping us to…'

'I swear I can never hold my head up in chapel again! Oh, the shame of it! When Mrs Chapman told me she had seen you and your sister talking and laughing with two dandies. That dreadful man nearly causing an accident with his antics, and Mrs Chapman, the sister of the Reverend Hickson himself, oh!' She clutched her bosom as if her heart would fly away in outrage.

Cassandra started to weep.

Isobel tried again.

'You see, Cassandra dropped her money, and Mr Douglas very kindly…'

'Oh, Mr Douglas is it? And who might he be when he is at home?'

Isobel thought quickly.

'He's an… a, a gentleman.' A pinch from Cassandra made her jump.

'A gentleman indeed! It is no-one I have ever heard of. And what gentleman, I would like to know, dances in the street, frightening Mrs Chapman's best horses?'

'He wasn't...'

Mrs Brite thrust out her hand in a defiant gesture.

'I do not want to hear another word from you Isobel. And as for your sister, well,' her voice perceptively softened, 'she should know better. But I suppose as usual she's been led astray by you. Really, Isobel, as the eldest you should be setting an example. Now, I'm not letting you out of my sight until you are safely home. Come along!'

Mrs Brite herded the girls in front of her, Isobel striding ahead, her chin in the air, and Cassandra two steps behind, her eyes on the ground, her cheeks as red as cherries.

'A tankard of best ale and a pigeon pie I think, barman!' said Frank Douglas, rubbing his hands together to get rid of the dust from the road.

Henry Hartley, sitting in a corner, inwardly groaned. He had hoped to have had a quiet hour with a pork chop and the latest edition of *Household Words* so he could catch up on Mr Dickens' latest instalment of *Nicholas Nickleby*. But already he could see out of the corner of his eye, Frank Douglas bearing down on him. It was useless to try to ignore him.

'Hartley, dear fellow!' he said as he sat next to him, while George Partleton apologetically took the seat on Henry's other side. They exchanged glances.

'About our little discussion last night; I think I have the matter in hand. The most beautiful girl you have ever set eyes on, my friend.'

Henry lifted a questioning eyebrow in George's direction, who shrugged and rolled his eyes. Frank did not notice.

Henry jumped as Frank clapped a hand on his shoulder.

'Do you know, Hartley, seriously speaking, old man, I think I may be planning to fall in love. What do you think of that?'

Henry thought for a moment.

'My thoughts turn to the young lady in question, and I wonder what *her* plans are,' he answered.

'Hartley, you old wag. Never worry on *that* score, I rather think her plans will concord with mine in the not too distant future.'

Henry sighed.

'And who might the lucky young lady be?'

'Her name, Hartley, burns in my heart. It is as exquisite as her beauty. It is a Miss Isobel Brite. Is that not the most delicious name?'

'A shoemaker's daughter, very young.' chipped in George, with a knowing look at Henry.

Henry banged his fist on the table.

'Oh, but really, Frank. Come now. The Brites are a respectable family. An innocent girl like that, surely you could have found someone a bit more...' he paused as the innkeeper's boy brought their food to the table, '...a little more, shall we say, worldly wise, for your conquests?'

'Oh, but innocence, my friends, is the icing on the cake, think you not? Or has marriage dulled your senses, both of you?' he asked with a wink.

Really, the man was preposterous.

'Marriage, Sir, when the match is a good one, on the contrary, can heighten and improve all the senses.'

'Ah, you are but recently married, I believe, Hartley. I would put a wager on it that you would not say the same in ten, no, even five years' time! What do you say? What about ten pounds?'

'I will happily raise it to twenty guineas if I could be certain we would still be acquainted in five or ten years, Mr Douglas. This business is not the best for lasting friendships.'

'Well, let us shake on it anyway, my friend. Who knows, we both may be treading the London boards and be meeting regularly in the taverns of Covent Garden.'

God forbid, thought Henry to himself.

After luncheon, the three of them walked back to the theatre. There was no performance that night; three times per week was the norm, the variety of the performances being very demanding for everyone, but they would be rehearsing all afternoon, improving scenes, working on new songs, dances and comic sketches for the following week.

They arrived at the stage door to find the theatre in an uproar. Henry Jackman, the company's manager, was pacing backwards and forwards across the stage, cursing, whilst a sorry little heap in the corner, surrounded by fussing women and the local physic, turned out to be Mrs Eliza Fenton, who played Ophelia, or had been doing so until now.

Caroline came rushing over and explained what had happened. Eliza had been practising a pirouette for her dance in the variety bill and had fallen right off the stage and broken her ankle!

Was there no-one of all of Jackman's other actress daughters who could fill the part of Ophelia by next week? There was not. Caroline was already playing Gertrude and Frances Partleton was not well enough after losing her third child earlier that year. The most obvious choice would have been Sophia, who was the right age, but she was slow to learn and had been very under the weather and was not felt to be well enough to play the demanding part on top of her variety show duties. Besides, of all of Jackman's daughters, she was not highly thought of as an actress in the classical roles, and was mainly given comic songs and dances. Harriet and Louisa, the youngest daughters, were far too young and untried for such a part.

Could they get up another play by next week? They could not. No other Shakespeare play was ready that could be put on with only one female, and there would be too many lines to be learned in the time.

It was a disaster. There could now be no *Hamlet* tomorrow night, and it looked as though next week would have to be cancelled as well, with a potential loss of revenue that would seriously affect everyone unless Sophia could take over the part.

Henry Jackman continued to pace and curse.

CHAPTER 3

A small frown hovered over the top of Mr Brite's spectacles while he read the morning local paper before breakfast. Isobel sighed heavily as she laid the breakfast table, and dropped her father's knife on the floor.

'Isobel, do take care, and don't disturb your father while he's reading the paper.'

Isobel sighed again, and went to the drawer for another knife.

'The new railway opens next month,' said Mr Brite grimly, 'I'm afraid it will ruin the coach trade in Daventry.'

Isobel sat down heavily and yawned.

'It can't be right,' said Mrs Brite, 'all this mania for moving about at inhuman speeds (Isobel, put your hand over your mouth!). Why, I've heard they can go up to speeds of 30, or even 40, miles in an hour! It makes you dizzy just thinking about it! No good will come of it, and that's a fact.'

She spooned out ladlefuls of porridge into seven bowls while Cassandra dished them out.

'What makes me rather more dizzy, my dearest,' said her husband, taking off his spectacles, 'is the trade we shall be losing. It would have been better if the railway had been planned to cut through the centre of Daventry, breakneck speeds and chaos and all, rather than bypass us completely. I am gravely concerned that it is going to affect us rather badly.'

'You really think it will have such an effect on the coaches? (Will, don't kick the table leg like that!) Do you really think that people will take to the railways instead of coaches?'

'It would seem so, my love. The Liverpool to Manchester has apparently proved very popular. Now, people will be able to journey from London to Birmingham in five hours. Think of it, no more need to stay at an inn overnight, and what else does Daventry exist for?'

'Shoes, Papa!' suggested Susanna, the youngest, who was nine next birthday.

Mr Brite smiled, in spite of his worries.

'Yes, my dear, but if the main trade comes to a close, who will there be to make shoes for? Thirty per cent of my boots are for the innkeepers and coachmen.'

Isobel stifled another yawn. She had not slept well again last night.

'Well, perhaps we should not talk of this over the breakfast table. It'll upset the children's digestions, and that's a fact.'

Mr Brite replaced his spectacles and went back to his newspaper, turning the page.

'Hmmm. The anti-corn law people are forming an association up in Manchester. I hope something comes of that.'

Isobel had finished her porridge and started to pleat the hem of her napkin. Saturday mornings were so dull.

'Good heavens!' said Mr Brite, as he skimmed through another page, 'this will interest you, Izzie!'

'Yes, papa?' said Izzie, not sounding interested at all.

'It seems we might be losing our theatre company sooner than expected.'

Mrs Brite made a scoffing noise as she got up from the table and fortunately did not notice the flush that had risen to Isobel's cheeks.

'Oh, really, papa?' said Isobel, not quite able to disguise a sudden tremor in her voice. Cassie looked quickly at her sister as she got up to collect the porridge bowls.

'Mmm, let me see… Ah, yes, it seems that Ophelia has broken an ankle and there is no-one to replace her: "*All future performances of Hamlet are regretfully cancelled.*" It seems they will be leaving Daventry tomorrow. That will be a blow for the management.'

24

'T-tomorrow, did you say, Papa?' came Isobel's small voice.

'Thank the Lord for that,' said Mrs Brite, 'I was always against that theatre being built, you know that. It brings nothing but corruption to the town, there's no doubt about it.'

'I'm sure they'll be back again, next summer, dearest,' said her husband, in a warning, yet condoling tone. But he winked at Isobel as his wife's back was turned.

'Next summer?' echoed Isobel, swallowing very hard.

'Hmph!' said Mrs Brite.

'It brings welcome relief to the labourers, Ann. Their lives are tedious enough; why should they not have *some* excitement?'

'Well, I'll not argue with you; I'm sure you know best. Izzie, whatever is the matter, you look ill, child! Perhaps you should have a rest for ten minutes before you start work.'

'Yes, Mama, I think I shall,' and Isobel scuttled out of the parlour and up the wooden staircase to her room, where she threw herself into the chair in the corner and propped up her chin with the back of her hand.

It's always the same, she thought, *just as soon as there is any excitement in my life, something happens and it comes to nothing. I am condemned to a dull life for ever!*

Later on, Mr Brite had just popped down to the store room, leaving Isobel on her own when Frank Douglas opened the door and entered.

Isobel looked up at the sound of the bell and her eyes widened when she saw who it was.

'I am delighted, Miss Brite, to be once again in your company,' said Frank.

Taken unawares, Isobel's eyes fluttered, and she looked to the ground.

'Mr Douglas, I… how nice. I… I shall get my father…'

'No! Please don't. I can order boots whenever I want to, but the chances of spending time alone with you are very slim.'

Isobel knew that she was blushing, and turned away, pretending to tidy some shelves. She was aware constantly that his eyes were upon her.

'I hear that you will be leaving the town tomorrow, Mr Douglas.'

'To my bitter regret, Miss Brite. Due to an unfortunate accident, I am afraid that is so. I would not, by choice, take my leave of our acquaintance so soon.'

Isobel smiled, slowly regaining her coolness.

'Mr Douglas, you flatter me! I do not believe you would remember my existence one second after you left Daventry!'

Frank shot his hand out and caught her wrist.

'Oh, but you must not believe that, Miss Brite. Do not believe that for a moment.'

Isobel's heart was now beating very fast, and Frank was looking at her so earnestly that it made her feel faint.

'Well,' she said, making a big effort to keep her voice level, 'it cannot be helped.' She gently removed her wrist, her heart skipping a beat as their hands touched.

'No,' he said, 'it cannot be helped...'

He suddenly looked intensely at her, with his eyes narrowed. 'Unless... unless... I wonder...'

Isobel blushed again under his scrutiny.

'Mr Douglas, my father will be back soon. If there is anything you wish...'

'Can you act?'

Isobel stared back at him, her eyes wide.

'Can I... forgive me, what did you say?'

'Can you act? Could you play a part? Could you learn lines within a week?'

'M-Mr Douglas, please, what exactly are you saying?'

'Allow me to be blunt, Miss Brite. I see a great deal of

passion within you, a passion that is wasted within these walls. I see great charisma. Yes, I can see it now, you could hold an audience spellbound. I foresee a great career, heralded by this chance meeting. Could it be that I, a humble strolling player, could have discovered a future bright and shining star?'

A strange, prickling sensation crept over Isobel's skin, and her stomach seemed to be turning over and over in an acrobatic kind of way. No-one had ever spoken to her like this before. She continued to stare, wide-eyed and speechless, at Frank Douglas.

'Miss Brite, an idea has occurred to me that would save the company, and bring indescribable pleasure to an otherwise disappointed audience. Of course, I will have to talk to Mr Jackman, and he will have to see you, but I do not see that he could possibly refuse. Oh, Miss Brite, do you think you could do it? Could you learn the part in a week and come to Northampton with us?'

Isobel could not speak for a moment, but she could hear the basement door open and knew there was no time left to hesitate.

'I… I… Oh, Mr Douglas, I do not know! Do you really think… but, yes, I think perhaps…'

'Then, I will speak to Mr Jackman and I will return later. Where can I meet you?'

Mr Brite's footsteps could be heard coming slowly up the stone steps.

'In Wagon Court - at half past five!'

'I will be there!' and Frank quickly darted out of the shop before Mr Brite appeared.

'Was that someone in the shop, Izzie? I thought I heard the bell.'

'Oh, it was just Mr Neal's boy, come for some shoe-black, Papa.'

'You know, I think your mother was right, Izzie. You don't look well. You look quite flushed. Are you sure you're not feverish, child?'

'No Papa, thank you. I am perfectly well.'

'My dear Frank,' said Henry Jackman, his chin high as he looked along the narrow ridge of his nose at him, 'do you intend to ruin me? My company has always prided itself on the talent and experience of its players. Why, most of the company were born and raised in theatres. My own daughters, sir, have lived, breathed and fed on the stage since the second they were brought into this world. All newcomers to this illustrious company come with the finest of references and histories before they are even allowed to audition. Yet you come to me with an idea to take on a completely inexperienced, untried and green *shoe*maker's daughter?!'

Throughout this speech, Frank nodded his head in agreement and acquiescence.

'Of course,' he said, as if chastened by this onslaught, 'I completely understand, sir. It is unthinkable, I see, to even contemplate taking on a complete unknown. It would be an insult, indeed, to your own daughters…'

'It certainly would, sir!'

'I quite see that, I quite see that. Forgive me for my foolish, insensitive suggestion. You see, I did not realise that you had already found somebody to take Mrs Fenton's place. I presume Miss Sophia, then, will be taking on the role?'

Mr Jackman, who had been busy looking through the accounts, and had resumed this job after his small speech, stopped in his tracks.

'Er… Sophia? Hmph. It may come to that,' he muttered under his breath.

'It would be, as you say, madness to even consider a rank outsider when you have already given the part to your own daughter. She is, of course, just the right age, and I am sure will be delighted to try such a demanding role.'

Mr Jackman opened his mouth to say something more, but nothing came out, so he shut it again.

Frank made a move to go.

'Well, I won't trouble you any further. You're a busy man, and you will be thinking about all the extra rehearsals that will be needed.'

'Er… umm…' Henry Jackman coughed and cleared his throat. 'Wait, one moment, Mr Douglas. You say this girl is handsome?'

'Extremely.'

'And, er, she has striking red hair?'

'Indeed. It would certainly make an impact from the stage.'

'Can she dance, and sing? Ophelia has to sing, you know.'

'Most excellently.' said Frank, crossing his fingers.

'Hmmm.' Mr Jackman drummed his fingers on the table. 'I suppose I could have a look at her.'

Isobel was worried that she might faint while she was waiting for Frank in Wagon Court, an alley that ran off Sheaf Street. She could not stand still. She flitted from one side of the alley to the other, her heart missing a beat every time someone passed by. She fiddled with the ribbons on her purse until they were crumpled and grimy.

'If he doesn't come soon I shall… I shall… well, I don't know what I will do, but I won't bear it. I simply can't. What will I do? What will I do? I shouldn't be here at all! Gracious, if Mama knew! But I won't think of that. Oh, I wish he would come… I think I will die if he doesn't come…'

She muttered to herself in a subdued frenzy, hoping that nobody, except Mr Douglas, would choose to walk up the lane.

She had just turned away, frightened that some people she knew were about to walk through the alley and discover her and engage her in conversation, so when she heard footsteps behind her she pretended to be on her way to the other end.

A hand caught her own and she gasped, turning to find Mr Douglas beaming in front of her.

'Miss Brite, forgive me for my lateness. It is extremely impolite to keep a young lady waiting, but it took so much longer to persuade the old man than I thought.'

Isobel couldn't speak. She looked down at the ground, wondering if he would catch her if she swooned. Her heart seemed to have stopped beating.

'I have succeeded in my mission, Miss Brite. At least, I have secured a meeting for you with the old… with Mr Jackman. Tomorrow at three.'

Isobel tried to take in this information.

'Tomorrow?'

'At three. Are you free? Oh, please say that you are, Miss Brite. I feel sure that he will decide to take you on the moment he sees you.'

'I…' Isobel thought quickly. Perhaps she could complain of a headache again, and ask to go out for fresh air, '…I think so. But what do I do?'

'Bless me, I nearly forgot. I have a copy of the part you are to read: Ophelia. Can you fain madness?'

Isobel felt quite sure at that moment that she could, without acting. She nodded slowly.

'But, must I learn all this? There is so much!'

'Don't worry. You may read from the page. But, perhaps if you learn some of it you will show him how quickly you can learn. That will put you in good reckoning.'

Isobel flicked through the pages and recognised some of the words from the play the other night. Perhaps she could remember how the actress said the lines and copy her.

Frank was watching her.

She flushed and looked up.

'Mr Douglas, you've been so kind…'

'Oh, please do not mention it, Miss Brite. The pleasure is entirely mine, believe me.'

He was standing very close to her. Far too close for decorum. She could actually feel his breath on her cheek. Why had Cassie tied her corset so tight this morning? She felt she could hardly breathe.

Was it her imagination or was he moving even closer?

'Mr Douglas, I have to go. My mother…'

He sighed, as if he, too, had been holding his breath and as though a spell had been broken.

She began to move away, though he was slightly blocking her path and it was necessary to almost touch him to pass. Frank did not move, but remained in front of her, his eyes watching her intently, almost hungrily.

'Until tomorrow, then, Miss Brite.'

She bowed slightly.

'Mr Douglas.'

But as she moved towards the end of the lane, he called her name again. She turned and saw his tall, sturdy figure silhouetted against the light from the other side. Excitement rose in her throat.

'Miss Brite, can you dance?'

'Can I… I beg your pardon?'

'Can you dance – and sing?'

'Why, yes. A little.'

'Good. Tomorrow, then. At three.'

He turned and walked back up the lane, and Isobel half walked, half ran back to the shop, and with a hurried, 'Good evening, Papa!' ran through to the back, up the stairs and into her room where she shut the door and leaned back on it, clutching the script in one hand and her head in the other.

'My goodness!' she said to herself.

And for a good ten minutes after that, she repeated those words over again, for she was unable to say or think

31

anything else.

CHAPTER 4

Isobel walked in a rush towards the theatre, her heart beating faster with every step. Looking over her shoulder, fearful that she would see Mama storming up behind her, she mumbled to herself over and over again the words of Ophelia.

She had not slept a wink. While Cassandra lay sleeping, she had crept out of bed, lit a candle and sat reading her part until she knew most of it by heart. But even when she finally crawled under the sheets, she could not relax enough to fall asleep. Her stomach would keep turning over and over, and her thoughts tumbled from one scenario to another.

Scared that she would make an utter fool of herself and be rejected as an actress, yet scared of what would happen to her if she was accepted, she tossed and turned for the rest of the night. She had not told a soul, not even Cassandra, for she knew she would try to dissuade her. Yet now, for the first time in her life, it was possible that she might leave home for a life that was completely new. It was terrifying, yet exciting at the same time. But what on earth would she tell her parents?

She would think about that only if the incredible happened.

Which it probably wouldn't. How could they possibly take a shoemaker's daughter who had never been near a stage all her life? The idea seemed impossible, almost laughable. Yet, Frank had said it was possible.

Frank. Oh, the way he had looked at her yesterday. The things he had said!

Oh, she *must* get the part! She would die if she didn't! She may never see him again!

But if she left Daventry, would she ever see her family again? How could she leave Cassandra?

No, it was no use worrying about that. It just was not

going to happen. It was impossible that her life could change so drastically after nineteen years of nothing happening at all! Her life was *bound* to continue as normal. How could she imagine anything else?

But, oh, not to see *him* again...

During the morning, red-eyed and yawning, she had sat demurely at her work, saying very little, but her mouth silently working away at the lines she was to say until her father began to throw her worried looks.

After lunch (at which she ate very little and her step-mother said she looked decidedly 'peaky') she sneaked into the store room for a few seconds.

At ten minutes to three she said to her father, 'Father, did you know we are all out of blue silk lace? I need some for Mrs Mercer's evening slippers.'

'Bless me! Are you sure? I would have staked my life we had plenty; it's not as if we use it very often.'

'Maybe that's why it's run out without you noticing, papa!' she said with a cheeky grin, 'But would you like to look yourself? Perhaps I was wrong, although I looked everywhere. But if you want to be completely sure...'

'No, no, Izzy. I am sure you are right. Emily,' he said, turning to one of his other daughters, 'go over to Mr Haddon's and see if they can make up some fine silk shoe lace...'

Isobel stood up hastily. 'Oh no, papa. Let me go. I need a little air. I have a slight headache again, and it may take a while for Haddon to cut it, and Emily will not be able to sit for so long without becoming impatient. I am quite happy to, really.'

Mr Brite looked with surprise at his daughter, but acquiesced, pleased at this unusual show of maturity.

She had run upstairs, taken off her dirty apron, and put on her best bonnet, making sure her hair peeped out in little tendrils, and scurried off towards the theatre, a ball of blue lace from the store room still hidden in her pocket.

When she walked into the theatre, she had a moment of utter confusion. Had she come to the wrong building? She had remembered the stage as a place of magic, glowing with lights with coloured scenery creating the illusion of castles or graveyards. The rest of the barn had been filled with people, and had smelt strongly of the sweat of farm labourers, orange peel and sawdust. It had had a special, strange, exciting atmosphere that she had breathed in at first with slight distaste, but then with relish. It had been like entering Aladdin's Cave.

Now, the benches were empty, some of them piled in corners to make way for a large table just in front of the stage. The stage was merely a slightly raised platform, bare and colourless, the broad light of day shining through uncurtained windows on either side. In the corners were piled strangely shaped objects, which Isobel recognised after a few moments as the screens that had stood on stage, representing castle walls or trees, now lying incongruously on their sides. A painted canvas of a castle courtyard still hung at the back, but seemed gaudy and out of place in the daylight.

There were some people on the stage, but there was no show going on. A young lady was practising a pirouette over and over again with nobody watching. A group of people stood talking towards one side.

In the space next to the table by the stage, Frank and another actor, about ten years older than Frank, were practising a swordfight, dressed only in loose shirts and britches. By the table was sitting a large man facing the duellists, giving comments and orders while he tapped out time on the ground with a walking stick.

'A little faster, Mr Fenton, we want to excite the audience, not send them to sleep. And when he lunges, try not to look like a startled sheep!'

As they were about to commence the fight again, Frank

suddenly held up his sword, shouting 'Hold!'

In several leaps and bounds over and around the remaining benches, he came towards Isobel. Isobel thought she had never seen anyone so handsome as Frank did in his wide-sleeved shirt and a cravat loosely tied under his neck, his hair long and tousled, his face flushed and animated with physical excursion.

Her cheeks were burning crimson as he took her hand and led her through the benches to the large table, where she felt the critical eye of Henry Jackman scrutinising her every move.

'Did I not tell you,' Frank said to Mr Jackman, 'that she would be here at three? And did I not tell you that she would be beautiful?'

Isobel could not prevent a coy smile, and inside she shivered with delight.

Henry Jackman looked her up and down.

'Hmmm, a pleasing figure. What is your name, child?'

'Isobel Brite, sir.' she answered, modestly.

'Speak up, child!' he boomed, 'If you want to be an actress you have to learn to make your voice reach the back of a barn.'

Isobel had never had anyone speak to her like that, except her step-mother. Nor had anyone looked at her in quite the same way, as if sizing up a piece of meat in a market. She felt a rush of indignation which rose up and made her forget her nervousness. Lifting her chin up, and looking down at him (he was still seated, which she thought very rude), she grew an inch taller, and announced in a loud and clear voice,

'My name is Isobel Brite.' This time she forgot the 'sir'.

She felt her voice echo around the building. The girl on the stage stopped pirouetting and stared at her, and the group in the corner stopped talking and turned around to see who had spoken.

Isobel felt everybody's eyes on her, but she stood her

ground. She rather liked the feeling of being the centre of attention. It was a little frightening, but also rather exhilarating.

Henry Jackman sat back in his chair and roared with laughter.

Isobel was not used to being laughed at. She didn't like it. It was really too much. Growing yet another inch taller, she turned abruptly and stormed towards the door, knowing that everyone was watching her.

Behind her, as she went through the door, she heard the booming voice of Jackman.

'Not only has she got spirit and presence, but she makes an excellent dramatic exit! Catch her, Frank, catch her!'

Isobel walked, not quite so quickly as she could have done, away from the theatre in the direction of Sheaf Street. When Frank caught up with her she saw that he was smiling from ear to ear.

'Miss Brite! You must return. The old man likes you!'

Isobel stopped walking. Of course, she was going to return. But she wasn't going to make it easy.

'Mr Douglas, I came here today to try a part. I did not come to be humiliated and… and… degraded!' She turned again to walk away.

'Miss Brite.! Isobel!'

She stopped. My word. He had called her by her Christian name. It was all very exciting.

'Mr Douglas?' she said, as calmly as possible.

'Please, please, come back. You must not mind old Henry. That's just his way. He's a theatrical; we all are! That's the way we are with each other. It's all meant in good faith, and in fun. It's something that you'll have to get used to in the theatre. I suppose that's why we're different from the rest of society. We don't pander to, how shall I put it, false etiquette?'

Isobel thought for a moment. She liked the thought of being different. It was something she had secretly felt all her life, that she was different. Saying and doing 'the right thing' had always bored her.

'Very well,' she said, 'I will return.'

Smiling, Frank took her by the arm and led her back to the theatre entrance. But before they went in, he stopped and whispered in her ear:

'You have just made your first dramatic exit. Now show them that you can make a grand entrance!'

Isobel grinned, and looked up at him, her eyes twinkling. 'Very well,' she whispered, 'Open the door for me, when I say.'

She stood by the door and at a nod, Frank pulled it open swiftly.

She stood in the doorway, knowing that her 'pleasing figure' would be silhouetted in the door frame against the afternoon sun. Taking a moment to make sure that all eyes were upon her again, she then walked with dignity and grace down the centre of the building towards the stage. Instead of stopping to speak to Mr Jackman, who was watching her every move, she swept past him without looking at him, climbed the steps up onto the stage and took the centre of it.

Again, she took a moment to make sure everyone was listening and then spoke, directly to Mr Jackman, but loudly enough for all to hear, including Frank. He was now standing at the back of the auditorium, leaning against the door, his arms folded, that now familiar grin on his face.

'Mr Jackman, I have reconsidered my departure, and I have decided to give you another chance. I believe you would like to see me play the part of Ophelia. I can do this whenever you are ready.'

Mr Jackman, looking both delighted and astonished, said, 'Indeed, Miss Brite, when ever *you* are ready.'

'I presume you would like me to take off my bonnet?'

'Indeed, I would, Miss Brite.'

Isobel undid the ribbon under her chin, removed her bonnet, and threw it towards one of the actors at the side of the stage, who managed to catch it with some surprise.

Then, Isobel removed the pins that were holding up her hair, and let it fall down, tossing her head so the curls cascaded in red waves around her shoulders.

Clutching her hands to her throat, and raising her eyes to the heavens, she began.

'Oh, what a noble mind is here overthrown...'

The flame of the candle flickered, casting great moving shadows around the dark room. Isobel shivered slightly, even though she was dressed in her day clothes and had a shawl wrapped around her. Outside, the moon was full, and cast a little light into the room and onto the bed where her sleeping sister lay. The sister she loved, and whom she may not see for a very long time.

Isobel dipped her pen in the ink pot and started to write.

My dearest Cassandra,

As you read this letter, try not to think ill of me, for I can bear the severest of criticism from Mama, or even Papa, but not from my own, dear sister. Please remember that I have no wish to cause anyone any sorrow, but the action I have taken is necessary for my own spirit. I am not like you - I cannot live the life that will no doubt be planned for me. I would rather die a thousand deaths.

My dear - I will be gone by the time you read this. Not far, but my life will be as different to what it is now than as if I had gone to the other side of the world. What I am about to tell you I have been unable to tell anyone for fear that I would be put under lock and key! Mama would give me up to the workhouse, without a doubt!

Isobel looked up and stared at the moon while she nibbled the end of her pen.

She remembered Mr Jackman's words after he had offered her a place in the company and she had been standing there feeling like she might take wings and fly:

'Of course, I will need to write a letter to your father. This is a respectable company and we would not want to cause any problems. I presume your family are happy for you to join our company?'

Isobel's heart had sunk to her boots and she cast a frightened look towards Frank. She felt her new wings were about to be clipped before she had even flown.

'Oh, that won't be necessary, Sir,' said Frank, 'I have spoken at length with Mr Brite and he is perfectly happy about it all. The family are great supporters of the theatre and will be most grateful.'

Isobel sighed with relief, yet could not help feeling slightly shocked at the ease with which he told such a brazen lie.

'Oh, really?' said Jackman, 'I am glad of it, but all the same, I feel I should write…'

'Perhaps from Northampton, Sir. Then you can also tell them what a marvellous performance their daughter has given at the same time.'

Isobel beamed at Frank. He really was very wicked, but so clever! Getting a letter praising her abilities would make it more difficult for them to do anything about it. And what could they do by then, anyway? They could not come and drag her away. She would simply refuse. She would give anything to see her stepmother's face when she read that letter!

'That's settled then. Miss Brite, welcome to our humble company. You will find us friendly, and quite respectable. We are, shall I say, a family affair. My wife and daughters, and their various husbands all tread the boards and sing or dance; whatever their capability. They will, I am sure, make you feel at home. We leave for Northampton, by the way, in two days. Friday morning at

five in the morning. And make sure you have your part.
We will commence rehearsals on Saturday and we open
on Thursday.'

She still couldn't believe it. Not just the fact that she
was now to be an actress, but her own performance at the
audition! What had got into her to stand her own ground
and behave the way she had? And the feeling that had
come over her when she stood on that stage! It was like
coming home. She knew she belonged there and this
feeling had given her the confidence to play the part as she
had felt it in her head.

Mr Jackman had been very nice to her afterwards. He
had said she was a 'natural' and had a true stage presence.
He told her that she needed to develop her technique and
timing a bit more but that this would come with time.

She dipped her pen again and continued writing:

*Cassie, I am to be an actress! Please try to be as excited
for me as I am for myself! I am as happy as it is possible
to be. You know very well that I have been fascinated by
the theatre since Uncle took me to see Hamlet - and the
very charming Mr Douglas has been so kind, and
arranged to get me an audition - and then to play the part
of Ophelia!! Now I will be on stage with him! I have to
keep pinching myself!*

Isobel stopped writing for a moment and hugged herself,
biting her lip to stop herself from laughing out loud.

Oh, if only she could tell Cassandra right now! If only
they could hug each other; she was so desperate to share
her good fortune. She imagined herself and Cassie
dancing round the room in delight.

She looked over to where Cassie lay asleep. Should she
wake her and tell her now? It seemed so wrong to go
without saying goodbye.

But she knew what her sister would say. She would not

41

stop her, nor would she run and tell their parents to stop her, but she would not be as delighted for Isobel as Isobel's fantasy would like her to be. No, she would weep and cajole, warn Isobel of the dangers of such a wild adventure and Isobel would no doubt have to leave her with tears and whispered reprovals, which would spoil everything.

She looked at the warm bed. She had grown up here; spent every night of her life in this bed. She felt scared. What was she about to do? Go out into the dark night to travel with a group of people she did not know to places she had never been, to act on a stage in front of people for the first time in her life. What madness!

She could still change her mind. She could destroy the letter, put out the candle and crawl into bed beside Cassie, and in the morning, no-one would know, and life would carry on as normal.

She took a deep breath.

Her mood slightly sobered, she went back to her letter:

So, my dearest, I have joined the Jackman Theatre Company, and my life will never be the same again.

I am leaving you the difficult task of breaking the news to Mama and Papa. I know this will be terrible, but really, I do not care what Mama thinks. As for Papa, please give him a kiss and tell him that I was never made to be a shoemaker's daughter. Perhaps some malevolent fairy swapped me at birth. Perhaps there is a miserable player somewhere, pining for a warm hearth and a quiet life!

But I will always be your adoring sister, whatever you or anyone think of me.

Please tell them not to try and follow me.

Please hug Emily, Tom, Susanna and Will. I will miss you all. But I will see you again. I am sure it will be soon.

Your loving and affectionate sister,

Isobel.

After carefully blotting the letter, she folded it and laid it on her own pillow. She went to the window and peered out.

The moon was bright, and she could just make out the shadowy figure waiting in the doorway of the baker's opposite.

Her stomach lurched. It was all real, and she had not dreamt it.

She turned to look at her sister, and softly touched her hair before whispering a farewell; then she picked up the candle and a bag she had packed earlier.

Taking a long look at the room she knew so well, she blew out the candle, softly lifted the latch and crept out. Downstairs, she let herself out by the back door and then tiptoed round the back, down through Wagon Court, to where Frank was waiting. Without speaking, he took her bag and took her by the arm.

Away in the east, at the top end of Sheaf Street, beyond the London Road, the first light of dawn was just beginning to lighten the sky.

They headed towards it.

CHAPTER 5

They met the rest of the company by the Wheatsheaf Inn at the top of London Road, and she was hastily introduced to her fellow company members. There were at least twelve people, most of them in their early twenties, plus some workers who were obviously stage hands, and a child of four. Isobel did not catch everybody's names, but she gathered that they were all family, mostly daughters of Henry Jackman, and their husbands. Some of the younger women and girls looked at her with sidelong glances and then turned, whispering to one another. Mrs Fenton, whose broken ankle had caused Isobel's sudden change of fortune, looked at her sulkily from her seat on one of the wagons, where a space had been cleared for her. For the first time it occurred to Isobel that she would not be welcome. Perhaps the others would resent her because she was an outsider, and make her feel unwanted, like an intruder. What did they think about her joining the company? Were they angry, or jealous?

She began to feel slightly sick. Here she was, Isobel Brite, a local shoemaker's daughter, running away with a troupe of players who probably all hated her, standing forlornly at 5 o'clock in the morning with no friends, leaving her family and all she knew behind her. Who on earth did she think she was? What had she done?

She began to wonder whether she could sneak back home, creep up the stairs without anyone noticing, tear up the letter to Cassie, and slip quietly into bed. For a moment, she yearned for the familiarity and warmth of her bed, with her sister beside her, her step-mother calling her for breakfast in an hour's time...

One hour! In one hour they would find her gone. Oh, what would they say? What would they do? Poor Cassie... How could she do this? She must return, go back and rise in an hour as if nothing had happened...

Then she was aware of someone by her side, and she turned to find herself looking at one of the kindest, most intelligent looking faces she had ever seen. It was a woman in her late twenties and she immediately took Isobel's arm.

'My dear,' she said, warmly, 'I am so pleased that you will join us and prevent us from closing. You are bound to feel quite strange at first, but just ask me anything you don't understand. Mr Hartley – that's my husband – and I will help you with learning your part. You can just treat me like a sister, and call me Caroline. Don't worry about the others, they are very impolite not to come and welcome you. But I am sure they will learn to love you in time.'

Isobel took an instant liking to Caroline Hartley. She decided, after all, that she would continue with this adventure. It was too late to go home now. Anyway, she had promised Frank.

Frank, who was busy talking to some of the other men, had put her bag onto a huge wagon piled high with bits of scenery and other strange objects, and for the first time she wondered how they travelled from town to town. She looked at the other two wagons, and noticed that they were all nearly overloaded with scenery and theatre properties. She looked around for more carts or carriages and horses, but there was nothing else. Every wagon was full, with no room for anyone other than the disabled Mrs Fenton.

'Where are the coaches?' she asked of Mrs Hartley, 'will they arrive soon?'

Unfortunately, she had spoken loud enough for some of the others to hear, and she was answered with peels of laughter from some of Caroline's younger sisters.

'Oh, she wants a carriage and four! Have we ordered the phaeton for her ladyship?', and these remarks were accompanied by a little pantomime from Sophia, Caroline's next youngest sister, who Isobel thought was quite ugly.

'Sophia! Really!' cried Caroline, 'it's not nice of you to be so rude! Poor Isobel is quite new to the theatre life. Of course, she doesn't understand, and why would she? Sophia, go and help my husband to tie up those props while I talk to Isobel.'

Sophia went off with a theatrical flounce, and Caroline turned to Isobel.

'My darling girl, we do not travel by coach I am very much afraid. That is one thing you will have to get used to if you are to join a circuit company like ours. Only those who can afford it – managers and stars - travel by coach – father and mother do. Mr Douglas could have done, but he has decided to walk with us today. Mr Hartley and I like to save our pennies as much as we can. Costumes, food and accommodation can all be very expensive, so we try and avoid the cost of travelling when we can.'

Isobel blushed at her own ignorance. She had been thrilled when Henry Jackman had told her she would be paid twenty shillings a week, but she had not thought of the things she would have to pay for out of that. Luckily, Ophelia's costume fitted her and only needed to be taken in in a few places, but if she was going to stay on she was dismayed that she would have to pay for her own costumes; and she had no idea how much it would cost to stay at an inn.

'I do hope your father makes strong boots!' continued Caroline, 'You will have to get used to walking long distances.'

Isobel stared at her. She had only been to Northampton once, when she had travelled with her father in his trap to buy leather and other stuff at the big market there. It had seemed to be a long and tedious journey, and she had not volunteered to go with him again.

'Walk?' she asked weakly.

Caroline grinned.

'Don't worry, you'll soon get used to it – if you stay for the rest of the season. We'll be travelling to Uxbridge, Buckingham, Banbury, Aylesbury, oh and lots of other places. Don't look so alarmed! An actor's life is very exciting and extraordinary. I know you'll love it. I can see you are just right for it. In fact, I thought the moment I saw you, "that girl's got spirit", and that's what you need in this business. Spirit, and lots of it.'

Isobel smiled and tried to forget her fears. What Caroline said made her feel a kind of delicious warmth about herself that she had not felt before. She had only ever been told off for having 'spirit', and she had never understood why this strong, excitable and ambitious part of her was something bad and wrong. Now, Caroline was saying that it was right: right for the theatre. So, if spirit was right for the theatre, then theatre was right for her.

They set off a few moments later, the wagons having been loaded with the baggage from the Wheatsheaf where a few of the older members of the company had been staying.

As they walked down London Road, Isobel looked at the new workhouse on her right: a wide, squat, gloomy looking building. She remembered her step-mother's words, and shuddered. What a hateful place to end up in.

And then she turned her face to the road in front of her and took a deep breath. She was leaving Daventry and her old life behind. She did not have to listen to her stepmother any more. She was free; freer than any girl or woman she had ever known. From this moment on everything would be an adventure.

After two hours, they reached the village of Weedon where they were to breakfast at the Globe Hotel.

Isobel was walking with Caroline and Henry Hartley, and as they approached the hotel, and the crossing with

Watling Street, Mr Hartley stopped and raised his arm, pointing south.

'There, Miss Brite! Take a look down that road and do not forget it.'

Isobel looked at the road that ran across their route, but saw nothing spectacular or memorable. She looked at him with puzzlement.

'That, Miss Brite,' he continued in explanation, 'is the road to London. The old Watling Street, the Roman road that goes straight to Londinium. That is the place where every aspiring actor should set his sights. Our life of travelling the circuits is a mere training ground, a time of learning the business and building your repertoire. But London – that is the place to be! That would mean success!'

Caroline rolled her eyes.

'Do not worry about my Henry, Isobel. He always does this every time we cross or travel a road to London. He is very eager to find employment in the London theatres, but, alas, it has not happened yet, and he grows more and more impatient.' Then she whispered, 'But don't tell my father.'

Caroline sighed, and Isobel saw a little frown appear for a moment on her face and realised that not everything was as satisfactory has she had thought in the Hartleys' life.

And Henry's words had also had an effect on her. When she had said yes to Frank's offer of a part with the company, she had thought no further than the excitement and glamour of playing a role with a theatre company and the freedom that would bring her. Now, she realised there could be more to aim for. Something to work for: an ambition. She again felt those fluttering feelings in her stomach that seemed to have become a regular part of her life since she had stepped inside the Daventry theatre.

They spent an hour breakfasting at the Globe, and Isobel was more ready for food and a rest than she had ever been in her life. Used to porridge every morning for as long as she could remember, she was amazed at the range of food that the company ordered and consumed. There were kippers, toast, eggs, ham, devilled kidneys and lots of coffee. Frank paid for her breakfast, and she dived in as if she had been starved for a week.

Frank was amused.

'Walking is good for the appetite, Miss Brite, as I see you have discovered.'

Isobel said nothing, because her mouth was full of ham and eggs, but she nodded vigorously, which made Frank laugh even more.

My Dearest Cassie

I barely know where to begin, my life has changed so much in these few days – can it really be only four days since I last saw you?

Firstly, I shall say that I hope you do not hate me too much for leaving in the way that I did. I know it will affect you and Papa much more than Mama – who will probably be <u>glad to see the back of me</u>. But, Cassie, I just could not have stayed. It is not in me. And I am finding out so much about myself, just in these few days, you would hardly recognise your old Izzie!

I have discovered that <u>the theatre is my home.</u> We started rehearsing almost as soon as we got here…

But first, I must tell you about life on the road. Do you know that most provincial actors <u>walk everywhere</u>??! At first, I was terribly shocked – you know I have never walked further than the back of St Mary's Churchyard – but I have now walked all the way to Northampton! But it took several hours and we stopped twice, once for breakfast, and once for luncheon, and the innkeepers seem to know everyone in the company and greet them like old *friends.*

Every bone in my body ached the first night where I am staying in a small inn which is right next to the theatre, and I thought I would not sleep from it, and being so excited, but I was so tired that I slept right away. Oh, and the theatre itself! That place at Daventry is just a barn – but this is a proper theatre with a gallery and boxes and an orchestra pit and <u>chandeliers</u>. Imagine!

The rehearsals have been fun – but I also have to <u>work very hard</u> – harder than I ever worked in father's workshop. But I enjoy it more, so it doesn't seem that hard. Mr Jackman is extremely particular and has to have everything just right, so we work and work until things are as perfect as possible, but I really don't mind, and I think he is a very fair man. I have learned so much already about the acting business, but I know I have so much more to learn, but Cassie <u>I do love it so</u>. There is just nothing like being on a stage and playing a part. I cannot explain it, but it just feels as though I have arrived home.

I have made some good friends in the company. Henry and Caroline Hartley have been so kind and helpful, especially as everything felt so strange and new to begin with, and the others (who are all related to Mr Jackman) I think were unsure of me to begin with, though I am sure that will become easier. Mr Hartley plays Horatio, and Caroline plays Gertrude – but she is much younger than that part in real life, but they use wigs and <u>make-up</u> to make them look older. And, of course, there is Mr Douglas, who has been very kind indeed. He hardly lets me out of his sight, but I try to pretend that I do not notice.

Tomorrow is my <u>big opening night</u>. Cassie, I am so nervous – but very excited as well. Imagine – I will be on stage in front of hundreds of people! I am sure I will not sleep at all tonight even though ~~Frank~~ Mr Douglas tells me I have nothing to worry about.

Cassie, I do hope that you will be able to come and see

me play one day. I am hoping very much that Mr Jackman will want to keep me on after <u>Hamlet</u> and cast me in the new plays. If he does, I will have singing and dancing lessons, so that I can take part in the early parts of the evening where the company puts on sketches and songs. Oh, you should see Mr Hartley when he does his comic song and dance – I have never seen anything so funny – I thought I would <u>die</u> I laughed so much.

I must close now. I really must try and get some rest before tomorrow, and I am writing this at night, as I have no time during the day. I shall send this by the first post tomorrow, and by the time you receive it your sister will have made her <u>stage debut</u> (that's a theatrical term for a first performance).

Give my love to father and tell him that I do miss him – and of course I miss you, Cassie. But you needn't say anything to mama – nothing I say would change anything she thinks about me.

Your loving
Isobel.

Isobel stood, shivering, in the wings. She felt sick and cold. She wished with all her heart that she had never heard of the theatre and that she was now at home safe and warm, having supper with her family. Why, oh why, had she ever decided to become an actress? What a stupid thing to do. Nothing was worth this dreadful fear and sickness.

Last night she had dreamed that she had gone on stage and found everyone speaking different lines to those she had learned. They had all rehearsed a new scene and no-one had told her! It was horrible, and she woke up in a cold sweat. It was the first indication of any nervousness about going on stage, and it had worried her. But when she told Caroline about it she had laughed and told her that everyone had similar dreams just before a first night.

Apparently, it was called the 'actors' dream', so she had felt better after that. Obviously, she was a born actress if she was having the actors' dream.

But now, standing in the wings waiting to go on, the first real nerves had started. She felt petrified. She couldn't go on. She was going to be sick, she was sure.

On stage, she could hear Frank's words as his scene came to a close, and next to her, Mr Partleton, who was playing Laertes, patted her arm.

'Almost time, Miss Brite. How are you feeling?'

'Oh, Mr Partleton – I… I don't think I can do it – I can't remember what I do, or what I say. I think I may be ill…!'

He patted her arm again.

'It will be all right, my dear. Take a deep breath.'

Isobel gulped in air, and held her breath.

'Now let it out, slowly.'

Why was it so difficult? But she tried to let her breath go slowly, though she wanted to scream and run away.

Henry Hartley came off the stage, leaving Frank on stage alone, and stood by Isobel.

'Are you all right, my dear?'

'I'm terrified, Mr Hartley – I can't do it…'

'Yes you can, Miss Brite. Just remember the rehearsals. Don't worry – we all feel like this our first time.'

'But…'

It was too late to run away now. Frank's lines came to an end, and he left the stage on the other side.

Mr Partleton gave her elbow a little squeeze and he led her onto the centre of the stage.

On her left the space of the auditorium pulled away from her. But now, instead of the wide open space she had become used to, she felt its fullness – a moving, breathing mass of people. They were not quiet: there had been a constant murmering as they commented on the action between themselves, and ate oranges and cracked nuts –

but as she arrived on stage there were some audible
'Hush's and they became very quiet. She could feel every
eye upon her: they knew this was her debut, and they were
waiting to see whether this new actress was worth
listening to.

It was a challenge. A spark of defiance lit inside her.

Mr Partleton turned and took her hands.

'*My necessaries are embarked; farewell: And, sister, as
the winds give benefit And convey is assistant, do not
sleep, But let me hear from you.*'

All at once the fear and sickness left her. She had done
this many times in rehearsals. She remembered the
warmth and love she must feel for her departing brother,
and how she had thought of Cassie during rehearsals, and
those feelings now, quite naturally, came through her
words:

'*Do you doubt that?*'

Her words came clear and strong, and there was almost a
perceptible sigh from the audience. She felt their
approval, and relaxed into the scene.

She had begun.

At last, the final scene was over. The curtain fell, the
dead rose from the stage and gathered for the curtain call.
The curtain rose, the audience applauded – and then, her
heart beating with a mixture of excitement, joy and
apprehension, Isobel was led onto the stage by Henry
Jackman himself to take a solitary bow as the new actress.
Would they like her? Would they be indifferent? Worse –
would they boo her off the stage? She didn't think the
latter would be the case – but you never knew... she had
already been told that audiences could be unpredictable...

She need not have worried.

As she entered onto the stage, there was a kind of
eruption from the audience area as they clapped, shouted
and cheered their approval. All of them were standing.

Isobel took centre stage, and offered a much-practised, low curtsey. As she paused at the bottom of her curtsey, she listened to the roar and the applause and the cheers and smiled to herself. She had never felt so happy in all her life. This was where she was meant to be: the centre of attention, a star! They loved her – Isobel Brite, a shoemaker's daughter! What would her stepmother say if she saw her now? She could barely stop herself from laughing as she rose graciously and stepped back to join the rest of the cast, and allow Frank to take his bow as leading man.

And then, unrehearsed, Frank turned and offered her his hand, and, feeling that she had reached the very peak of happiness, she took his hand and he brought her forward again as the crowd exploded again into joyful approval.

Off stage, she felt she was walking two feet off the ground as other members of the cast (but not all) congratulated her. Henry Hartley shook her by the hand and said, 'Very well done, Miss Brite, well done indeed!' and Caroline Hartley hugged her and told her she was a delight.

As for Frank, after he had led her off the stage, he had whispered privately in her ear: 'You are beautiful; the night is yours; you have captivated the audience, and others...' and he had left her to be surrounded by the rest of the cast, while his words hung in her ears, so that all she could hear as they all spoke to her giving her their congratulations, was 'you have captivated the audience, and others, and others, and others...'

What did he mean? Who did he mean? Surely, he did not just mean the rest of the cast, or did he? Or did he mean *one* other person? Did he mean himself, or was she just being hopeful?

For the rest of the evening, she felt over-excited and euphoric. Henry Jackman suggested that she went to bed early for there was work to be done the next day and he was calling a meeting first thing in the morning.

But Isobel found that sleep was impossible. Her state of excitement continued and she did not want to sleep, she wanted to dance and sing and laugh. All night she heard Frank whispering: 'you have captivated the audience, and others…', she heard the congratulations of Henry and Caroline, the cheers of the audience; she saw the gas lights in front of her, and the looks on the faces of the nearest onlookers and other members of the cast as she sang Ophelia's 'mad' song. The normally raucous audience had become hushed. She was sure there had been tears in Caroline's eyes.

But not everything had been wonderful. There was another image that kept coming back to her. Sophia, Caroline's sister, had been watching from the wings. She had been deemed not well enough to take over the part of Ophelia, but for some reason Isobel had an idea that she perhaps had not been thought good enough to play the part.

Tonight, she had seen Sophia as she came off the stage, and her face was a picture of hatred.

It had not worried her, because everything else was just so delightful and she had not thought about it until now.

Isobel lay in her bed and wondered why Sophia had taken such a dislike to her. Was it because she had taken over the part she had wanted, or was it something more than that? Was she jealous of her friendship with Caroline? Or was there some other reason…?

Isobel decided not to think about it. Life was far too good to be spoiled by the petty feelings of someone else. Besides, there was Frank to think about…

CHAPTER 6

Over the next few weeks Isobel felt as though she was caught up in a whirlwind. Jackman was pleased enough with her work to offer her a formal contract, and she officially became a member of the Jackman Theatre Company, which filled her with enormous happiness.

They played for two weeks at Northampton, and then they moved to Aylesbury; a two-day journey which left Isobel again with blistered feet. This was unfortunate because she was being given dancing lessons as well as singing lessons by various members of the company, and her feet were so sore for several days that they would bleed. Caroline showed her how to mix up a remedy of candle tallow and spirits to rub into her feet every night, and it did help a little, but as each day wore on it would get worse again until she was in agony. Yet, she was determined not to complain or show weakness. She was intelligent enough to realise that her success in Northampton was not enough to prove to the rest of the company that she could cope with this new kind of life. She wanted them all to see that she may be a shoemaker's daughter, but she was quite capable of leading an actor's life too. If she was to make a success of being an actress she would need to win over her fellow players, and it would not do to cry off rehearsals for a few blisters. She would have been laughed at. She wanted to prove herself: to Frank because she wanted his admiration; to Henry and Caroline because they were so kind, to Henry Jackman because she wanted to play more parts, and the rest of the company so they would accept her as one of them. But most of all, she wanted to prove to herself that she could do it, that she hadn't left her home and her family for nothing.

So, she threw herself into work with a kind of wild passion. They were rehearsing a new play, called *The*

Ocean of Life in which she was to play the part of the spoilt and scheming Miss Jemima Jenkinson. When they were not rehearsing her scenes, she would practise her dance steps in the wings, or practise a song for the intervals. Henry Jackman had also given her the part of Kate in *The Taming of the Shrew* to read as he was planning on getting this up for the next summer season and he wanted to see if she was up to this part.

She rehearsed all day, and performed with all the energy she had at night, and returned to her room at the inn tired and aching, but with a feeling of fulfilment that she had never experienced in her life. She fell asleep almost as soon as she had lain down and slept more soundly than she could remember, until each morning the knock on her door told her it was time to rise to face another day of gruelling rehearsal and performance.

It was lovely to play a new part, and the character of Jemima Jenkinson was so different to Ophelia. There was a completely different way of playing such a character, with comic and loud asides to the audience and she learned to use some of her own personality to enrich the part, and developed a certain toss of her head that became an integral part of the character and which made the other actors watching howl with laughter.

Furthermore, she was learning a comic duet with Henry Hartley which was enormous fun, if only Mr Hartley did not make her laugh so much that she could not sing her part.

And Frank was never far away. If he was not in the scene she was rehearsing, he was watching her from the auditorium; if she was having singing lessons in a room at the inn, she would find him at the bar when she finished; if she was practising a dance step in the wings, she would look up to see his shadowy figure in a dark corner.

At Aylesbury, she received a letter from her sister, sent

on from the post box number she had supplied her with.

My dearest Izzie

It has taken me several days between receiving your last and starting to write this letter, for I have hardly known how to begin or what to say. Indeed, Mama has forbidden me to write, so this will be necessarily brief.

I am sure it will not be news to you that our mother and father were very shocked and dismayed - I should even say hurt - by your disappearance and your decision to join the theatre. And, Izzie, I too was greatly saddened to lose you.

Mama refuses to hear your name mentioned and does not appear to acknowledge your existence, but perhaps, in time, she may soften.

As for father, Izzie I am very anxious for him. He misses you very badly, but he is also very worried about the fall in trade we are experiencing in Daventry. I do hope that this is temporary, but father seems to think the worse. I am glad to say, however, that he did smile when he read the letter from Mr. Jackman, and I think that secretly he was quite proud to hear you are doing well. All the same, he looks very sad much of the time, and your departure has troubled him, I am sure.

Dearest Izzie, I still do hope that you have made the right decision. Your last letter did sound very happy, and it is clear that you have a talent for the theatre, but I really do not know what to think. Please be careful. I wake at night and think of you walking from town to town and without the protection of your family. I wish I could come to see you, but you must understand how impossible that is.

Mama will be returning from the market soon, so I must take this letter to the post immediately.

Your loving sister,
Cassandra

Isobel felt a pang of remorse as she read Izzie's words concerning her father, but there was nothing to be done, especially if Mama had virtually disowned her.

Not that I am hers to disown anyway, she thought.

No doubt at some point in the future the theatre company would return to Daventry or Northampton, and perhaps she would be able to arrange to see her father and Cassandra then. She did not care about seeing her stepmother.

From Aylesbury, they travelled to Buckingham, where they opened *The Ocean of Life* to an appreciative audience, and Isobel had her first benefit performance. Each actor in the company had their own benefit night from time to time, and it meant that they received all the profits from that night's performance, in return for work put in to promoting it. The days leading up to her benefit night saw Isobel walking from house to house, putting leaflets through doors, putting up playbills and selling tickets in the town square. It was hard and rather tedious work, but when she saw how much she had earned in profits, she was delighted, and she immediately went out and bought a new bonnet.

By the time they had played at Uxbridge and Banbury, Isobel's feet had toughened up and she no longer walked or danced in agony.

At Christmas they put on a pantomime, *Jack and the Beanstalk*, and the audiences were loud and sometimes unruly. In many places, it was almost as if the audience was not interested in seeing what was happening on stage as long as they had a warm place to spend the evening, talk and laugh with their friends, eating and drinking as merrily as if they were at home or at the pub. On nights like these it was hard work to get their attention, but Jackman would never pander to the growing trend for the spectacular such as bringing live animals on stage or other such gimmicks, as other managers sometimes did. He believed that if you could not grab the attention of an audience with your talent, then you had no business on the stage in the first place.

With her natural charisma, striking red hair and the intensity of her acting style, Jackman saw very well that Isobel was often able to quieten an audience by her presence where sometimes his own daughters could not.

Rehearsals were long and arduous, and several members of the company grumbled about the cold conditions they had to work in. There was a lot of sneezing and red noses; the children caught colds and spread them round the company, and Isobel began to realise that life in the theatre was tougher than she had even imagined on that day in August when she had been mortified at the thought of walking from Daventry to Northampton. It seemed such an easy thing now, looking back. Yet, she had no regrets. The joy of performing and the thrill of the applause were worth all the hard work, sore throats, sore feet and cold, shivering rehearsal mornings.

On a rare bright and crisp morning in January, Henry Hartley and his wife took themselves for a walk along the canal in Banbury. The company was playing at the Davenport Theatre, a venue Jackman leased for the winter every two years.

'Well, my love,' said Henry, taking his wife's arm in his, 'tell me what you think of our new starlet.'

'Oh, dear Isobel. She is a natural actress. I sometimes find it hard to believe that she has never been on the stage before, yet, there is a naivety and rawness about her work which is both alarming and charming at the same time. I think that is what is so appealing to an audience; they feel ever so slightly *unsafe* when she is on the stage, yet she never fails to deliver. She's exciting and engaging. I shall never forget the first time she played the mad scene in

Hamlet; I really believed her. Of course, she has lots to learn: her voice needs to develop; it can still sound a bit thin in the larger houses, and her delivery of comedy is sometimes a little contrived, but I think she will do.'

Henry, who had been nodding all the way through her speech, gave her arm a squeeze.

'I agree with everything you say, my dearest, and I am glad that you have taken her under your wing. That naivety of hers is natural and very *un*contrived, though I believe she would like us to think her sophisticated, as do most girls of her age who have not spent their lives in the theatre!'

'You are so right. She does need someone to look after her, and sadly some of my sisters feel put out by her presence and have been rather unfriendly. A guest star from London is one thing, but a shoemaker's daughter without any theatrical experience is a little difficult for some of them to swallow. I would be very distressed if she became the victim of jealousy or revenge.'

'Or worse...' said Henry, thoughtfully.

Caroline looked up at her husband.

'You think she really is in danger? Do you think his intentions are so bad? He always seems so charming, and quite a gentleman.'

'Oh Caroline, I sometimes think you are half infatuated with him yourself! He is a good actor, both on and off the stage! The man is a complete scoundrel. My love, I hate to worry you, but have you not noticed that his attentions were lately directed at your Sophia, until Miss Brite arrived last August? Then he dropped her like a dog drops a stick for a bone...'

Caroline stopped walking and her arm slipped out of her husband's.

'Henry! Really, you cannot mean... Our Mr Douglas, in love with Sophia!'

'Now you are showing your own naivety, my dear. I do

not think love had anything to do with it.'

'Oh, but…! It cannot be! How could this happen without my knowing? Why, Sophia has never said anything to me! And, furthermore, if you really believe such a thing, why have you never said anything to me? Sophia is my sister; she may be spoilt and silly, but I do love her, and I would have thought…'

'My dear, I did not want to worry you, and I was not that sure. But I am now. Ever since Miss Brite arrived with her innocent green eyes and voluptuous red hair, Frank has only had eyes for her while he is in the theatre, and Sophia is looking daggers at her and is more out of countenance and disgruntled-looking than ever before. Surely you must have noticed that?'

'Yes, I have. But I put it down to the fact that Isobel is a newcomer and has taken parts that Sophia had hoped to play. Not that she would have been given them, anyway, but I am sure she does not see it that way.'

'That is true. But I do believe it is more than that. Sophia may not be as naïve as Isobel, she has been brought up in the theatre, after all, but no young woman likes to be rejected by a suitor, however disreputable his intentions might be. I have seen the way she looks at Frank, and it is not a mere admiration of his acting ability.'

They stopped on the bridge and leaned on the parapet watching three moorhens paddle past beneath them.

'Am I right in thinking that Frank has made some visits back to Northampton lately?'

'Yes, and I believe that a lady is in the case there too. I've said it before, but the man is a complete scoundrel, and if Jackman found out he would not be happy.'

They were silent for a while.

'Do you think I should speak to Sophia?' asked Caroline.

'It may be as well to let it pass as far as Sophia is

concerned. I do not think she is in any danger of Mr Douglas's attentions any more, and she may not appreciate you showing any knowledge of such a thing.'

'No, she is not easy to talk to at the best of times.'

'It will probably be best just to keep an eye on her. I think the one we have to be more vigilant about is Isobel. I know her parents to some degree; I have had boots made by her father, and very good ones too. They are respectable people, and I feel a responsibility towards them. But I have a feeling that talking to her would be as equally an unfortunate a move as talking to Sophia.'

Caroline laughed. She linked her arm in his and they moved on.

'Oh, Henry, you are a very good judge of character. It has just occurred to me that, hate each other though they do, their characters are very much alike!'

Henry chuckled too, but he had a frown on his face.

'Very true, but that leaves us with the problem of what should we do about the honour of Miss Brite?'

'There are some within the company that would probably advocate doing nothing; that she needs to be taught a lesson about the kind of life some actresses lead.'

'…and are you of the same opinion?'

'Henry, you should know me better than that. Although, in many ways she will never be really a part of the theatre until she fully understands the dangers and choices facing a woman in the business. But if Mr Douglas is the rake that you seem to think he is, and already has a romantic interest in Northampton, then we should certainly do our best to prevent her going down that route. I would not mind so much if we knew he was somebody more trustworthy. I shall heed your advice, my dear, and take on the office of chaperone, if I can do so discretely and without her realising it. It could be my most challenging role.'

'I am sure you will rise to the challenge, as you always

63

do in all your roles, dear heart.'

Isobel hurriedly put on a thick pelisse and the blue bonnet she had bought with her benefit earnings, trimmed with feathers. It was so lovely to be able to buy her own clothes with her own earned money, and not have things bought for her. Her benefit night had earned her an extra £2 of income, and wearing her new bonnet, bought with those proceeds, always filled her with the most exquisite feeling of autonomy and independence. Why didn't more women join the theatre if this was the kind of life you could lead? She had decided that most women, content to be owned and ordered around first by their fathers, and then by their husbands, were just plain stupid. In her new life, she was able to choose everything from the clothes she wore and the food she ate, to the man she wanted…

Pinching her cheeks quickly and applying a little rouge to her lips, she raced down the steps from the dressing room to the door of the theatre.

She had seen Frank go out this way a few minutes ago, and she had a good idea of where he was going. He would be on his way to his favourite chop-house in Banbury, and if she was very quick she might be able to catch him up and spend a few minutes alone with him before anyone else.

She knew Frank was interested in her. It was impossible not to read the signs in her favour. He was always where she was, he watched her as much as he was able, and he was so much more attentive to her than he was to any other of the female members of the company. For a young girl who had been brought up in a small town under the strict protection of her stepmother, this was exhilarating and extremely exciting. In her days working for her father, she had never been allowed very near any of the young men that came into the shop. Her father would always come to deal with customers himself, and if anyone had ever shown signs of attention outside, during visits to church or social visits, her stepmother would always speak for her or even lead her away if the man was deemed 'undesirable' in any way.

Now, she had the chance to accept the attention of someone on her own terms. And she would play things her way this time.

But it was not so easy, even now, in this new-found freedom. The company stuck together much of the time, and there never seemed to be ever a time when she found herself alone with Frank.

So, she thought, if it will not happen naturally, I shall have to make it happen. Since having that thought, she had looked out for opportunities to 'accidentally' find herself alone with him, and this morning had presented just such an opportunity. She had seen Frank head for the outer door, just as she had broken from her own rehearsals. He had caught her eye as he went, raising an eyebrow, and she was quite sure that the look on his face had said 'follow me'.

Which was why she was now rushing through the same door.

But just as the door swung shut, she heard a voice calling her name from within.

'Isobel! Oh, wait for me!'

Caroline Hartley. Isobel rolled her eyes heavenwards and inwardly swore an oath that she had learned only recently and would never have dared say out loud.

It wasn't that she did not like Caroline's company. She loved Caroline dearly, and she appreciated her friendship. She was the only one of the company, apart from Mr Hartley, who had been really kind to her.

But it was just too unfair that Caroline should choose this moment to want to speak to her. A similar thing had occurred a couple of times recently, to Isobel's frustration. But how could she be annoyed with her? It was very useful to have a female companion. She needed Caroline, and without her she would have felt isolated and out of place.

Isobel allowed the stage door to shut behind her. Perhaps, if she hurried, she could be gone before Caroline caught up with her, and later she could pretend that she had never heard Caroline call her.

She walked as fast as she could to the corner of the street, but just as she turned the corner, she heard Caroline's voice, and knew that she had hesitated for a second too long.

'Isobel! Oh, I'm so glad I've caught you!' said Caroline as she joined her, 'Henry is going to practise his hornpipe and I am left with an hour with nothing to do. Please let me join you. It is, after all, not quite the thing to dine alone. Oh, I *do* like your bonnet!'

Isobel took Caroline's hand and kissed her on the cheek.

'It's my benefit bonnet! No, of course you are quite right. It was very rude of me to rush off like that, but really I am so hungry I could eat a horse, and I just did not stop to think.'

'Where are you off to?'

'Well, I had a sudden fancy for a lamb chop. What do you say to Mrs Brown's Chop House?'

'In such a nice bonnet?'

'Oh, well, I was in such a hurry it was the first one that came to hand. Oh, come on Caroline, I am *so* hungry I will faint. In fact, I nearly did just now doing those pirouettes.'

Caroline took her arm.

'Oh, my dear. Come then, let us go to Mrs Brown's. I think a lamb chop sounds very good!'

They linked arms and walked at a pace down the road, their skirts swaying in unison, until they reached Mrs Brown's.

Through the small, mullioned windows Isobel could see

Frank sitting at a table by the fire, already with a tankard by his side. It looked warm and cosy inside. Just right for a triste. What a shame she was not alone.

Well, at least she would get to see him, and perhaps there might be a moment they could somehow steal together…

The bell tinkled as they opened the shop door and Frank looked up. His eyes met Isobel's and a little smile played on his face. Then he looked past her and registered the fact that Isobel was not alone.

Without a moment's hesitation, his expression turned to one of social delight. Isobel thought that no-one would ever have guessed that he might be disappointed at Caroline's presence. His acting talent was so sublime.

'Why, Miss Brite, and Mrs Hartley!', he cried, standing up immediately, 'How very delightful! Please do come and share my table with me. It would be a very great pleasure to share my dinner with such lovely and charming company.'

Caroline, for the first time since she had known Frank Douglas, felt a little shiver of distaste run down her spine. Was this just because her husband had suggested things to her, or was Frank really a sham? Had there been a brief moment of eye-contact between the two of them before Frank realised she was here too?

Isobel was also doing her best to dissemble. The feathers in her bonnet trembled in flirtatious animation as she spoke.

'Mr Douglas! Well, this is a surprise! I had thought you were dining with the Partletons. How very pleasant for us that you are not.'

Frank bowed and pulled out two chairs for them.

Caroline bowed her head and greeted him with a short 'Mr Douglas' as she took her seat. Her thoughts were racing.

There was no reason for Isobel to expect Frank to be

dining with the Partletons. I am sure she knows they are visiting family today. No, it is quite obvious that she expected him to be here, and it explains the bonnet. Yet, I am surprised she did not change venues when she met me; did they have a prior arrangement, I wonder, or is she really so naïve that she does not think I will notice? Or doesn't she care?

It was three quarters of an hour later that the three of them returned together to the theatre. Caroline, who had linked arms with Isobel and placed herself between her and Frank, noticed only too well how flushed Isobel was looking, and how Frank regarded her with an almost hungry look which alarmed Caroline considerably. How was it that she had not noticed what was going on before? Henry had been right. Isobel must be protected at all costs.

Later, in her room at the Reindeer Inn, Isobel took out from the pocket in her pelisse, the small, folded piece of paper that Frank had managed to pass to her at luncheon, and read it for the tenth time that day. It was a note, hastily scribbled no doubt when Frank had gone to find Mrs Brown to pay his and their bills:
Tomorrow night. 10 o'clock pm. The Unicorn.
Isobel put it under her pillow and sighed happily.

CHAPTER 7

Isobel could not concentrate all day. In rehearsals she forgot her lines and did not enter when she was meant to. Mr Jackman became increasingly impatient with her, finally exclaiming, 'Miss Brite! We are not here for your pleasure and it is not your prerogative to arrive on stage when you please and speak your lines as if you were still a shoemaker's daughter!'

A sudden hush filled the stage, the wings and the auditorium, and everyone turned to look at Isobel.

Isobel stood stunned, as if she had been slapped in the face. If she had not been feeling so ecstatically elated about the coming evening, she would probably have burst into tears and run off the stage. All the same, it was the very comment that she most dreaded, and it brought her to her senses quicker than a whiff of smelling salts.

If she was to be thought of as a professional, she could not allow her personal feelings to interfere with her stage work. This was dangerous ground. No matter how difficult, she would have to make sure that she put her emotions to one side.

Knowing that everyone was waiting to see how she would react, she stood her ground and dissembled her feelings of distress. She knew they were expecting a storm, but she would not give them one.

As calmly as she could bring herself to speak, she said, 'I am very sorry, Mr Jackman. I do confess that my concentration seems a little lower than my professionalism would normally allow. Please forgive me, I will endeavour to work harder from now on.'

It was quite possibly the most difficult piece of acting she had done so far.

Mr Jackman bowed slightly.

'Well then, let us take it from the top…'

The atmosphere relaxed, and Isobel focused her mind on

the job in hand.

By the end of rehearsals, she felt drained and exhausted, but the thought of seeing Frank later kept her going into the evening's performance.

She was only in the first half of the programme, so she was able to slip out of the theatre and to her small inn room for a few moments of preparation and thought.

She lay on her bed and took some deep breaths, just as she had been taught to do before going on stage.

Frank was going to ask her to marry him.

That was the only reason she could think of that he would have asked her to meet him alone in such a way.

They had very rarely had a chance to be alone together, but that was quite normal in any circumstances, and she was quite aware of his attention towards her. There could be no other explanation.

Jumping up, she looked in the mirror. It was a good thing that she was meeting him at night: candlelight much improved what she knew was a tired and pale complexion. Her sleepless night last night and the demands of the day had taken their toll.

She put on a salmon-pink gown that she knew would warm up her skin, and reached for her new bonnet.

When she looked in the mirror again, she would be an engaged woman!

She wrapped her pelisse around her, blew out the candle and stepped out into the night.

'Henry!' hissed Caroline, as he came off the stage.

'My dear, it was a good night tonight, don't you think? The weather has been kind to us this week and the audiences are venturing out. I do hope...'

'Oh, do be quiet Henry! This is important!'

Henry paid attention. It was not often that his wife spoke to him like this. She was generally calm and self-contained. Something must have happened.

Caroline took him by the arm and led him to a corner of the wings out of earshot of anybody else.

'Henry, I am very worried about Isobel. She is not in her room at the inn, and she has been very distracted all day. You must have noticed what happened in rehearsals earlier today. Both she and Frank are free tonight. I think she may be meeting him. What can we do?'

Henry frowned. After his observations of the past few months it was certainly possible, but perhaps they should not jump to any conclusions.

'Are you sure, my dear? Perhaps she has just gone for a walk.'

'Oh Henry, now you are being silly! What woman in her right mind would go out for a walk alone at this time of night? I am sure that something is up. She shot off after her last scene tonight. I spoke to her and she did not even notice me. She certainly had something on her mind.'

'Hm. Well, you certainly have changed your mind about our Mr Douglas. Perhaps we should be alerted. When I am dressed I will go over to the Unicorn on some pretence and see if he is there.'

'Oh, please hurry, Henry! I feel you were right about Frank now; I don't trust him. Isobel doesn't understand what he wants, I am sure. I don't think he is the marrying kind.'

'Well, we can only do our best. But I certainly cannot go out into the streets in this costume. I will have to take my call and then change. Don't worry, my pet, I am sure in the end whatever will be will be for the best.'

Caroline was not so sure that he was correct in this case, but there was nothing she could do except to wait and see what would happen.

Frank was waiting for her. Isobel was glad that he had

71

been thoughtful enough to meet her outside of the inn, it was not really very seemly for a woman to walk into an inn on her own, though goodness knows why. She would have walked in just the same, but it was nice to think that he was concerned about her reputation.

He took her hands as she joined him, and his hands were warm and firm. She took a deep breath, and laughed to cover up the nervousness she felt.

'Isobel Brite!' He said her name with relish, as though testing the name on his tongue for the very first time. He looked searchingly at her face in the dim streetlight, while she tried to look demurely down at the pavement. He drew her arm around his and led her into the inn.

They entered a candle-lit snug and sat opposite each other across a table stained with ale and wine.

Frank had already ordered a flagon of ale and two tankards.

'So, you came,' he said simply as he filled her tankard with foaming liquid.

'Of course,' she said, smiling at his doubt.

He met her eyes and then looked away with a slight laugh.

'Not every woman would.'

'Well, you may as well know, Mr Douglas, that I am not every woman.'

He laughed again, this time with spirit.

Oh, I can see that, Miss Brite. You certainly are not, indeed.'

It was going very well. How free she felt: free and grown up, sitting here in an inn with her young man. How shocked her stepmother would be if she knew, how she would go on about ruined reputations and how they were a *respectable* family and she would try to put the fear of God in her and talk about paths to ruin and the workhouse! Just because she was in an inn unchaperoned with a man, and she an actress. What on earth did any of it matter?

She was happy and free, unlike any of the women she knew back home, and why couldn't she do what she liked? What a romantic and exciting life she was now leading, just because she had thrown away those stupid rules that had no reason but to provide gossip for lonely and bitter old women?

'You are looking very pleased with yourself,' said Frank, 'what are you thinking about?'

'Oh, I was thinking how different my life is now, and how my stepmother would tell me off for sitting here with you!'

He looked at her through narrowed eyes.

'Isobel Brite, you really are a very wicked woman.'

She pouted, ever so slightly.

'Oh, you don't really think so, do you? I don't think I'm so wicked. And anyway, you are one to talk. Who was it who persuaded me to run away from the bosom of my family and join...' she put on a mock shocked expression, '...the theatre!'

Frank looked even more intensely at her, and gently laid his hand on hers as it lay on the table.

'As far as I can remember, my dear, you did not take much persuading.'

'Ah, well,' she replied, pretending not to notice the touch of his hand, 'you did so much to flatter me, Mr Douglas; how was a poor, innocent girl like me to have a chance against such charm?'

His fingers curled underneath her hand until he had hold of it tightly and lifted it off the table, pulling it slowly towards his mouth. But he stopped, and looked into her eyes above their joined hands.

'And now?' he said, 'how far is the innocent Miss Brite open for further persuasion?'

She dropped her eyes. Her heart had suddenly started to beat very fast. Was this the moment? Was he about to ask the question?

'I… you will have to explain yourself, Mr Douglas. I do not understand you.'

He took her hand in both of his and played with her fingers.

'Oh, I think you are toying with me, Miss Brite. Isobel. I think you know exactly what I mean. You know very well that I did not invite you here this evening just to share a tankard of ale.'

She blushed.

'Well… I…'

'The night is yet young.'

Not understanding this last comment, Isobel said nothing, but waited patiently. Why did he not just ask her? His manner was not one of a shy, inexperienced youth who did not know how to propose…

'Well, Isobel?'

'Well…?'

'Shall we…?'

His eyes shifted upwards in a gesture that was lost on Isobel.

Feeling that something was not going quite the way she had anticipated, Isobel decided to take action. It was hopeless waiting for the man to propose. She would have to take control of the situation.

She leaned towards him so that she could not be overheard; she did not mind people seeing them together, but a proposal of marriage should be a private affair.

'Mr Douglas, am I to take it… I mean, am I to believe… oh good heavens, Mr Douglas, are you asking me to marry you?'

He looked at her for a few moments as if he did not understand her. Then the word that she had spoken – that very private and wonderful word – seemed to sink into his consciousness. The word was repeated, soundlessly, on his lips. And then again, this time with a sound, a slightly hesitant, questioning whisper.

And then he leaned back and laughed.

Isobel felt the heat rush up to her cheeks, and turned slightly to see if anyone was watching them. A few heads had started to turn.

Frank was laughing; no, guffawing, now.

Isobel leaned towards him.

'Mr Douglas… please… people are watching…'

This seemed to make him laugh even louder.

'Marry you!' he cried, in a voice which Isobel was sure was echoing round the inn, and possibly out onto the street. She could not even bring herself to see how many people were now watching.

'Mr Douglas… Frank… please be quiet!'

At last, his laughter subsided to a few involuntary chuckles.

'Miss Brite, my dear Miss Brite. I owe you an apology.'

Her eyes lowered with anger and embarrassment, she answered, 'I think you do, Mr Douglas. Please explain yourself.'

But he was unable to. For just at that moment, they both became aware of a third person who was standing at the side of their table.

'Miss Brite,' said Henry Hartley, and then gave a slight nod of acknowledgement to Frank, 'Mr Douglas.'

Isobel looked up at Henry and saw that he was barely able to contain his feelings of contempt for the man sitting opposite her. He turned back to Isobel and offered her his hand.

'Caroline was worried about you. If you would care to join me, I will escort you back to your room.'

Isobel turned back to Frank, who was grinning at her.

'Your knight in shining armour has arrived, Miss Brite, to rescue you from the wicked rogue. Well, it has been an interesting evening I must say, but I see I will have to bid you a good night otherwise my friend Hartley here might throw down the gauntlet and it would never do for one of us to be wounded or killed. What would Mr Jackman do to replace us?' and he smiled widely at her, baring his white teeth, as if the whole thing were a good joke.

Isobel slowly got to her feet as the colour rose around her neck, her ears and her cheeks until she felt that her head would burst. Between Mr Hartley's arrival and Frank's sarcastic repost, the truth had dawned on her, as if she had been looking through coloured glass, and now the glass in those few minutes had broken all around her, and she was left staring at the garish truth. A roaring in her ears confused her senses.

Unable to look at either man, she placed her hand on Henry's outstretched arm, dimly aware that as she did so, Frank had got to his feet and was making a dramatic bow, still looking completely amused at the whole scene.

When they got out into the fresh, cold air, Isobel breathed it in gratefully, glad to be out of the way of the staring and mocking glances of the strangers in the inn.

Henry stopped for a moment and looked at her with concern.

'Are you all right, Miss Brite?'

Embarrassment was swiftly turning to irritation; knowing that she had made a complete fool of herself, she became defensive and cross.

'I am perfectly well, thank you,' she answered shortly without returning his look.

They turned and walked in silence down the street to their inn.

Isobel did not sleep that night. The scene in the Unicorn, with the staring faces of onlookers and the appearance of Henry Hartley, played over and over in her brain, intensifying her humiliation and embarrassment.

It had not been helped by Caroline and Henry, who had treated her with nothing but kindness and understanding, had not forced her to discuss her relations with Frank and had only been gentle in their communications with her. Caroline had fussed a little about Isobel's well-being, until a sharp look from Henry had silenced her. Yet, all this only sharpened Isobel's sense of self-ridicule and stupidity.

How un-sophisticated and naïve she had been, when all the while she had wanted to prove herself the opposite.

She turned over in her bed, trying to put the memories of the night out of her head. But then she started thinking about the last few months and her interactions with Frank. What did he think of her now, after she had led him on, flirting and making him think…

She turned over again, but only to start thinking about the rest of the company. She thought now of Sophia and the way she looked at her. Was this the reason why she gave her such hateful looks? Was she assumed to be… Isobel could not bring herself to form the word that might be used to describe such a woman as she might be seen to be. Did the rest of the company know how she behaved with Frank? Did they think she…? Did Mr Jackman think…? No. He always said that he ran 'a respectable company'. He would not tolerate that kind of behaviour.

Twisting to try to find a comfortable position, her thoughts irrevocably turned to Frank. Still, his smile, his eyes and his sensuous mouth excited her. Strange how the events of the night had done nothing to quell her attraction towards him. Should she not dismiss him, refuse to talk to him, behave like a wronged woman? She imagined how this would only make him smile or laugh with amusement, as if he could see deeper inside her to something else, something she did not even recognise herself.

Throwing the bedclothes off her, she sat up, rubbing her eyes and trying to hold back the thoughts that now were beginning to trickle into her consciousness.

Out of the blue, she heard her stepmother's voice from that night she had first been introduced to the delights of

the theatre: 'nothing but a den of sin and corruption...'
and then, 'I seriously doubt whether any *decent* young
man would take you.'

Had her stepmother been right? And even if she was
right, did Isobel want to give in to the humiliation that
would entail; to go home with her tail between her legs,
having failed to prove that she could look after herself,
having fallen prey to the first man that threatened to ruin
her?

Isobel sat straight up in her bed.

She was damned if she would.

Yet, as she sank back under the covers, questions arose
in her mind that demanded uncomfortable answers.

Who, then, am I to be?

Am I to be the worst kind of actress, the kind that causes
people to joke and sneer behind cupped hands. If so, how
much does it really matter?

Or shall I be pure and virtuous, unobtainable and aloof to
all suitors, including Frank?

She saw clearly that, as an actress, this was her choice.
Both choices had their attractions, and both had less
appealing consequences. If the former, she could live
fully the exciting, sophisticated life that had attracted her
to the acting world in the first place. She could be with
Frank.

She giggled to herself suddenly, for the first time
without feelings of embarrassment at this idea.

However, she would also let herself open to gossip,
jealousy, and perhaps even the disapproval of Jackman.

If she chose the latter, she would gain respect, perhaps,
but would her life be half as fun?

She pulled the covers over her face, grinning to herself
in a way that Frank would understand.

She would not decide now. She would sleep on it.

Eventually, she fell into a restless slumber, her dreams
feverishly revolving around Frank's smile, and Henry

Jackman's disapproving frown, while his words echoed in her head: 'this is a respectable company… a *respectable* company…'

CHAPTER 8

Daventry
April 3rd

My dearest sister

I am writing this quick note to give you two pieces of news, one bad, the other much better. I write with haste so that I do not miss the post and I do not know how long this will take to reach you.

The bad news first.

Father is ill. He has not been himself for some time – I think this is partly due to the loss of business that started to become apparent ever since the trains started and people don't stop here any more. The coaches run, but every week there are fewer people on them and so all the businesses here are suffering. But Doctor Meadows also says that his heart is weak and he must not get over-worried or work too hard.

Dear Isobel, I think it would be such a tonic for him to see you. I know Mama would not like it but she does not know I am writing this, and I am so worried about father. Please – if you can – try to come home, even if it is just for a while. I too would dearly love to see you. I miss you so much.

Onto better things.

Izzie – what do you think? I am to be married! Do you remember John Duncan, who used to pass through Daventry on business from London and always came into the shop for boot repairs? Well, he was here in March and he came to tell us that it would be the last time as he would be taking the train next time (like everyone else!) but he stopped for a while here, and we met at church (Izzie – do you ever manage to get to church??) every Sunday and we talked so much, and he is such a good man, and then he asked me to marry him last Wednesday! Mother and Father are very pleased, except Mama is worried about having fewer of us to work in the shop than before – but Papa thinks it won't matter so much with business being so slow. Of course, it means that I will be going to live in London, which is rather frightening, but it won't be until autumn so perhaps I will be used to the idea by then.

Oh Isobel – I do hope that you will be able to come home soon – my wedding is in September. I am sure Mama could not begrudge you being here for that. But I think you should come home sooner – for father.

With all my love and blessings.
Cassie

Isobel folded up the letter slowly with a mixture of feelings, most of them disturbing, and put it in her pocket.

Cassie to be married! Such an event had never really occurred to her. It was always herself that she and her sister had discussed concerning romance or marriage. Isobel was to be adored and overwhelmed with suitors. She had always, if she had thought about it at all, assumed that Cassie would stay at home, at least until she, Isobel, was married and settled.

She realised she no longer counted since she had chosen to leave home in such a way. Cassie was the elder sister now.

She told herself she was pleased for Cassie; of course, she was. Yet, she found it hard. Cassie was to be married and to go and live in London. Cassie, who was of average looks, wouldn't say boo to a goose and had no sense of adventure, had had a proposal of marriage, while she, Isobel, beautiful and outgoing, had just been rejected… well, in marriage anyway. Cassie was going to London, a place of light, night life and the best theatre in the world, where she would hardly appreciate the benefits, while Isobel was treading the boards in the provinces. It just didn't seem fair.

The fact of her father being ill was also disturbing, but Isobel did not set too much store on Cassie's fears. She was always worried about something, and Isobel was sure that father could not be ill enough to warrant her rushing home. It was impossible for her to go home now anyway. They had just arrived at Woburn Abbey Theatre and were busy with rehearsing the next Shakespeare for the summer season: *The Taming of the Shrew*, with Isobel playing Katherina and Frank to play Petruchio. How very gratifying it was to play the shrew opposite Frank right now! In fact, their stage relationship spilled over into their every day relationship, and made each day very interesting indeed.

Isobel had decided to be quite cross with Frank after the events of Bedford. At least, that was the impression that she wanted to give him; that she was not a woman to be toyed with, and if he thought that she was that kind of woman, then he could look elsewhere.

Secretly, and almost afraid to admit it to herself, she was waiting for his next move. For she knew without a doubt that there would be one. And then she might, just might, decide which way she was going to go.

The company was particularly busy right now because Frances Partleton was expecting another child and so was unable to work or perform, although she spent a lot of time sitting and repairing or making costumes. Frances was just about Isobel's age, and over the eight months that Isobel had now been with the company, they had formed a light-hearted friendship. At first, they had been very wary of each other, with Frances being resentful at Isobel after taking the role of Ophelia from her, and worried that she would take other parts that should have been for her, but Henry Jackman was by no means a stupid man, and he was not going to let his own daughter be superseded by the newcomer. Frances had been given several important roles to play, including one at first that meant she could spend the whole time sitting down while her ankle was till in plaster. She had also become quite a celebrity among the audiences of Aylesbury and Banbury by coming onto the stage on crutches to sing 'The Sailor's Return' which brought the house down on several occasions.

Isobel was still very friendly with Caroline and Henry, but they were several years older than her and their relationship was more parental towards her. With Frances she could giggle in corners and talk about bonnets and lace trimmings. She also had gained favour with Frances by helping her with the baby from time to time, having had plenty of experience of looking after her own half brothers and sisters. Frances also told her about the company, how her father, the nephew of the eminent Irish playwright, Isaac Jackman, had become an actor manager at the age of nineteen, and had had many interesting and well-known actors as guest actors in the company, including the great comedian, Henry Compton. She told her how proud her father was of his company, how professional and business-like he was, that he would never take unlicensed premises or do anything even a little outside of the law.

Jackman's other daughters, Eliza Fenton (the eldest), Sophia, Harriet (aged 14) and Louisa (aged 12) were friendly (except for Sophia, who refused to have much to do with her), but with a detached coolness, as if they wanted to remind her that she did not really belong. She was not one of the family.

There were also two sons of Henry Jackman's in the company: Henry, who was a brilliant musician and arranged many of the songs and musical interludes, and Charles, who was nineteen, and had a slight infatuation for Isobel, which Isobel found both irritating and amusing, but had no intention of encouraging because she found him awkward and immature.

Frank, on the other hand, had behaved towards her with

impeccable politeness and grace. He had not, as she had
thought he might, mocked her, in either word or look, but
had only smiled or nodded with the kind of respect that
she felt had perhaps been wanting before. This was even
better than before. By pushing him away and telling him
that she was not interested in what he had to offer, his
behaviour towards her had changed, but she was sure his
feelings had not diminished.

In March they had had great excitement at Aylesbury
when it was discovered that Charles Dickens was in the
audience. A well-known theatre-lover, and one who had
trodden the boards himself, and put on his own
productions, he often attended the smaller provincial
shows, as well as those of the West End in London. At
Henry Hartley's suggestion, Isobel had been reading the
monthly instalments of his novel, *Nicholas Nickleby* with
much enjoyment. She had never read anything like it in
her life; it was so real and full of life, she felt that she
herself had embarked on the adventure with Nicholas. She
particularly loved the theatrical section, which made her
laugh out loud often, so much did she recognise the scenes
and characters.

So, when Dickens himself introduced himself to her
afterwards and commented on her delightful acting skills,
she was uncharacteristically robbed of speech and could
only bow her head and say, 'Thank you, Sir, you are very
kind.'

Just as she had anticipated, it was not long before Frank
made another move.

After the evening performances, it was the usual practice
for the unattached women of the company to walk to their
inn or boarding house accompanied by at least one
married couple. This was a rule laid down by Jackman,
who insisted on respectability within the company, and

who did not want any member of the public having an excuse to slur the reputation of his female actors. Isobel sometimes walked with Caroline and Henry, and sometimes with Frances and her husband. Quite often they would all walk together.

On this particular evening, Frances had retired early to rest, and George Partleton had set off to join her immediately after the curtain had fallen. Isobel had arranged to meet Caroline and Henry at the stage door. They had been delayed because a member of the audience had insisted on talking to Henry about a comic ballad he had written, which he thought Henry would like to buy, and was attempting to press the rather grubby copy into his hands. Henry, protesting that he did not have the authority, and that he should apply to Jackman, had some difficulty in getting rid of the gentleman, and by the time they set off from the theatre, everyone else was gone.

The evening was unusually warm, and just before they reached the inn, Isobel removed her gloves. They had got back to their lodgings and Isobel had said goodnight to the couple and gone to her room, when she discovered that she had dropped a glove. As it was her only pair, and the nights could still be cold, she was anxious to find it. It could not be far, so should be easy to find.

She stepped out of the door and started to retrace her steps. In the dim light of the oil lamps it was difficult to see, so she was proceeding very slowly with her head down in concentration, when a figure stepped out from the shadows and said:

'May I assist?'

Isobel screamed in alarm and fright.

Before her was the figure of a man in an evening cloak. He was holding something out towards her. She looked at it.

It was her glove.

She looked back at his face, and could just make out the

grinning face of Frank.

'Were you looking for this?'

Isobel, bristling back into composure, snatched the glove from his hand.

'Have you been following me, Mr Douglas?'

Frank shrugged.

'Is this the thanks you give me for retrieving your glove, Miss Brite? And you out in the dark on your own? I could have been anyone, lurking out here, waiting for some innocent young lady with evil intent, as you apparently were expecting judging from your alarm at my presence. Or, perhaps you knew it was me. Was it *my* presence that alarmed you so?'

The man was completely insufferable, mocking her like this. Isobel experienced the usual strange mixture of extreme annoyance and extreme excitement whenever Frank spoke to her like this. Nevertheless, he was not going to get round her that easily.

She turned to walk away, hoping that in the darkness he could still detect the contempt that she was attempting to show.

'Isobel, wait!'

Something in his voice brought her to a halt. He was no longer mocking, and there was no grin in his voice. Instead, there was a gruffness that suggested a sincerity that she had never heard before.

'Well?' she answered, without turning round.

He did not answer, and the silence that followed caused Isobel to wonder whether he had walked away.

She turned round, but he was still there and the intense way he was looking at her made her heart turn over. He seemed unable to speak, which was unlike him, and then he looked down at the ground as if uncertain for a moment. When he did speak his voice was different, low and unsure.

'Dear Isobel, I cannot get you out of my head. You have

done something to me that others have not done. I am without words, I know not what to do. You see, you have quite overthrown me. For the first time in my life I am at a loss.'

He laughed at himself and looked awkward, as if he did not know how to be himself.

Isobel was herself unable to speak. She was used to the ready quip, the witty repost, when dealing with Frank, but this sudden change disarmed her.

'What am I to say?' she eventually asked.

Frank took her hands with a sudden urgency.

'Tell me that I am yours, and you are mine. That is what I ask.'

Then suddenly she was in his arms and he was kissing her with a passion she had never imagined. All kinds of sensations were thrilling through her body, but when her knees started to weaken and she felt in danger of fainting, she pulled away, realising how easy it would be to be completely carried away. She mustn't lose the control that she seemed to have over Frank…

Breathlessly she said, 'That is the second time you have taken a liberty with me, Mr Douglas. Do not expect that it will happen a third time.'

Frank said nothing, but in a gesture that was more like the Frank she knew, he took off his hat and bowed low.

Then he was gone. He disappeared into the night as if he had never been there, and Isobel was left to shakenly find her way back to her digs.

It was April, and the glowering skies and chilly, blustery tantrums of March had given way to warm, bright days full of hurrying, unthreatening clouds. The long walks between theatres began to be a pleasure, and everybody in the company seemed cheerful and spent the travelling days with good humoured chatter and joking, with the occasional break out into uncontrollable laughter.

Isobel's heart was light as they walked the distance from Woburn to Uxbridge. Her feet no longer hurt after five miles, and she turned her face to the sun to enjoy its warmth. The birds were singing everywhere, reflecting Isobel's internal song, her delightful secret that Frank was in love with her.

She had known since that evening when he found her glove. His attitude towards her had changed subtly, but surely. He was gentler, less sure of himself around her. She looked at him now, strolling by the great horse, Falstaff, who pulled the cart just in front of her, and gazed longingly at that fair hair and the strong, muscular arm that occasionally he raised to stroke Falstaff's neck.

As if he felt her gaze, he turned suddenly, and their eyes met and lingered for a second or two before he grinned and turned away.

She was giving herself away, she knew. But dissembling was no use on a day like today. Her heart was all too eager to be known. Her eyes danced, she turned her face back to the sun, and skipped a little phrase from the jig she was learning for Northampton.

For eight months she had waited for Frank, but despite her impatience, she knew now that it was the right time. Thank goodness, she had not given in to his earlier plans, for he had not known her then, but now she had him in the palm of her hand. Oh, she knew the kind of man he was. She was no longer the naïve Isobel of eight months ago. She knew he had known other women. But what he had said that night, she knew was true. He felt something different for Isobel that he had never known before. She had caught the wayward player and it would not be too long now before she could call him hers in the eyes of the world. Perhaps she would get to be married before Cassie after all.

After a short term in Uxbridge they were back in

Northampton in June. It was good, yet somehow strange to be back, where, only eight months ago her acting life had begun. It felt more like eight years ago. She had been so green then, so inexperienced and scared. Now she returned as a real actress. She had proved herself in every way. The audiences loved her, and Jackman was pleased with her. There was still a slight unease with some of the others but what did it matter? She, Isobel, would not always need this company. One day, she would walk the stages of London. Then, how much more envious would they all be! And, not only that, but she would be married to Frank!

Her hopes seemed to be becoming reality when, on a day in early May, she received a note from Frank.

My dearest Isobel

If you would do me the great honour of meeting me at the Fish Inn (Fish Street) at nine o'clock this evening, I have something to say to you that I can put off no longer. Believe me, my offer this time is of a serious nature. I am

Yours in hope and anticipation

Frank

The tone of the note was clear. He had something to propose. And this time it was to be of a respectable nature.

With the joy of certainty in her heart, she left her room at the Shakespeare Inn with the confidence of a woman, remembering such similar circumstances only a few months ago when she had left for a similar assignation with the silliness of a young girl. How strange it was that she was only but a few months older. Smiling smugly at her own younger self, she stepped onto the street, intending to find a cab to transport her to Fish Street in the centre of town. After all, if she was to be treated with respect, then she must treat herself so too.

No cab prevailing at that moment, she decided to drop in to the theatre next door to enquire if any post had been left for her. She was hoping to hear from Cassie any day now since her reply to her last letter. The small anxiety that lay at the back of her mind in having no news from home since Cassie's last letter had been locked away in preference to her great, more agreeable, anticipation of Frank's proposal.

The doorman of the theatre shook his head at her enquiry.

'Sorry, Miss Brite. Nothing for you today.'

Isobel turned to leave, but was called back.

'Oh, Miss Brite. Would you by any chance be seeing Mr Douglas before tomorrow? There is a note for him here. The young lady said it was urgent. She wanted to see him, but he has not been in all afternoon. Not that there's any reason with all the stage being built today and no rehearsals, but, as I say, the lady was most insistent on seeing him and wrote a note to be passed on as soon as was possible. But perhaps you will not be seeing him...'

Isobel held out her hand.

'Give me the note. I believe I shall be seeing Mr Douglas this evening. Some of us are meeting for supper...'

'Oh, that is grand. I am sure the young lady in question will be most pleased. As I say, she *was* very eager to...'

'Yes, well, I shall be happy to pass it on' said Isobel, with a brief smile.

Outside, she hailed a carriage, and once inside, took a look at the folded note.

It was still just light enough to see the *Mr F. Douglas* written on the front with a feminine hand, and underscored twice, as if the writer wanted to be sure it fell into the right hands. The paper was of a cheap kind, not the kind of paper that a woman of means would use, though the hand itself was elegant enough.

Isobel stared at the name. Another woman had written to her Frank and dared to write his name. The temptation to open the note and read it was almost too much.

She turned it over. The word: *Private* had been written across the back in the same hand.

Private! What cheek! Who could be writing private notes to Frank?

She attempted to reason with herself.

Of course, there was nothing to fear. Frank had told her that he felt differently about her than he did any other woman. Even if someone from his past was writing to him, it could mean nothing to him. Anyway, it was probably – and Isobel smiled to herself – it was probably just some young lady who had come to see the play some months before and been so taken with Frank's handsome features and his acting talent that she had taken to writing letters of admiration. Why, he probably received notes like this all the time!

She would not open it. Frank and she were close enough now to share the fan letter, and perhaps have a laugh at the poor girl's expense. She would wait until Frank opened it and then it would be done with.

But wait. The doorman had said that the lady had wanted to see him and that it was very urgent. That sounded too forward for a young and innocent girl who just wanted to show her admiration.

Well, perhaps it was someone that Frank knew from the past. What of that? Frank was hers now.

There was no time to speculate any further. The carriage dropped her outside the Fish Inn, and there was Frank, waiting outside the Inn, and coming forward immediately to pay her fare before she could argue with him.

He helped her down from the cab and stood so that she could not avoid falling into his arms as she stepped down. He looked into her eyes without speaking and she smiled back at him. Nothing could spoil their happiness now.

The carriage moved away, breaking the spell, as Frank whisked Isobel out of the way of the wheels and led her into the small and dark inn and to a corner where they could sit at a table unseen.

He took both her hands with his immediately.

'My dearest Isobel. I cannot say how completely delighted I am that you have chosen to meet me again. I will call the barman in one moment, but first…'

'Wait,' interrupted Isobel. She wanted to get the matter of the letter out of the way before he proposed to her. She wanted nothing to spoil the moment. It was best out of the way first so that she could accept his offer of marriage with nothing unanswered between them. She released one hand and took the note from her purse.

'This came for you. It was at the stage door. A young lady, I believe,' she said, raising one eyebrow mockingly.

He took the note, giving her a sheepish grin. He looked at the writing on the front, and then opened it quickly, still smiling.

Isobel watched his face change as he read the note. His smile slowly disappeared, and she felt her hopes fade with it. His skin turned pale and he sat, seemingly stunned, for a few moments before he looked at Isobel again. She knew from his look that there would be no proposal tonight.

'I have to go' he said, standing abruptly.

'But Frank,' answered Isobel, standing as well, 'what is it? Can't you tell me? Is it bad news?'

For a moment, he stood and looked at her.

'We cannot meet again. I am sorry; I am so very sorry.' He put a hand up to a wisp of hair that had strayed from her bonnet and fingered it for a moment. And then suddenly he was gone.

Isobel sat down heavily on her chair. Things had changed so suddenly that she could hardly think for a moment; she could only look at the empty chair opposite her and feel numb.

Then her thoughts began to tumble into her head in a rush.

She should not have given him the note. She should have let him propose first. Why hadn't she read the note? Why did she had to have to give it to him at all? Now everything was spoilt. What could this young woman possibly have told him that he should so suddenly bring everything between them to a halt?

Isobel went cold.

No. It couldn't be.

How long ago were they in Northampton? Oh God. It almost nine months.

She felt sick.

Rising quickly, she ran to the pub door and out into the street, looking for a cab to hail. Rain had started to fall, and the cobbles were shining and the street was empty. She ran down to St Giles and looked up and down the street. The sudden rain had caused people out on the street to take all the available cabs. No matter. She would make her way back to the theatre herself. She was not going to wait; she had to find out now.

The rain was getting heavier, but she did not stop to shelter; she ran to the bottom of St Giles, past the great All Saints church where a few people were huddled in the doorway under the pillared canopy, and down Gold Street. Half walking, half running, her bonnet ruined, and her hair straggled around her ears, she reached the theatre door.

Sophia was standing talking to the doorman. As she turned and saw Isobel she let out a gasp of almost hysterical delight.

Isobel ignored her. She turned to the doorman.

'That young lady,' she gasped, trying to catch her breath, 'the lady who left a note for… for…'

'For Frank?' said Sophia. She was obviously enjoying herself. Isobel found herself itching to slap the stupid grin off her face.

Isobel continued to address herself to the doorman.

'Was she… I mean, what kind of… was she…'

The doorman coloured, and cleared his throat. Sophia giggled.

'I think I can answer your question, Miss Isobel. I happened to be standing right here when the young lady in question came to deliver her note. A young lady I have seen before.' As she said this, Sophia's voice became hard and bitter. 'Yes, I have seen her before, and others too. But that is no longer my concern.'

Isobel looked at her. The smile had returned to her face. 'It is obviously of your concern, so I will tell you.'

Isobel looked her firmly in the face.

'Well?'

'The lady was with child. Very heavily with child. Oh yes. She must have been quite desperate to have come out on a night like this. I would say that her time was due at any time. She must have been very desperate indeed.'

CHAPTER 9

The following morning, after a sleepless night, Isobel arrived at the theatre for rehearsals feeling sick and exhausted, but determined to pretend to all and sundry that nothing was amiss.

As she entered the stage where most of the company was gathered, she became aware that a lively buzz of conversation had abruptly stopped at her entrance. She caught Sophia's eye, who smirked and looked away, turning to whisper into Harriet's ear. The two girls giggled and turned away. She looked towards Frances, her friend, but could not make eye contact.

So, Sophia had no doubt been spreading the news throughout the company, not just about Frank, but about her own attachment. Isobel, with a brief and wild look about her realised that Frank was not present, and neither was Henry Jackman.

Caroline was coming towards her with her usual kind smile.

'Darling Isobel, we appear to be all in a muddle this morning. My father has had to go to an important meeting and we are left to our own devices. We must all practise our parts and we were just discussing what we should do. Perhaps,' she said, turning to Henry, 'as we now have our parts for *Nicholas Nickleby*, we should start to look at…'

'My dear,' interrupted her husband, 'it might be difficult without Nicholas himself, after all, he is in nearly all the scenes…'

'Perhaps Miss Brite should give us a rendition of her favourite song, "The Married Bachelor",' said Sophia, accompanied by explosions from Harriet.

'Girls! Please!' replied Caroline, her face drawn with anger.

She turned back to Isobel with a quick, nervous smile.

'Well, let's you and I go over our lines for tomorrow

night. We'll take a corner of the wings. Sophia, why do not you and Harriet get together a dance for next season?'

The rest of the cast had already begun to busy themselves with practising scenes or sword-fighting, and Henry also wandered off to speak to George Partleton.

Caroline drew Isobel by the arm to the wings, out of earshot of the others.

'My dear, you must not take any notice of my younger sisters…'

'I don't,' Isobel lied, 'why should I?'

She looked away from Caroline, feigning nonchalant interest at what was happening on the stage.

'Well, of course there is no need. But I do understand that you might be sensitive to comment at this moment.'

Isobel said nothing. She watched Sophia and Harriet practising jetés. Caroline took her hand.

'Dear Isobel, forgive me if I speak of things that are painful to you. I… we… Henry and I have been aware of a certain attachment of late…'

Isobel watched Partleton parrying with Henry Hartley. They were practising with walking sticks instead of the blunt swords that were stored in the wings. It looked very silly.

Caroline continued: '…and last night, Sophia told us what happened. I am afraid, my dear, that Frank has been careless with… with his… his… relations with our sex. Even with my own sister…'

Isobel turned sharply and looked straight at Caroline.

'You mean Sophia?'

'Yes, that is why…'

'…she hates me.'

'I am afraid so. You see, she has always been fond of Frank, ever since he joined the company. I'm afraid he never took her seriously, and she noticed the attention he has given to you.'

'I see,' said Isobel. There seemed little else to say.

After a pause, she said, 'well, shall we try our lines?'

But at that point the door to the auditorium burst open and Henry Jackman, his face the colour of a boiled ham, thundered across to the stage.

'We will rehearse tomorrow's performance. Unfortunately,' he said, his voice gruff with scarcely repressed rage, 'Mr Douglas is unable to be with us for the next few days; he has been released until next week. Mr Fenton will take his part, and the rest of us will have to fill in as necessary. Mr Fenton, your script!'

Here he handed the bemused looking Fenton a tattered looking roll of paper that was Frank's part.

Isobel could stand it no longer. She did not care what anyone thought or did. She could not wait, wondering, until Frank returned. She turned to the door off the stage, shaking off Caroline's hand as she tried to stop her.

'Isobel, you mustn't!' Caroline whispered.

'I don't care. I have to see him!' and she ran out towards the stage door, leaving Caroline to explain her absence to her irate father.

She saw him half way down Gold Street.

'Frank,' she shouted, not caring whether people turned and stared at her or not, 'Frank!'

He turned and saw her coming, but then turned and walked away from her. She caught up with him.

'Frank,' she gasped, catching his arm, 'where are you going?'

'To the Devil,' he muttered, determinedly, walking on and trying to shrug off her hand.

'Please stop and talk to me.'

He sighed and turned to her, then, looking up and down the street, he pulled her into the semi-privacy of a shop doorway.

'Go back to the theatre. If Jackman finds out you're with me, you will be in big trouble.'

Isobel stamped her foot.

'I will *not* go back to the theatre until you tell me what is happening.'

He leaned against the side of the shop's window. It was a small tobacconist's. The door opened, bringing with it a waft of tobacco smells, and a small, stout man came out. He looked suspiciously at the two staring at each other on either side of the shop porch, and walked briskly away, lifting his top hat in a gesture to Isobel as if he was not sure whether to be polite or keep his hand where his wallet was.

Isobel ignored him and waited until he was gone.

'Well?' she asked, her arms folded in front of her.

He grinned in his old sardonic way, but which now seemed a mockery of previous grins that used to have charm and fun behind them.

'You must congratulate me, my dear, for I am to be married. A young lady I met when we were in Northampton last.'

She felt her legs weaken beneath her.

'Married…? But, but…'

'It seems that it was going to happen one way or another. But unfortunately for you, or perhaps fortunately, somebody else has claimed my affections first.'

She could do nothing to stop the hot tears that were spilling down her face, and the tight, painful feeling in her chest.

'But you can't, you can't…!'

'I'm afraid I must. I do not have a choice. A young lady's honour is involved. If I do not do the honourable thing, her parents will disown her, and she would be for the workhouse, and…'

'…and what?'

'My friend Jackman has made it very clear to me where I stand. "I run a respectable company, Mr Douglas!"' he said, giving a good imitation of Henry Jackman's oft repeated phrase, 'to put it quite clearly, if I don't marry the lady in question, I will no longer have a job.'

'Oh, but Frank, it's so unfair. I mean, you love me! You love me! I know you have been, well, a… a…' she stopped and blushed, unable to think of an appropriate word.

'A bit of a rake?' he suggested.

'Well, yes, I suppose so. But, but, well, I forgive you. I don't care about the past. It can go hang! Why can't we go away together? I don't know, there must be some way…!'

Frank laughed, and then his face became serious.

'Dear Isobel. If only that were possible…'

'But it could be!'

'No. You know very well that it would be the end of both of us. The end of both our careers, and the end of your reputation. Even I cannot do that to you, my dear. No,' he said, 'I have to face the consequences of my past, and you must continue to be the actress that you are.'

'But I can't…'

'You have to. Now, go back to the theatre and do your work. I have to go. Everything is arranged. Goodbye, my dear. When you see me next, I will be quite the respectable husband, and father!' His smile faded again. 'How one's life can change on the turn of a sixpence.'

And then he smiled at her again, shrugged his shoulders and left her, walking quickly across the street, between passing coaches and disappearing down a side street.

Isobel slowly made her way back to the theatre, hardly seeing where she was going. At the stage door she left a message for Caroline saying that she was ill and could not rehearse that day.

Then she pulled her shawl around her shoulders and walked out of the theatre. She did not think about where she was going or in what direction, she just walked, without seeing the people passing her by, or the coaches that rushed past. She walked for hours without speaking to anyone and without knowing where she was. All she could think was that something had happened to her that did not make sense. Frank loved her, that was certain. He had also been about to propose to her. That, too, was certain. And now he was to marry someone else. Someone he had known after he had met her, Isobel, and had obviously visited over the last year. This was an undeniable fact, but she could not bring her mind to understand it.

How was it that Frank only just knew of this lady's condition now? She thought back. It seemed likely that Frank had realised his deeper feelings for Isobel before the lady herself knew that she was with child. It was possible that Frank had dropped all contact with this woman quite suddenly, and she may have had difficulty tracing his whereabouts. For a moment, she thought of the anguish and fear that the poor woman must have gone through, and she cursed Frank for his treatment of them both. Yet, was it not terrible timing, a terrible joke that fate had thrown down on them all, just as Frank had turned a corner, knowing where his heart lay, to thus take away all chance of happiness for them both?

She sat down, exhausted, on a seat in a park, not knowing what park it was.

Another thought began to enter her mind.

Frank would come back to the theatre a married man. She would have to see him every day and no longer share little glances, or meet him in secret. His wife and his child – his child! – would come to visit, perhaps even stay with the company. She, Isobel, would be forced to view him as just another member of the company. She would have to work with him, share intimate scenes with him on stage, knowing that none of it was real and would not be replicated off the stage.

She did not know how she would do it. It was unbearable. All her happiness seemed to have been swept away with one blow. How could she enjoy her work now? How could she try to forget Frank and concentrate on her career when he would be there in front of her every day? It was not possible.

Isobel sat with her head in her hands, not caring about passers by, not caring about what time it was or whether Henry Jackman would be angry that she had missed rehearsals. All she could think of was that her world, the one she had fallen into with such joy and hope just under a year ago, had come to an end. It could never be the same again.

She did not know how long she sat there, but she at last was aware that the air had grown chilly. She must go back, but not to the theatre. She would return to the inn and pack her things. But where would she go?

Perhaps she could audition for another theatre group?

The thought lifted her spirits only slightly, and then she fell into a pit of despair again. She knew nothing of other theatre groups, and they knew nothing of her. Yes, she may have had some small success within this circuit, but who would know her in other parts of the country? She did not know where to go to or who to see. Even if she did, surely Mr Jackman would never give her any references if she left him without notice?

Oh, if only she'd taken more notice of the practicalities of being in the theatre. If only she'd listened to Mr Hartley when he spoke of other managers, other theatres. Her head had been too full of Frank and her own day by day existence. She had never thought she would need to think of leaving the Jackmans and going somewhere else, or, if she had it was to be some vague time in the future, when she would be happily married to Frank.

Could she ask the Hartleys? No; they would only try and get her to stay. And anyway, she was too young, too unknown for anyone else to look at her. What was the point?

As she slowly walked back through the streets she realised that she had lost more than a future husband and her joy in her acting career; she had lost her new-found freedom. She knew nothing other than her father's shoemaking shop and the Jackman Theatre Company.

So, if she could not stay with the Jackmans, she had only one option.

I'll go back home, she thought, *I'll go back home and look after father. Cassie said he was not very well. It will cheer him up if I return home, and Cassie will be glad that someone sensible will be there if she is going to be married...*

Tears welled in her eyes again. How cruel life was. Cassie was going to marry and go and live in London, while she must return to the very place she had tried to escape from, without the man she loved. Why, Cassie had not even wanted to leave home!

Back at the inn she got out her small bag that she had packed so excitedly when she first left home, and started wearily to fill it with her possessions. Apart from the bonnet she had bought with her benefit profits, there was very little. Her salary did not go far after buying costumes, food and the occasional travelling fare when the weather was inclement.

She jumped when there was a knock at the door. Her heart started beating fast. Could it be Frank? Could he have changed his mind? Or was it Caroline, or someone from the theatre wanting to know why she had missed rehearsals? One she would have answered with joy, the other she did not want to answer at all.

'Who is it?' she called briskly.

'It's the innkeeper's son, Miss. I have a letter for you.'

A letter? Who could this be from?

She opened the door and took the sealed paper.

She looked down at it, and a strange chill shivered up her spine. It was edged in black.

She opened it slowly, hardly daring to read the contents.

My Dearest Izzie

I am so sorry to be the bearer of terrible news. I can hardly bear to think of the shock you will experience on receipt of this letter, but please think of me as being with you to weep with you as you read it.

Father died on the night of June 3rd...

Isobel dropped the letter and sat down on the bed heavily. For a moment she thought she might faint, and her breathing became fast, feeling the need to gasp for air. When she bent down to pick up the letter she saw that her hands were shaking. She took up the letter again.

It was quite peaceful in the end, but his thoughts were muddled, and he imagined you there in the room.

We held the funeral three days later. There was no time to tell you as I did not know where you were, but I saw in the paper that you are back in Northampton this week, so I sat down to write to you immediately.

Izzie please come home. Our stepmother is in a terrible state of mind and the children are very unhappy. My dear John has been wonderful, but we need you at home. He must travel to London, and I have been at home trying to sort things out and see what is to become of everyone. Father did not leave us much, and mother is saying she and all the children will be in the workhouse soon. Oh, Izzie, please come.

Isobel did not know how long she sat there holding that piece of paper. It seemed that she could not move, that all vitality had gone from her.

103

It was only when she realised that someone was knocking on her door and calling her name that she knew that she was still alive, still flesh and blood. Yet, it seemed strange to her to be still part of the world, that someone was knocking on her door.

'Yes?' she croaked, and was surprised even to hear herself speak.

The door opened slowly, and Caroline's head appeared.

'Izzie, dear, I came to see… Oh dear, what is it? What has happened?'

Caroline sat by her side and put her arm round her. Isobel said nothing, but handed her the letter, which Caroline read, her hand over her mouth.

'Oh, my poor girl, my poor Isobel!'

She wrapped her arms around her and held her against her.

The sympathy was too much for Isobel. The tears welled up and she sobbed uncontrollably onto Caroline's shoulder, while Caroline repeated words of consolation.

'I wasn't there…' Isobel sobbed.

'But, of course not my darling. How could you have been? You weren't to know…'

'But I did,' Isobel moved away and sat up, 'I did know! That's just it! Cassie told me he was ill, and I took no notice! I thought she was just worrying too much. Oh, Caroline, I am a terrible person. How could I have been so thoughtless? My dear father… My dear, dear father! I will never see him again…' and she broke down again into more sobbing that seemed to rack her whole body, leaving her breathless and gasping for air.

She was only vaguely aware of Caroline shouting down the hallway: 'Henry! Henry! It's Isobel, she's not well. Bring some brandy!' and then she was aware of Caroline kneeling on the floor, holding her hands, saying, 'Isobel, please… you mustn't blame yourself, please try to calm yourself…'

And then there was someone else, and a glass held against her mouth and a burning liquid going down her throat that both shocked and soothed at the same time. She coughed and gasped, and she felt her face being wiped with a lavender scented handkerchief. Her sobs turned into long drawn out gasps. She took some more brandy and welcomed the slight numbing effect. Somebody helped her to lie down. Slowly she calmed down, so that she was breathing normally and only weeping silently.

She heard Caroline and Henry talking in a low murmer, but she did not care what they were saying. She felt utterly exhausted, not caring what happened next or what she was to do. All she wanted was to sink into oblivion and to wake up to find everything was returned to normal. She shut her eyes and the world seemed to swim around and away from her.

CHAPTER 10

'What is to become of us? What is to become of us, Izzie?'

Isobel stared blankly at her stepmother. How was it that she was once so afraid of this woman, who now seemed so helpless and feeble?

'Izzie?' Cassie was sitting next to her, and now took her hand in hers, 'Izzie, in five days John and I are to be married, and then I will be joining him in London. But, but if you think… if you think I am more needed here, then perhaps we should cancel the wedding.'

Isobel turned and looked at her sister.

'Cancel the wedding?' she repeated, without comprehension.

'I don't want to leave you all without… well, I don't know what we are going to do, but you will need help with the children, and…'

Isobel cut her off.

'Oh, don't be silly Cassie, of course you cannot cancel the wedding.'

But her voice was weary and without emotion. The last thing she felt like doing right now was to see her sister getting married to the man she loved. The day was going to be painful enough for everyone without father, but for Isobel, it would be like a knife twisting in an open wound.

'But Izzie,' said her stepmother, 'what are we to do? There are bills to be paid, debts, food to be bought, the rent…'

'Mother, John won't let you starve,' said Cassie.

'Oh, but he cannot afford to keep us all!' wailed her mother,'Oh, we are for the workhouse, I just know it!'

Isobel wanted to slap her. Since she had arrived the night before she must have heard her stepmother use the word 'workhouse' at least twenty times. But something else had just permeated her consciousness.

'Debts?' she asked, 'what debts?'

Her stepmother sniffed.

'Well, of course; what do you know about how things have been for us here? You go off without a word with those people...'

'Just tell me. Please.'

Mrs Brite looked down at her hands and spoke in a low voice, as if she did not want the neighbours to hear.

'It has been a terrible year. The railways have taken away the coach trade from Daventry. There have been fewer mending orders and the coach drivers don't come to us any more. They are facing ruin themselves.'

'But surely,' said Izzie, 'one year cannot have made such a difference?'

'You don't understand. It is not just this year; not just because of this ridiculous craze for travelling on those God-forsaken locomotives, or whatever they are called. The Northampton manufacturers have been robbing us of our trade for some time, what with their faster machines and fancy "French" styles. It is impossible for us to compete, and we have relied very heavily on passing trade. That would have been enough, just; but now the passing trade is dwindling and...'

Isobel had a vague memory of her father frowning over the newspapers and saying something about the railways bypassing Daventry, but she had not thought it important at the time. Her head had been full of other things: her own concerns about Frank and the theatre. She had never thought seriously that her father's livelihood could have been in any danger. In fact, she had not really thought about it at all.

She looked at her stepmother, who was sitting at the table with her head in one hand, and Cassie sitting next to her, holding the other.

For the first time in her life, Isobel found herself feeling sorry for her stepmother. She was not young. She had married her father at a time when her chance of marriage would seem to have passed, had borne him four more children and was now, in her mid-forties, a widow without any inheritance or income, and no family to fall on. Izzie's Uncle George, her father's brother, who had taken her to the theatre what now seemed like a life time ago (could it really be only ten months?) was in no position to provide a living or income. Too old to enter domestic service, it did seem that the only option might be to throw herself upon the mercy of the parish. The workhouse might be more of a reality than Isobel had ever thought.

'Whom do we owe money to, mother?' she asked, in a voice that was softer than usual.

'Some of our suppliers; the tanner, and then there's Doctor Meadows. Susanna had a fever last month. Oh, it's not so bad, but I cannot see how I am ever going to repay anyone…'

'And is anyone pressing for you to pay these debts?'

Cassie looked at Isobel and shook her head.

'Everyone has been very understanding, Izzie, especially as father was such a well-loved man…' She swallowed, and looked for a moment as if she might cry, and then took a deep breath to steady herself. 'But they cannot wait forever.'

Isobel thought of the money she had earned over the last year, and the frivolous little bonnet she had bought with her benefit money. It had not once occurred to her to send money home. She had not earned very much; a travelling actor's wage was barely enough to cover her own expenses, but a few pennies might have been possible from time to time. Why had no-one told her? But then she checked herself. Cassie had told her at least once in a letter that father was worried about business. She had chosen to ignore it, choosing to believe that it was just Cassie being over-anxious. She had not wanted to think about anything except herself.

She bit her lip.

'Well,' she sighed, 'I had better look at the accounts and see what needs to be done.'

Mrs Brite lifted her head from her hand and looked at her in astonishment.

'You, Izzie?'

'Yes, me, mother. I have had to look after my own affairs for the last year. I do know the difference between a pound and a shilling, and I can add up a line of figures as well as subtract. Let me see them.'

Looking slightly bewildered, Mrs Brite said, 'Cassie, go and find your father's ledger books.'

Isobel sat at the back of her father's shop with a single candle, the large account books and a pencil.

She licked the tip of the pencil and frowned. Things were not quite as bad as her stepmother had described, but they were not good. They needed an income.

With Cassie getting married and moving to London, the onus would fall on herself. The oldest of the four younger children, Emily, was just about old enough to be sent into service, but that would bring in very little money, and would not solve all their problems. But what could she, Isobel, do now, if she was no longer to be an actress? The thought of going into domestic service herself appalled her, yet it seemed as if it might be the only option. But would that still be enough to feed and clothe the rest of the family? As for a place to live, they would have to move away from the shop and move into some small cottage, or encumber themselves onto Cassie and her husband in London…

The door creaked open and Cassie came in.

'I have brought you a piece of mutton pie and a tankard of ale, Izzie. Mother has a headache and has taken an early night.'

Isobel laid down her pencil.

'Thank you, Cassie. You are kind.'

'How goes it? Are things really as bad as mother says?'

'Well, not quite. But something will have to be done. I can pay the doctor and the tanner out of my last bit of wages, so we do not need to worry about them. The others can wait a while. I will have to think of something…'

'So… is there any danger of the workhouse?'

'Oh, damn the workhouse! I wish everyone would stop talking about it!

Cassie's eyes widened.

'Izzie! Don't let mother hear you swear like that!'

'Oh, for goodness sake, Cassie. I have heard far worse over the last year I can assure you. And as for mother, I am not a child any more and she will just have to put up with me. And, no, there will be no question of the workhouse. Not if I can help it.'

She was sitting up, looking through into the shop. The shutters were down, and the room looked sad and neglected. Shelves of unfinished boots and slippers looked silently back at her. A ray of late evening sunlight had escaped through a gap in the shutters and spores of dust danced in its golden beam.

For a moment, she remembered a day when the door had opened and in had walked a handsome young actor, and her life had changed…

Cassie's voice broke into her thoughts. 'I just don't want to be worrying about you when I am in London,' said Cassie.

'No, no, of course,' said Isobel. Not without a little struggle she brought her thoughts back to the present. It was no use lingering in the past now. It would do none of them any good.

She looked at her sister, and fondly took her hand.

'But once you are in London there will be so much for you to think about, and think of all the sights you will see,' she said, not without some envy, 'all the entertainments, and the fashions…'

'Oh, but Izzie, I will be thinking of you all the time, and will…'

'Wait a minute!' interrupted Izzie, 'let me think.'

Cassie patiently waited while her sister thought for a few moments and then hastily did some sums at the back of the ledger.

'Cassie, how is Emily at making ladies' shoes now?'

'Oh, very good. Mrs Taylor always asks for Emily's shoes specifically, and…'

'Good. Cassie, I have thought of a way you can help us all.'

'Yes, Izzie, of course. If you wish me to cancel my plans and stay here with you I will…'

'Oh, do stop it, Cassie! Of course not. In fact, my idea is completely reliant on your being in London.'

Cassie looked questioningly at her, eyes wide. Isobel continued.

'I shall turn this shop into a ladies' dressmakers, with fine ladies' shoes to match and…'

'But, Izzie, Mrs Applebee makes…'

'Mrs Applebee makes dresses for old women and frumps. We, on the other hand, will make gowns for young ladies of fashion. You will be my spy, Cassie. You were always good at drawing. You will send me drawings of the latest London fashions and I will copy them. Do you think you could do that?'

'well, I think so. But Izzie…'

'For the last year I have had to make all my own costumes for the theatre, and I have learned how to make up a pattern from a picture or an idea and turn it into something real. I can adjust a waistline, add a lace or a ribbon here and there to give a desired effect. I have also seen how certain choice of colours can make the most of a person's features. Cassie, mama and the children cannot make men's heavy boots, but they can sew and make

ladies' evening shoes and slippers. I shall teach them all I
have learned and nobody need starve, or go to the
workhouse.'

'But…'

'Oh, do stop "butting", Cassie. We must do something
and that is my answer. If you have a better idea then
please say so.'

Cassie was silent.

'Of course, we will all have to work hard, but that is
nothing new. There will be new skills to learn, but it is
not outside the bounds of anyone's capability. Why, I
have spent the last year working hard and learning new
skills. It was not all just acting and singing; I had to make
my own costumes, and keep my own accounts.'

Cassie was looking at Isobel as if she did not quite
recognise her. She put her hand on Izzie's and looked
earnestly at her, trying to catch her eye.

'Isobel, my dear. Does this mean… Are you…? I mean
to say…'

'Oh, do say whatever it is you want to say, Cassie.'

'Are you to stay here now? Are you not, then, returning
to the theatre, Izzie?'

Isobel looked suddenly away, back into the empty shop,
but the light had died, and she could see nothing. Yet a
mist was there in front of her, and eyes suddenly felt
moist.

She snatched her hand away from Cassie's and stood up,
under pretence of putting away the ledger into her father's
bookshelf. Away from the light of the single candle, she
hastily she wiped her eyes and took a deep breath to
steady her voice.

'No Cassie, I shall not be returning to the theatre. You
can tell mother in the morning. I am sure that she will be
delighted.'

CHAPTER 11

Uxbridge

October '39
Dear Isobel

I thought it was time I sat down and wrote you a note and give you all the latest news. I have chided myself several times for not having set pen to paper and write to you, but now we have the penny post there really is no excuse, though I have to say that Henry and I have been kept extremely busy with the new Nicholas Nickleby and (I am sure you know) a new production of Hamlet with Frances back in her old role of Ophelia. We have a new star cast member for the role of Hamlet – Mr H. Betty. Frank is very busy with the part of Nickleby and so is not at all put out. In November we are due to return to Daventry. I do hope this will not trouble you too much dear Isobel.

More news of a much graver nature. It is almost unbearable to write, but I am very much afraid to say that poor George and Frances lost their daughter Helen in a terrible accident. While they were at rehearsals, Helen's nurse gave the infant a dose of laudanum to help her sleep, but the pharmacist had accidentally given the wrong dosage, and the poor child was dead within a few hours. Poor Frances was distraught and could not perform for several days. The business was a terrible blow for the whole company and left us all in a low state. Do send a letter to Frances – I am quite sure that she would appreciate some words from you.

Henry is leaning over my shoulder and sends his love. We both of us hope that one day you will decide to return to the theatre. I know things cannot be easy for you, but father often mentions you and asks when you will be

*returning. After the terrible tragedy your family has
experienced, he was very sympathetic, and completely
forgot his anger about the day you walked out of
rehearsals. He really does have a lot of respect for you,
my dear, and your abilities as an actress. I know he can
be gruff and loud at times, but that is only because he is
such a perfectionist, and he misses you – we all do.*

*Oh dear – there is so much more that I would like to tell
you, but I am afraid I will miss the post, and Henry is
pacing the room as we have a dinner engagement and he
does not like to be late.*

*Do please write and let us know how you are getting on.
Perhaps we will see you in November when we return to
Daventry?*

Yours ever,
  Your friend,
    Caroline Hartley

Isobel could not help smiling as she read Caroline's
letter, and thought of her and Mr Hartley fondly. But the
news about Frances shocked her, and she wished she could
have been there to comfort her old friend. She frowned
when she read that they would be in town in November.
The thought of a chance meeting with Frank, with his new
wife and child in tow would be more than she could bear.
No. She would arrange to go to London and stay with
Cassie for the time the company would be there. Besides,
it would give her a chance to see the London fashions and
perhaps get some further ideas for her dressmaking
business. It would be sad that she would not see the
Hartleys, and her poor friend, Frances, but it could not be
helped. Caroline would understand.

She looked at the clock. It was already gone nine
o'clock and she had several letters to write: a reply to
Caroline, a condolence to Frances and a letter to Cassie
telling her to expect her for a visit. Yet, there were dresses

to get finished, and customers to speak to. She wished there could be two of her, there always seemed to be so much to do.

In the few months since she had had the idea, once Cassie was married and settled in London, they had all had to work extremely hard to adjust the shop, make announcements in the paper about the change of business, and start working on ideas that Cassie immediately began to send. All the children were involved, with the younger ones putting up posters around the town. John Duncan generously lent Isobel a small sum to buy materials needed to get started, and by the end of September they were properly in business with almost more work than they could handle. This success had been helped somewhat by her father's good reputation in the town, and her new and imaginative ideas for gowns, bonnets and shoes appealed to the fashionable ladies of Daventry and the surrounding area. However, many people had come to her shop wanting to see, out of curiosity, the girl who had run off to the theatre and returned to become a respectable dressmaker. Isobel knew by the way they looked at her that often they had come there just to look at her and gossip amongst themselves afterwards. But she did not care about that, just as long as they ordered a gown or an adjustment and she could make enough money to keep the family in food and a roof over their heads. She was so busy that she hardly had time to think from day to day, which was a blessing. It meant that she did not have to think too much about her father and how she had never said goodbye, or about Frank, and how she came so close to being happily married.

Going into the workroom, she looked at her sister Emily, her head bent over a pair of dancing slippers, sewing ribbon onto the uppers. She was still very young, but there was no other way; she would have to look after the shop while she was away.

Mrs Brite herself was being useful by making up or adjusting day and evening gowns to suit the new fashions, and actually seemed to be quite content, despite her continual state of mourning and the occasional wave of anxiety. Isobel doubted, however, her abilities with management, and thought Emily had by far the more sensible head on her, despite her young age.

'Emily, I am going to London next month. I'm going to stay with Cassie for at least three weeks. You will have to be in charge.'

Emily looked up sharply.

'Me, Izzie? But I can't…'

'Oh, don't fuss, Emily. You will have Mama to help, and you will only have to take orders and make sure that everything is being done on time. I will ask Uncle George to come by and look at the accounts from time to time.'

Emily's cheeks flushed. 'Yes, of course, Izzie, if you think I can. I am sure I will manage.'

'Good girl. That's settled then. I will write to Cassie and let her know to expect me, and I have some other letters to write too. Do you think you could finish Mrs Gery's ballgown today? She will be calling this afternoon.'

Emily bit her lip, but nodded. 'Yes, Izzie. I am sure I can manage.'

Isobel smiled. Emily was a good worker, and never complained about the amount of work she was expected to do. In fact, Isobel thought that she actually enjoyed it, probably more than Isobel did herself. Isobel enjoyed this new work insofar as it kept her busy and it was fun to create new styles, and keep up with the London fashions, but she knew that when she went to bed at night, though she was tired, she did not have the same sense of satisfaction and achievement that she had done when she was in the theatre.

But it was no good thinking about that now. That was

behind her. She folded up Caroline's letter and went to her father's desk to sit down and write to Cassie, and then to Frances, and Caroline. After that, she would not think about the theatre any more.

From the first moment she stepped out of the coach at the inn of the Angel at Islington, Isobel knew she would love London, and when she arrived within the city itself, she felt that three weeks was not going to be enough. As they drove through the streets in John Duncan's carriage, she stared out in excitement at this city that was alive with bustle and noise; everywhere something happening, from street vendors, to flower girls and market stalls, from street urchins to men and women dressed in the finest of fashions.

For the first time since that terrible day when she had lost Frank and read of her father's death, she began to feel again the blood running through her veins, and an excitement in her guts that she had not felt since she had last stood on a stage.

Here was life and adventure. Here, perhaps, was something she could move forward into. Daventry now seemed quiet and dull. Without its coach trade it would be dead before long. But London! The very air was rich with life; smells, some good, some distinctly unpleasant: food from street vendors, animal excrement, drains, flowers and herbs, sweat, horses, human effluence, rotting fruit and vegetables, and as they neared the River, the stench of the Thames. Isobel breathed it all in. And the noise: the constant sound of horses, carriages and the shouts of the carmen, the cries and songs of the street vendors, children begging, the chimes of church bells.

John ordered his carriage to take them through some of the interesting parts of London so that Isobel could see the new Trafalgar Square with its magnificent monument to Admiral Lord Nelson, the newly built Houses of

Parliament with the great clock tower, the River Thames, full of all sizes of boats and ships.

Cassie and her new husband lived in a small townhouse on Red Lion Square, a pleasant, fashionable square on the southern edge of Bloomsbury. It was a four-storey terraced house with a basement kitchen and two rooms on each floor. The Duncans, it seemed, could afford two servants, a general maid and a cook. Isobel had never even thought of what kind of marriage Cassie had made, but now she realised that she had stepped up in the world, and she could not help feeling amazed at how Cassie, her modest, self-effacing, sweet, shy little sister, had managed to make such a successful match for herself. She was pleased for her, but she was also aware of a rather more uncomfortable feeling of being the older spinster sister, disappointed in love, disappointed in life. She was only twenty, but so far, she felt her life was a failure.

Isobel's bedroom was a charming little room on the third floor overlooking the square. The window had a little window seat, and it was perfect for sitting and spending a little time to herself and watching people pass by, and for checking the latest fashions. It was just right for her purposes, but it also suited her general mood of melancholy.

Cassie, not used to this quieter, more thoughtful Izzie, discussed her with her husband.

'I know she has done well with the new business, and it has given her something to do, but poor Izzie has just not been herself since father died. I think she feels a sense of guilt, you know, that she wasn't there when he was ill. But, I don't know, I think there is something more than that. She will not talk about her time in the theatre, and that is strange because her letters were so full of information and enthusiasm. She seemed so happy. Since she came home she has not said a word about it, and she has shown no desire to go back. I feel sure that something has happened. I was very concerned about her obvious infatuation with one of the actors in the company. Do you think she has perhaps been let down in some way?'

'It sounds more than likely, my love,' said her husband, who was ten years older than his wife and had seen more of the world, 'theatre people are…' he struggled to find a word that would not offend or alarm his young wife, '…well, they are not like us normal folk. They are little more worldly; a little less, er…'

Cassie grinned.

'Are you trying to say they are not quite respectable, John? My dear, I am not quite so naïve as all that. My mother quite convinced me that all actors and actresses are bound for the devil, and she has never held back from saying so.'

John smiled at her.

'And now you have spent a few months in the city and been to see a few plays, what are your own thoughts?'

'I have to confess to feeling a little wicked every time I set foot inside a theatre, yet I cannot really believe that it is all as sinful as my mother believes. And from Izzie's letters, it seems that the theatre manager was quite strict about respectability.'

'Hm.' John thought for a while, while Cassie returned to mending some stockings. 'Do you think that Isobel would enjoy a trip to the theatre? Or would that be a bad idea?'

Cassie put down her work and frowned a little.

'Oh! That's quite a question. Oh, dear. I really don't know. I know what mother would say.'

'We are not asking her my dear…'

'Oh, I know, but I am so used to hearing mother's voice saying what should and shouldn't be done, you will have to be patient with me. I am not quite sure I have a mind of my own. Not like Isobel. She has always known her own mind.'

John laughed and kissed Cassie on the forehead.

'In that case, the best person to ask is probably Isobel herself.'

Isobel looked at her brother-in-law and back to Cassie. They were sitting in the little dining room at breakfast.

'The theatre?' she repeated, putting down her knife and fork, 'the theatre,' she repeated, staring at her coffee cup. Her skin was prickling all over, and when she picked up her fork again she noticed her hand was trembling. She put it down again.

John exchanged a glance with Cassie.

'It's a new play by Bulwer-Lytton, at the Haymarket. We thought you might like to see the great William Macready who is playing in it. It's called *The Sea Captain*. Is this something that you would like to do?'

'I…'

'Dear Izzie,' said Cassie, putting one hand on hers, 'do not feel that you must if you would rather not, we just wondered…'

'Oh, but no… I mean, yes! It is something I would like to do. Very much, I think. When is it?'

'Tomorrow night.'

Isobel's eyes widened. What did she have to wear? She was still in mourning, but perhaps it was time to move on and wear something a little brighter.

'I can wear my benefit bonnet,' she said, hardly realising she had spoken out loud, 'and I can make some adjustments…'

Cassie grinned at her husband and he winked back. Cassie then turned back to Izzie.

'Pardon me, dear sister, but what on earth is a benefit bonnet?'

Accustomed to small theatres and fitted-up barns, Isobel was astounded by the size of the Theatre Royal, Haymarket, and she knew that this was small compared to

Covent Garden or Drury Lane. She of course had known that London theatres would be much grander than she was used to, but even so she had not quite expected this palladian building with its pedimented six-columned portico.

Inside was even more breath-taking. Never had she seen such luxurious fittings, from the red plush seats to the sparkling chandeliers. And all around were theatregoers in their very best finery; there, not so much to see a play, but to be seen at a play, to be at the most fashionable theatre, seeing a new play by one of the most popular playwrights and acted by one of the best actors of the times.

Cassie leaned over to Isobel and whispered in her ear.

'Are you looking at all the gowns and thinking of all the new fashions you can introduce at home?'

Isobel smiled to herself. She had completely forgotten for the moment that one of the reasons for her to be in London was to note the new fashions and transfer them to the ladies of Daventry.

She had barely even thought of Daventry since she had been in London. It seemed so dull and backward compared to the excitement of the city; and in the last few minutes she had been in too much of a daze, and so very agitated at being inside a theatre once again, albeit as part of the audience instead of on the stage. Strange to think of her naïve excitement at her first visit to the theatre in that draughty little hut in Daventry, when she felt she had been at the very height of entertainment. Why, it could not possibly compare to where she was now.

Could that have been only a little less than eighteen months ago? It seemed like another world to her now.

After the play, which, despite the wonderful performance of William Macready, was a little disappointing, they stood in the foyer, waiting for their carriage. Through the crowd's noise came a booming voice.

'Why, if it isn't Miss Brite!'

Isobel turned, and standing before her was Charles Dickens, accompanied by another young man.

'It is Miss Brite, is it not? I saw you in the play at Aylesbury. We met very briefly. How delightful to see you here!'

Isobel bowed and smiled.

'I am equally delighted, Sir. How kind of you to remember me…'

'Oh, pf! It is my honour. I thought then, and I will say it now, as I should have done then, but did not for fear of offending others' he said with a wink, 'you were the best thing in the play, without a doubt.'

Isobel blushed and bowed her head again. She became aware suddenly of her sister who was tugging her sleeve.

'Oh, may I introduce my sister, Mrs Cassandra Duncan, and my brother-in-law, Mr John Duncan. May I present Mr Charles Dickens.'

'And this is my good friend Mr John Forster, a great man of words. We are just off to see Macready round the back. Heaven knows what we'll say. It's not the best Lytton has come up with.' Isobel grinned in agreement. 'But Miss Brite, please tell me that you are here in London on business? Tell me where are you appearing and I will make it my priority to come and see you at the first opportunity.'

'Oh,' said Isobel, 'but I am afraid my visit to London is mainly a social one. I am afraid to say that I no longer am attached to the theatre.'

As she said this, Isobel's throat felt as though it would close up, and to her mortification, tears sprang to her eyes.

Mr Dickens caught her hand and looked straight at her with a candour that went straight to her heart.

'My dear Miss Brite. Forgive my forthrightness. But

please allow me to say this. The theatre has lost something. Whatever it is that has taken you from it, I beg you to reconsider. You belong to the stage…'

'Charles…' said Mr Forster, looking at this pocket watch.

'Yes, yes. I know. Macready will be pacing and growling. One minute, my friend, and then we shall pacify the bear. Miss Brite, I hope very much to see you on the London stage in the near future. Promise me you will think about it.'

Isobel stammered, 'I… yes, yes, I will…'

Mr Dickens and his friend bowed and at once swept out. Isobel swayed slightly, overwhelmed by a desire to go with them back stage, to be with real theatre people again. She looked around her and realised how out of place she felt on this side of the house. All evening she had felt not quite right, and it was because she was here amongst the audience, not back stage where she knew she belonged.

Cassie squeezed her arm and looked at her with wide eyes.

'Isobel, was that really Mr Charles Dickens, the author? I cannot believe it! You never told me you had met him!'

'Oh, yes, we met only briefly. I am surprised he remembered me. Really, it was very kind of him.'

'He appears to be rather a fan of yours,' said John, offering an arm to both women as they stepped out into the cold night air.

Dickens' words echoed in her head all night: *You belong to the stage.* She knew he was right. Yet what could she do? It was the old dilemma. Without the backing of Jackman's Company, how could she ever get anywhere in the theatre? But while Frank was there, how could she possibly return?

For days Isobel turned the question over and over in her head, saying nothing. Cassie watched her with concern,

123

for she too had heard Dickens' words and wondered what her sister would do, but she did not dare broach the subject. It was obvious that Isobel did not want to talk about it.

They worked together, often making drawings of the London fashions they had seen, and sending them back to Emily at the shop. They went to balls and strolled in the pleasure gardens at Vauxhall and at Hyde Park, and then they went home and made notes on what they had seen.

From time to time a young man might take notice of Isobel and ask to call, but she showed no interest in receiving any callers. She would dance if someone asked her, but none of the gentlemen she danced with filled her with any interest or excitement. To her they all seemed dull, and she did not like the way everyone, men and women alike, viewed her as marriage fodder. She no longer felt any interest in 'catching' a husband. She had tasted a life of independence and free-thinking; a life so strange and unreal to most women of her age that many of them would have been shocked if they knew her past history. But it had left her with a will to live her own life. Her year as an actress had made her different to all the other women she saw at dances, giggling behind their fans and blushing at some fatuous compliment made by a dance partner. She wanted to slap their blushing little cheeks and tell them what it was like to stand on a stage with your hair around your shoulders and pretend madness, while a whole audience became hushed because they were moved and entranced by your performance; and to stand there in front of an applauding, cheering crowd. That was real, that was life lived. Not this simpering false modesty and shy looks made to attract a wealthy man so you could make a 'good' match and then hand over every bit of property to him and spend your life bearing his children. No, she had no interest in these fashionable London men who thought they were doing you a huge favour just by asking you to dance.

But London she loved. She loved its noise, its busyness, its dirt and grit, its smells and colours, its contrasts. Its dark, poky little alley ways, and its green, open parks. She breathed all of it in, and for the first time in her life she felt at home. The heartbreak, sorrow and confusion of her soul began to find some peace amongst the noise and confusion of the city.

By the end of December, Cassie had announced with quiet joy that she was expecting her first child, and Isobel thought this excuse enough for her to say in London a little while longer. She wrote to Emily saying that as her mother and she was doing such a good job of running the shop, she felt confident enough to leave them to it and would stay in London for a few more months.

In March she had a letter from Caroline telling her that she and Henry were going to be in London for a couple of days as Henry was meeting some friends here, and she suggested that they meet at the Bell Savage Inn on Ludgate Hill, where they were staying.

It was with a mixture of emotions that she anticipated this meeting. She was of course looking forward to seeing Caroline and Henry again. Her friendship with Frances had been pleasant, but not deep. The Hartleys, on the other hand, had become her closest friends during her year in the theatre, and apart from her own sister, Caroline was the sweetest person she knew. But the meeting would also touch on raw nerves. The last time she had seen them she had been brought to the lowest state she thought it was possible to be, and seeing them might bring it all back, after having spent nearly a year trying to forget. They would talk about the theatre, and would she be able to bear it and not feel the bitter loss of the best time of her life? And, would they mention Frank, and his wife and child? She hoped they would not be so insensitive.

Spring was beginning to show itself as she made her way to the inn along Chancery Lane. Despite her trepidation, the rare early warmth of the sun made her smile, and passers-by raised their hats and greeted each other in mutual acknowledgment of the unusually warm early spring weather.

Henry and Caroline were waiting for her outside.

'We had an inkling that you would arrive on foot without a chaperone, and here you are, my dear Isobel!' said Caroline, taking her by both hands and kissing her on the cheek.

'My sister is in confinement and it was far too beautiful a day to use a carriage,' said Isobel.

Caroline continued to hold her hands and stood back, stretching both their arms open.

'Look at you. It is so good to see you in such good health, and quite your old self again. Obviously, London suits you well.'

'Oh, it does indeed,' said Isobel, 'I feel quite at home here.'

Henry took her hand. 'My dear Miss Brite, this is a happy day indeed! Come on in, we have had a luncheon prepared for us in the back room.'

Isobel had not laughed so much since, well, since she had been in the company of Henry Hartley in the happier times of her theatrical career. In fact, she was not sure she had laughed at all for nearly a year.

The Hartleys had not mentioned Jackman's company at all, but about their visit to London where Henry was meeting some London managers. While he was telling Isobel about this he told a few anecdotal tales of some of the actor-managers he had met in London, standing up to give his impressions of them. In particular, his impression of Alfred Bunn, the pompous manager of Drury Lane who was currently going through the bankruptcy courts, was particularly funny. Although she did not know him, she recognised his bombastic type, and it reminded her a bit of Henry Jackman. Henry told Isobel, with embellishments, of William Macready's assault on Bunn, with whom he had been involved in a long-standing argument for several years regarding Bunn's love of melodrama and spectacle, and Macready's contempt of the same. Apparently, they had a fight in Bunn's rooms at Drury Lane, with Macready still in his costume as Richard III, ink and oil lamp flying across the room, and Bunn bit Macready's finger. However, it was Bunn who won damages.

When she had finished laughing at this strange scene, she was reminded, with this talk of Macready, of her meeting with Charles Dickens, which she related to Henry and Caroline. They were delighted with this news, particularly at Dickens' comments on Isobel's belonging to the theatre, and after exchanging glances, Caroline laid her hand on Isobel's and said,

'Isobel, my dear, we have something to tell you.'

Isobel felt a little sick. She knew by Caroline's face that she was talking about Frank, but what could she possibly need to tell her that she needed to know? She half pulled her hand away, but Caroline gripped it tighter.

'Isobel, he has left the company. Frank is gone. For good.'

Isobel stared at them both. Henry nodded his confirmation.

'Where…?' Isobel managed to ask.

'We do not know. But he's gone, and won't be coming back. Too many arguments with my father,' grinned Caroline; 'there has always been some tension between them since… well, anyway, there was a bit of an explosive disagreement between them and Frank walked out. My father was furious and has sworn he will never have him back. And we wondered… My father has asked after you… He misses you dear Isobel.' Caroline and Henry again exchanged glances; 'we wondered whether you would be at all interested in returning to the theatre?'

PART II

1844 – 1849

The friends thou hast, and their adoption tried,

Grapple them to thy soul with hoops of steel

William Shakespeare, *Hamlet,* Act 1, Scene 3

CHAPTER 12

Isobel sat with the baby on her lap and coo'd over her, shaking a rattle and watching the tiny hand make a small jab at the air. It was a rare night off and Isobel was taking advantage of it to spend a quiet night with her friends, the Hartleys. The nurse had also been given the night off.

'She is just perfect, Caroline. She has your nose and just the biggest eyes I have ever seen.'

'She also has a good pair of lungs,' said Henry, who was standing at the window of the lodging room, looking out over the Northampton street, 'she may be a good singer in future.'

Caroline yawned, and gently shook her two-year-old son, who was asleep on her lap, thumb in mouth.

'Time Henry Charles was in bed. Come on, Lambkin, say goodnight to Auntie Izzie.'

Henry Charles sleepily waved a damp hand to Izzie as Caroline carried the barely awake boy into the next room and closed the door.

Despite the dim early evening light, Isobel had noticed how tired Caroline looked as she passed by the lamp. There were dark circles under her eyes and her skin looked taut. It was not that motherhood did not suit her. No-one could have been more happy and more loving than Caroline. The first few years of her marriage seemed to have been barren, but she had been delighted when at last she had become pregnant and produced her first child, Frances, three years ago, who was currently staying with Henry's sister in Oxfordshire; this was followed by Henry Charles, and then last month baby Clara had arrived. She was happy to be a mother, but it had been a difficult two years for the Hartleys. Caroline had had bad bouts of ill health as well as the two pregnancies, leaving Henry often in a permanent state of worry, and the company constantly having to find ways to cover for her.

With so many married couples in the company, and Jackman himself having produced a large family whilst working the circuits, they were used to having to fill in whilst the female members went into confinement, often using temporary guest players to stand in for a season. The arrival of children could be planned for, but illness was usually unexpected and could sometimes leave a company without a star player with very short notice, resulting in huge changes which would put everyone under strain.

Isobel rocked baby Clara on her knee, watching as her eyes began to flicker and close. She looked up at Henry.

'Is Caroline feeling quite well, Henry? She looks a little tired today.'

Henry sighed and moved away from the window, closing the curtains and sitting heavily onto the chair Caroline had just vacated.

'In truth, we both are,' he said wearily. He sat forward, resting his head on his hands.

'My dear girl, there is something that Caroline and I wish to discuss with you.'

Isobel felt a chill across her shoulders. Since she had returned to the Jackman company four years ago, she had once again felt at home, knowing that she was doing what she was born to do. She was happy once again; happy to focus on improving herself as an actress without the distraction and excitement of being in love. She had concentrated on learning the finer details of her art, had practised her singing and had worked her body into the very peak of fitness. At the age of 25 she had lost all the awkwardness and naivety of her younger self and was now a woman in the height of physical condition. Every night men waited to greet her at the stage door, hoping to gain her favour, but every night she politely turned them away, feigning tiredness, and on most evenings she went to bed early, making sure she would be awake and bright the next day for the rigours of rehearsals or the change of theatres. She had fallen back into the theatre life so easily and quickly she could barely remember she had spent a whole year away from it. Her stepmother and Emily now were doing a good job of running the dressmaking business, while Cassie was busy being a mother to her own two children, with another on the way. Life, at last, felt good.

And, since her return to the theatre, despite her continuing friendship with Frances Partleton, her relationship with Caroline and Henry had deepened, and it was them that she spent much of her spare time.

But with Henry's words she felt the wind of change, like a creeping draught, chilling her neck and shoulders and bringing her out in goose bumps.

It was not just the look on Henry's face that alarmed her. She knew in her heart of hearts that things in the theatre were not all perfect. She had seen the look on Jackman's face when he saw the reports of audience numbers, declining steadily over the last two to three years, and she had not failed to notice the change in some of the coaching towns and inns that were now losing their bustle and busyness to the new railways. This was reflected in audience numbers as people chose to travel in relative ease and comfort to bigger theatres in the larger towns.

Isobel had felt the change, but had tried to ignore it, scared to face the growing reality that her life as a travelling actress may be under threat. But when Henry now looked at her, she knew the time was approaching when that threat would have to be faced.

'You know, don't you, 'said Henry, 'that audiences are dwindling and it does not look as though the circuits can survive this time.'

Isobel's heart sank hearing Henry say the words she had already suspected.

'Are you sure, Henry? They've survived in the past.'

'Oh yes, but that was just a case of legalities, and the

theatre itself was still, and always will be, popular in one form or another. No, it is not that people no longer want the theatre, it is that they no longer need the theatre to come to them.

'Also, I am tired of the game and I wish to be more settled. You probably do not know that I nearly left Jackman's a couple of years ago. Jackman found out. He was not happy. But he is now realising the days are numbered. The Fentons have gone already. He has seen the writing on the wall. The railways are here to stay, and they are taking our audiences to the large town theatres that have their own resident companies. Jackman's no fool. Just last week he said to me: "Henry, my boy, our time has come. The circuits will be dead within a few years." He's thinking of retirement and the likes of you and I must make other plans if we are to survive.'

Isobel stared at the floor, wondering what would become of her. It seemed so cruel that this whole way of life that she had come to love should be so shattered just because of the wheels of progress in the greater world. Would she now have to go and live with her sister and play housekeeper and nursemaid to her children; or, worse, go back home and live under the thumb of her stepmother? She shuddered.

She looked down at the sleeping baby in all its trusting innocence, and suddenly was conscious that this was not just about her, and not just her problem. Henry and Caroline had a growing family now. Their situation was worse than hers. At least she had a choice of home to go to if it came to that.

'Oh, Henry, what will you do?'

At this point Caroline came back into the room and took the baby from Isobel.

'I'm just going to put her to sleep now. Go ahead and tell Izzie our plans, dear. I will be back in a short while.'

'So,' continued Henry when they were alone again, 'we

have decided to give London one last push. I am writing to all the London managers to see if they have an opening for a comedian of my type.' He paused. 'London theatre has changed. Covent Garden and Drury Lane no longer have the monopoly on the legitimate drama, so the smaller theatres can now put on Shakespeare and other dramas. The opportunities for a low comedian who can sing and dance may be fewer than they ever were, but I feel I must take a last try.'

He sighed, and then sat up and slapped his hands on his knees.

'And if that doesn't work, Caroline and I have decided that we will take a public house somewhere and run our own entertainments. Either way, we will be settled in one place, which is a blessing. The circuits may struggle on for a few years yet, but we feel the time is right for us to make a change, one way or another.'

Caroline had come back into the room while Henry was speaking.

'If we do take on an inn, dear Izzie, then we thought that you could come and help us run it too, if you don't find other work, that is. Sophia has already said that she wants to stay with us.'

'Oh,' said Isobel, trying to sound enthusiastic, 'thank you.' but her heart was sinking by the minute. The thought of spending her days in a public house, singing and dancing to small audiences of pub punters in a small provincial town made her feel stifled. And her relationship with Sophia, Caroline's sister, had remained cool since those black days several years ago. She knew in that moment that she wanted her life to be more than that.

As if he had read her mind, Henry grinned.

'But before you need to think about that, Isobel, why don't you come to London, and I will see if I can get a few introductions for you. I think you may be ready to try

London. You know that I have been trying for years to get onto the London stage, and this will be my last try, but if, as I suspect, no-one wants an old packhorse comedian like me, they may be more interested in an actress who can perform the classics, and perform them well. You have a dramatic fire that may very well suit the London audiences, as long a we can find a manager intelligent enough to recognise it,' he said with a wink.

She felt her stomach turn over and a tingling feeling that was a mixture of fear and excitement. She remembered the first time she had felt that feeling. It was when Frank had first suggested that she left home and joined the theatre. She had made the leap then, and despite all the ups and downs since then she was glad that she had. Was it now time to make another leap? Could she do it? She had to. The alternative seemed bleak. Her world as she had come to know it was ending and the choice had to be made: to try for London and sink or swim in that theatrical world of harsh rivalries, or to be safe, and sink into an inevitable world of obscurity. She knew enough about herself now to know that she was never going to take the safe option.

'Oh Henry,' she said, her heart thumping loudly, 'please take me to London with you!'

Henry helped her to write some letters to several London managers and before long she was in the city again, catching two days between venues.

She and Henry travelled down by railway. Caroline had decided to stay with the company and be with the children. For them all to go would have been too expensive, and Henry would not allow any of them to travel in the open third-class carriages, which were notoriously uncomfortable and open to the wind and rain. It was the first time Isobel had been in a railway carriage. She had been uncertain about it; after all, it had been responsible for effectively destroying her father's business, and now, it seemed, her own, but as Henry pointed out, it saved them much time and one cannot ignore progress. 'Progress always creates change', he said, 'and change is not always comfortable, but we must go with it, or get left behind.'

In the event, she found the experience an interesting and exciting one. She watched the countryside fly past, at a speed she had never imagined, from the relative luxury of a closed second-class carriage, though it was hardly comfortable. Henry had paid the twenty shillings for her fare out of his benefit night pay, for which she was extremely grateful; if the wooden seats of second class were bad enough, the more basic seating and crowding in the third-class carriages must be miserable.

They had boarded the train at Weedon in Northamptonshire, and arrived in Euston Station in just three hours. Having refreshed themselves at the Victoria Hotel, Isobel found herself once more in the streets of London, and she felt again the same sense of excitement that she had felt when she lived there four years ago. Once again, she happily breathed in the heady mix of smells and felt its rush and busyness sweeping her along while the sights and sounds teased her senses.

Oh, if she could work and live in London. Surely her life would be complete.

The first meeting they had planned was with John Medex Maddox, the manager of the Princess Theatre in Oxford Street. Henry had informed her that he specialised in opera, but also put on the occasional comedy and drama.

They were shown into a small room which appeared empty of human occupation but full of theatrical paraphernalia of all kinds. On a desk at one end of the room were piles of what looked like manuscripts, along with separate piles of letters, music scores, playbills and invoices. In fact, there seemed very little space on the desk with which to do any work. As for the rest of the room, it was difficult to move across it. Isobel found herself squeezing past a wooden painted tree, and sat down on a chair next to a rack of costumes.

'Hartley!' said a voice from behind the piles of paper, making Isobel jump, as she had thought there was no-one in the room. A dark-haired man with Jewish features in his mid fifties suddenly appeared above the papers as he stood up to greet his visitors.

'Well met, well met indeed!' he said, shaking Henry's hand vigorously, whilst in his other hand he waved a letter he had just been reading, 'it is refreshing to have so intelligent a visitor after the utter foolishness I have to deal with. Just look at this! No, I will tell you; this lady, who believes herself a "star" player, is upset because I have cast her in the chorus and threatens to resign; I have been sent three manuscripts in the last week, all of which are complete *schlock*; my stage manager tells me the scenery paint won't be dry in time for tonight's performance, and the costumes they have sent me are… Ah! My dear lady, I did not see you there… forgive me!'

Henry introduced Isobel to Mr Maddox, and he moved a few piles of paper in order to half sit on the edge of the desk.

'Well, Hartley,' he said, offering him a cigar, 'Oh, do have one, my brother Samuel owns the cigar shop over the road; you will find them the best in London. You do not mind, dear lady, if we smoke? Hartley, my dear fellow; Miss Brite, well, you know how it is. The manager's lot is not a happy one; I have three plays going into production and all of them are cast. So much pressure from all sides, and we have to try and keep everyone happy, but it's an impossible job, eh?'

He looked at Isobel with the same look she remembered Henry Jackman giving her when she auditioned on that very exciting day nearly six years ago.

'Charming, charming,' he said, 'it is a pity I have already cast the heroine of my own play. But your looks, your presence, would do well at the Lane. A pity Macready is in America, but are you seeing Bunn? I presume you can act?'

Isobel was not sure how to answer the last question, but Henry answered it for her.

'She most certainly can. She is our company's greatest asset. It is a pity you cannot see her; there is a piece we have prepared…'

Maddox threw his arms in the air.

'Ai! What can one do? I am fully cast, but I will write to you if I have an opening. Of course, we have the legitimate drama now so there may be more openings in future for dramatic actors, but go and see Bunn if you can, though he is more for the opera these days, too.'

He held out his hand to help Isobel out of her chair and started ushering them out of the room, where, waiting outside were several people waiting to speak to Maddox, and as he hurriedly said goodbye, he was already turning his attention to the problems they had brought him.

'Good to meet you. I hope you have better luck. Now, Beamish, I wanted to speak to you about that music score; it needs seeing to…'

Isobel and Henry made their way to the stage door and came out, blinking, into the sunshine, Henry still puffing away at the cigar.

'Well,' he said, 'how did you like your first London manager?'

'I thought he might have at least seen us do our prepared piece. I hope they are not all as rushed as that. I feel rather deflated; we barely met him at all.'

'Welcome to the London stage,' grinned Henry, 'but, no, they are not all quite like that. But they are all harassed and under constant pressure. Taking on the management of a London theatre is not for the faint of heart, but we may find one or two who will give us a second look.'

'And are we seeing Bunn?'

Henry finished his cigar and threw the butt into the gutter.

'The last time I wrote to him he told me he was only intending to put on opera and ballet, but that was at Covent Garden. Perhaps it would do no harm to pay him a visit, if he will see us at short notice.'

For most of the day they followed up appointments that Henry had made, and sometimes managed to act out their prepared piece, but mostly it was the same story. The plays coming into production were already cast, or the productions were not the right kind.

Late in the afternoon they stopped for a chop and an ale at the Lamb and Flag near Covent Garden, and discussed everything that had happened that day. Isobel felt very despondent that no-one had offered her a part immediately. Henry patted her hand.

'Do not worry about it. We have achieved much today. We have introduced you to several London managers. They will not forget you. It may not have brought any work our way today, but it may do in time, when someone is looking for a Beatrice or a Lydia Languish, they may think about the beautiful young actress they met today.'

'Oh, I am so impatient I just want everything to happen at once. But what about you Henry? Surely it is about time that someone took you on here?'

Henry sighed and leaned back in his seat, pausing to look out of the window before he spoke.

'I think my time in the theatre has come to its natural end, Isobel. The London theatres are putting on operas and the legitimate drama. That is good for you, but for a low comedian like me; well, they are just not interested in what I have to offer. But do not let that upset you,' he added, smiling, as Isobel frowned, 'I have known this was coming for some time. I told you this would be my last try in London. I am tired of the game. I have a growing family. No, Caroline and I will set up in a public house and put on entertainments. I think that will be jolly, don't you?'

Isobel agreed, but she knew that Henry was putting on a brave face. His dreams of treading the London boards had failed and he was having to make the best of it.

And what would happen to her? Even if she got work in London, or in a provincial theatre, the thought of starting again on her own, without her friends, filled her with fear. Yet, the alternative was also unthinkable.

'Oh Henry,' she said, 'I will miss you and Caroline so much. I so wish we could all be in London together. Could you not find an inn here in the city?'

'That would be far too expensive,' he said, 'no, it will be somewhere in the Midlands, perhaps near to my home town of Chipping Norton; I am already looking for leases. But, Isobel, you will be welcome to come and stay with us any time. Never think that you do not have somewhere to go, whether it's for work or just somewhere to escape to when the going gets rough. You can always come to us.'

Isobel smiled, and felt a bit better. 'Thank you, Henry, that means so much to me.'

'Well,' he said, draining his tankard, 'shall we go and beard Bunn in his den, and see what he is up to?'

The great, solid edifice of Drury Lane Theatre, with its grand, square porticoes both on Catherine Street and Russell Street, felt almost intimidating to Isobel. She had been past it before, but never with the thought of any possibility of playing there. Now, as they approached, she imagined that perhaps one day she may be one of its actresses, and she felt hot and cold all over, hardly daring to believe that this could possibly happen. Outside, the posters declared the unusually long run of several months

for *The Bohemian Girl*, an opera by Balfe and Bunn.
Isobel remembered that Frances had recently sung one of
its popular arias, 'I Dreamt I Dwelt in Marble Halls'
during their stay at Uxbridge, but she had not known that
it was from an opera at Drury Lane, or that Bunn was its
librettist. She suddenly felt small and inadequate. There
was so much she did not know. She had gone along,
learning her parts in each play, singing songs, enjoying her
life and career without really knowing anything about the
playwrights or the songwriters behind each piece. Now
she was to meet one.

'Oh, Henry, I am so ignorant. I did not know that Bunn
was a librettist and we had actually used his work.'

Henry chuckled. 'He is a little bit of everything, our Mr
Bunn.'

They found that Bunn was indeed to hand and were
directed to his office, where they found two gentlemen in
intense conversation. One of them with thick, curly hair,
sideburns and large, hooded eyes, the other a thick-set
man with dark, thinning hair and a large, potato-like face,
but a rather kind expression, so Isobel thought.

'Why, Mr Hartley, my dear fellow,' said the first man,
'what brings you to London, as if I didn't know!'

'My last round this time, Mr Bunn,' replied Henry, 'I'm
settling down in the provinces after this, unless you have
something for me?'

Bunn shook his head. 'Sorry old fellow. Things are
much the same as when last I wrote to you. As you can
see, we are tied up with the opera, and have nothing in
your line. But, do introduce me to your companion.'

'This is Miss Isobel Brite, a very talented actress who
has been in our company for about five years. She is also
looking for a place.'

The other man was looking at Isobel with great interest.

'But where are my manners?' said Bunn, 'Allow me to
introduce Mr Benjamin Webster, the manager of the

Theatre Royal Haymarket.'

'Tell me, my dear,' said Webster, after all the niceties had been taken care of, 'have you played Kate in *The Taming of the Shrew*?'

'Why, yes, I have sir,' said Isobel, remembering with a little frisson the time she played opposite Frank, as Petruchio.

'And, tell me, how soon are you available?'

Isobel exchanged a glance with Henry. For the first time, she thought of the unpleasant task of informing Jackman of her leaving the company.

'Well, I...'

'Two weeks,' cut in Henry, 'that should be enough notice.' He winked at Isobel.

'Then could you come to see me in, let's say, sixteen days' time, and we will see what you can do? I have a leading actress who I am not too pleased with. Bunn and I were just discussing the matter when you walked in like an answer to a prayer. If you fit the bill, I will put you in her place and you will be paid £20 per week.'

Isobel's eyes widened. She had never heard of so much money being paid to anyone. Her father might have made that much money in about six months in a good year. She answered slowly.

'And, if I do not "fit the bill?"'

Webster smiled, and his eyes crinkled pleasantly.

'I will find another part for you and pay you £5, and we will work on your acting until you are able to play the starring role.'

Isobel stared at him, not quite believing what had just happened. After the exhausting, tiresome day where nobody seemed to be interested in her, this had happened so suddenly and so unexpectedly. She felt rather sorry now that she had likened his face to a potato.

'You seem to be very confident about my abilities, Sir, to take me on with such little knowledge of my work. I have to say, I am a little overwhelmed by your generosity.'

He shook his head.

'Not generosity, my dear child; generosity would get me nowhere in this business. No, I can see you have something. You have a presence. I could see that even as you walked into the room. The way you hold yourself, and your, if you will pardon me, your figure and beauty. I would be confident to put you in front of an audience in some capacity. You have already worked for a company for five years, and your friend here has already told us you are talented, and why should I disbelieve him?'

Isobel looked back at Henry, who smiled and nodded his approval.

She swallowed. Her life was about to change again.

'Then, I accept your offer, Sir. I will be at the theatre in sixteen days' time.'

CHAPTER 13

To Caroline Hartley
Golden Lion Inn
Stratford-upon-Avon

London

June 1845
My dear Caroline

Forgive me for not writing sooner. I have been so busy
with some new parts, and I have been spending some time
helping Cassie with her growing family.

But enough of my excuses – it really is time that I wrote
to congratulate you and Henry on your new career as
innkeepers. What a change for you! But it must also be a
relief to settle down in one place, especially with the
children. I hope it was not too much of a wrench leaving
the company and your father – but I wish you both well as
the 'master and mistress of the house'. My regards to
Sophia too.

There has been much excitement here at the theatre. The
Queen and Prince Albert attended our performance last
night and sat in the new royal box. I believe they enjoyed
the play, but I was so nervous knowing they were there –
though there was something quite delicious in knowing
one was performing for royalty, and in the end, I so
enjoyed the experience I think I gave one of my best
performances! But, as Henry would say, I say it as one
who shouldn't! I bowed very low towards the royal box
when I took my call, and I am sure that I caught a glimpse
of the Prince leaning to say something to the Queen as
they applauded. I do wonder what he said!

My salary has increased to £25 per week – I never
thought that I could earn so much – and I have been able

to move recently to slightly larger rooms – much more convenient than the poky little place I had before, and much closer to Cassie, so I am able to visit her and the children nearly every day. John Robert is now five years old and is red-haired and lively. I think he takes after our real mother, whereas Frederick is quieter and probably is more like my father. How I wish father had lived to see his grandchildren. The youngest, Katherine, is just teething, so she is a little grizzly at present, but she is a pretty little thing and Cassie thinks she will take after me! (I am not sure whether she means the prettiness or the grizzlyness!)

Caroline – it is difficult for me to take in how my life has changed in the last year. I was terrified when I took my first step onto the London stage, but the audiences were kind, and Mr Webster has been very encouraging. He has worked with me to lose a few, what he called "provincial habits", and to give my acting some extra "polish" for the London audiences. It seems that there is always something else to learn.

You asked me in your last letter whether I had made any new friends here. I cannot say with any honesty that I have any friends that are as dear to me as you and Henry, and of course my own dear sister. It is strange, is it not, how life repeats itself? When I joined your father's company, there were some there (I will not mention their names) who perhaps looked down on me because I was a shoemaker's daughter. Now, here in London, I fear there are some who look down on me because I am an actress from the provinces, and there are some who have been jealous of the parts that Mr Webster has given me and it caused some "difficulty" with his other leading ladies. But, do you know, I find I am quite happy without their approval. I seem to be a person who needs only a few good friends to feel satisfied, so do not think from the above words that I am unhappy or without

145

companionship. While I do miss you and Henry, I find life in London to be enjoyable, and I cannot say that I miss all the travelling between venues, even though we did have some fun, did we not? Without it, and because all the scenery painting and get-ups are done by others, I have more time on my hands and I have taken to walking around London, looking at the wonderful buildings here and visiting the parks and houses. Last week I visited the National Gallery and I was so bewildered and amazed by all the wonderful paintings there that I was nearly late for the theatre! Really, I had never known there were such wonderful things in the world. Have you seen Rubens and Claude? The next time you come to London, we must visit together.

Life is funny, is it not? Some years ago, I remember sitting in my little room above my father's workshop contemplating what my life would be, and it seemed that the only choice I had was either to marry and spend my life keeping house and bringing up children, or to remain a spinster, housekeeping for my ageing stepmother. Neither of these options filled me with any joy, and now, here I am leading an independent life in London with a salary I would never have dreamed of. Back then I had not even known that such a life was possible for a woman. Of course, it is hard work – and I have the constant worry – as we all do in this profession – of whether I will have work next year, or even next month! But I find it best to live day by day, and I know I have family and friends to rely on if ever a time comes when I need them, so I am content.

Give my love to Henry and the children. I hope to see you all soon.

Caroline – the most incredible thing has just happened, and I just had to delay sending this letter so that I could tell you. I was just on my way to buy a stamp to send this

*to you on my way to the theatre, when who should I meet
but Mr Alfred Bunn on his way to Drury Lane. He told me
that he had been to see me last week and was so impressed
with my performance that he wanted to cast me in his new
production of As You Like It. He is focusing on opera, as
you know, but in between, he wants to put on the drama,
and thinks I would do well there. He will also give me
small parts in the opera, as I can sing quite well.*

*I know that Drury Lane has not had the success in recent
years as the Haymarket or Covent Garden – but, Caroline,
the thought of playing on that historic, great stage fills me
with such excitement! What do you think? He would
match Webster's salary, and perhaps increase it for any
further plays, though it is not so much the money that
attracts me. I live very comfortably with what I have, but I
do think it would be an experience to play at the Lane, do
you not agree?*

*I must rush now to post this, but I would like to know
what you and Henry think of this proposal. Bunn wants
my answer within the week, but I hope it does not spoil
things with Webster. It is so difficult to not upset people in
this business – do you not find that?*

*With love – I am in haste now for the post office!
Isobel*

It was a warm day, and Isobel strolled her way back to
the theatre along the Strand, as usual avoiding the poorer
areas around the Seven Dials where it was not advisable
for a woman on her own to walk at any time of the day or
night for fear of pickpockets or worse. She already
attracted odd looks and stares as an unaccompanied
woman on the streets as it was, but she loved the freedom
of walking on her own and was not a person to
compromise her own enjoyments for the sake of social
niceties or what other people might think.

As she walked through Trafalgar Square she pondered

the last words of her letter to Caroline, and the difficulty of following a theatrical career without at some point upsetting someone. Or perhaps it was just that following your own path was always going to be unpopular with someone, whether it was your own family, or those who were jealous of your progress. She thought of Sophia, and could not help but feel a little sorry for her. She had seen Isobel as taking away the parts that she should have played, but in reality, she just was not a very good actress. Now, she was working as a barmaid in her brother-in-law's inn. She wondered if she was happy, or whether she still felt bitter about her career and the fact that she, too, was still a single woman.

When it came to men, Isobel had made the decision that she would be married to her work, and that men were just an unwelcome distraction. Night after night, men waited for her at the stage door, hoping to gain favour, expecting any actress to be willing to give a little bit more than just her companionship for an evening. She despised them. And as for her fellow actors, they were hardly any different. She occasionally attended social events with her fellow actors and actresses, and tried to be friendly and sociable enough, but declined any deeper relationships with either sex. More and more, she found she preferred her own company.

Occasionally, she allowed herself to think about Frank, and wonder what he was doing and how married family life was suiting him, but it was still so painful to think of him in this way that she would quickly find something else to do; practise her part, or take a walk.

She knew she was not popular. Because of her quick rise to success at the Haymarket, she was unpopular with other actresses who gossiped amongst themselves, making up scandalous stories as to how she had managed to curry favour with Webster and how she had come along and 'stolen' the part of Kate. And the men saw her as cold and detached, unresponsive to their attempts at friendship or anything else.

Would the same thing happen if she worked at Drury Lane? *Probably*, she thought, *but I really don't care. As long as I can be the best actress that I can possibly be, I don't care what anyone thinks, and I will do what I can to achieve fame and success, and then what will my stepmother think? Ha! Workhouse indeed! That would show her that I can look after myself.*

Yet, the Haymarket was currently the most popular theatre in London. Was it foolish to let go of her attachment to that theatre in favour of the Lane, where, despite its history and status, it had not fared so well in recent years, with even the great Macready's time there not being financially successful. Bunn had managed to create a long running production, but even he still struggled with bankruptcy, and his focus on spectacle, at the expense of dramatic quality, was despised by many actors. The plays he was planning on were an attempt to increase struggling ticket sales. So, if she failed there, would she have burned her bridges with Webster, or anyone else?

In her heart she knew, though, that if she turned down Bunn's offer, she would somehow regret it. Every time she walked past Drury Lane Theatre, she felt a tingle of excitement. It was as if she felt that the theatre somehow belonged to her, and whether or not it was the most successful theatre of the day, it still seemed to be the place to aspire to with all its history. Surely, the ghosts of Garrick, Grimaldi and Kean walked its stage and corridors, and of course, the great Sarah Siddons. What a thrill to walk in her very footsteps!

It was no use delaying her decision. She knew what she wanted to do. Whether it was foolish or not, her heart and soul told her to take the next leap, and hadn't she always listened to her heart and soul? And despite some pitfalls along the way, here she was, a successful, independent woman with a salary. If she had followed her head from the beginning she would probably still be living with her stepmother, working every possible hour just to try and get by.

Her steps quickened a little. She would write to Mr. Bunn as soon as she got to the theatre. She had time before the day's rehearsals started. She slowed a little as she thought of the conversation she would have to have with dear Mr Webster. He had been so good to her, but surely he would understand. This was the theatre world; underneath its veneer of joviality and comradeship it was a cut-throat business world of disappointments, heart-ache and frustration. If you wanted to succeed you needed to have a tough skin and not be afraid of disappointing others.

She picked up her pace again. She was going to act at Drury Lane! Her stomach flipped over as she picked up her skirts to run the last few steps to the theatre. She had to write that letter at once.

CHAPTER 14

July 1847

Sitting in solitude in her dressing room, Isobel smiled as she put down her copy of *Punch* magazine where she had been reading the latest instalment of *Vanity Fair*. She could not help liking the character of Becky Sharp, despite her place as the anti-heroine, and found her much more interesting to read about than the milk-and-water Amelia. Selfish and manipulative she may be, but she was intelligent and witty, able to make her way in the world without worrying too much about what people thought of her.

Standing, she moved to the small window, and peered out. By the dim light of the gas light on the street, she could see that the crowds had all but gone by the stage door. It was safe for her to leave the theatre without being jostled by the men who waited by the stage door every night, hoping to catch a glimpse of what the papers were calling 'The Brite Star of our Time'. Her performances and charisma at Drury Lane had revived the declining ticket sales since she had signed the contract with Bunn, and that vast auditorium was once again filled to capacity on most nights. But, while Isobel delighted in her new fame, it had brought with it new difficulties, the worst of which was having to make her way through the men who thronged around the stage door to catch a glimpse of her, bring her baskets of fruit or flowers from Covent Garden, or even ask to escort her to some club or inn. She had no interest in them, and hated the nightly push through the crowd, or the reliance on other actors to escort her to a waiting cab. So, every night after the performance she had taken to sitting in her dressing room, reading the latest works by Dickens or Thackeray, and then only venturing out of the theatre when the stage door keeper had found a hansom cab that would take her safely back home.

She pulled a silk shawl over her shoulders. It was a warm night, and she did not need anything thicker. Downstairs at the stage door, she nodded to Old Tom, the stage door keeper, and he stepped outside to hail a cab. She heard him shouting 'Clear orf!' to the prostitutes that stalked the streets, and a response from one of them that would have made her sister blush, and after a few seconds, an 'Oi! Cabby!'

Pulling her shawl tighter around her, she thanked Tom and stepped out to quickly enter the waiting cab, but as she did so a man came running out of the darkness and, not seeing her for looking over his shoulder, ran right into her, almost knocking her over.

''Ere, what's your game?' cried Tom, turning to help Isobel, 'why don'tcha look where you're going?'

'Oh,' cried the stranger, turning to make sure she was not harmed, 'Oh, I am sorry, Miss. Did I hurt you in any way? To be sure, I meant no harm…'

Something in his accent caught Isobel's attention and made her take a short gasp. She looked at the stranger, who was looking over her shoulder in dismay. She looked behind her and saw a peeler running in their direction, his truncheon in his hand.

She looked back at him, and she could see the desperation in his eyes. Tom had hold of him by his sleeve, so he was unable to run.

He looked at her, his eyes appealing for help.

'I'm sorry,' he said again, 'I would never harm anyone, I promise. I only wanted a bit of food for my sister.'

Isobel turned to Tom.

'Never mind, Tom,' she said, 'I am quite all right. Let him go.'

She turned to the stranger, who looked like he might run again, but the policeman was catching up. He would see him soon, and the young man did not have a chance of getting away. Tom had turned away, grumbling under his breath.

'Get into my cab,' she said, 'you'll be safe there.'

The stranger's eyes widened, but he lost no time in climbing into the cab and leaning back into the shadows, while Isobel remained on the pavement and waited for the peeler to reach her.

The policeman slowed down, holding onto his tall hat and puffing like a steam train.

'Excuse me, Miss,' he said, 'but did you see a young man run past here – a dirty ruffian…'

'Oh, yes I did indeed,' said Isobel, her hand on her breast, leaning against the carriage, as if she was in shock but masking any sight of the man, 'the scoundrel nearly knocked me off my feet, a horrible looking individual he was; he bumped right into me and swore at me, and then ran right off round the corner into Drury Lane. I am quite overcome…'

'Oh, thank you Miss. There's terrible people out at this time of night; you shouldn't be on your own now, really. Get home as quickly as possible and to safety. I'll see to this thieving little beggar!' and he ran off again, waving his truncheon. Isobel watched him until he had disappeared round the corner, and then got into the two-seater cab to sit next to the stranger.

'It's all right, he's gone,' she said.

The man took his cap off.

'God bless you,' he said, 'it's good to know there is some kindness…' he stopped, looking down at his feet. Isobel thought he might cry. 'I'm not a thief,' he said, 'but I was desperate, reduced to begging on the streets. I must go,' he said, making to open the short wooden door.

'No,' she said, 'please. Let me take you to where you need to go.'

His eyes widened, and he looked at her, his eyes resting on her silk gowns and shawl.

'Oh no, Miss. You'll not be wanting to go there. 'Tis not a place for the likes of you.'

'Well, at least tell me where that is and then I can make up my own mind,' said Isobel with a smile.

He turned his cap over and over in his hands, his head down.

'We live in Ivy Lane, but it is not as pretty as it sounds. They call it the Rookery, Miss, in the parish of St. Giles. The worst kind of place to live you can possibly imagine, if you can call it living. Not far from here. I can walk, really I can.'

Isobel had heard of the rookeries, the slum areas of London, and the place he was talking about was one of the most notorious. It was not the first time she had been warned against entering its streets. But having rescued this man once, she somehow did not want to leave him to go back to such a place without food, to have to continue to beg. It would only be a matter of time before he was caught and ended up in Newgate or worse. And there was something else about him, something about the way he spoke that made her think of her mother.

'You're Irish, aren't you?' she asked.

He looked up then, with tears in his eyes, and all he could do was nod, and look out into the streets, as if he was seeing a far different place, a green land of clean air. Isobel saw a look of such longing and grief that her heart went out to him.

'What's your name?'

He turned back to her.

'Joe, Miss. Joseph Denny.'

'You look hungry, Joe. Let me at least take you somewhere where I can get you something to eat.'

'Oh but, I, I can't...' he stopped, and she could see him battling with himself. He was hungry, but was it pride or something else that stopped him?

'I have to get back to my sister,' he said at last, 'she is

154

not well. I don't like to leave her too long in that place.'

'Well, would it not be better to go back late with food, rather than back now empty handed, Joe? Please, I can buy food for both of you.'

He leaned back in a mixture of relief and resignation.

'God bless you, Miss, I don't know how to thank you.'

'It is no matter, and please, my name is Miss Brite.'

She knocked on the trap door above her head and called to the driver.

'Take us to the Strand – the Trafalgar Square end,' she ordered. Sitting down again she said, 'there's a pie man who is usually at Charing Cross at this time of night. We can get a pie each, and one for your sister. I would take you to a public house, but there's not many a female should set foot in at this time of night, male companion or not.'

'I understand, Miss,' he said, touching his cap.

They sat by the fountains at Trafalgar Square where Joe ate his steak pie in almost two gulps.

'What happened, Joe? Tell me how you came to be living in the Rookery with your sister.'

Joe took a long time to reply, staring into the water with tears in his eyes. There was a chill in the air, and Isobel pulled her shawl tighter around her. Suddenly, Joe spoke, his eyes looking into the distance, seeing past the fountains and noble buildings to something else.

'It was like a vision of Hell. The black, withered leaves as far as you could see. The potatoes rotted where they grew. No-one knew what was happening, or why it should be so. Many saw it as a punishment for our sins, though for the life of me I don't know what we'd done.

'We sold our cows and our one horse in order to survive that year, but then the blight returned the second year and we had nothing to sell except for a few bits of furniture. We fell behind in the rent. They stopped providing us with corn. The English government did nothing, and exports of oats still left the country leaving its people with nothing. Nothing but turnips and blackberries. People starved to death one by one all around us. Last year it looked like there might be a harvest, but then there were the blackened leaves again and people sat down and wailed in the fields. It was a terrible thing. A terrible thing.'

He stopped for a moment, and Isobel shivered, imagining the fields of black, withered crops, waiting for him to continue, and when he began again, his voice was quieter.

'My youngest brother, little Patrick, was the first to die; he had always been a little weak, you see. It was too much for my mother, and she took to her bed and never got up again. The rest of us carried on as best we could, but then last winter the snows came, the blizzards caused drifts higher than our cottage. My other brother Dermot dropped dead as he worked to try and earn a penny breaking stones. My pa caught a fever, and then Mary, my older sister. They hadn't the strength to fight it. Lord save us, there was not'in on them. Like skeletons they were. They were thrown in an unmarked shallow grave on the hill. No-one had any strength to make coffins or dig proper graves.

'So, then there was just meself and my sister Bridget left. We had no money to pay the rent and so we were evicted, not that there was anything left for us there, but you know, it seemed so cruel, all the same.

'We heard there were soup kitchens being set up in the nearest town where you could get soup and porridge and bread. We walked twenty miles, pulling what roots we could from the ground and eating nettles and weeds. When we got there, there were so many people trying to get the soup there was barely enough to go round, and everyone was still just as hungry and dying.

'What to do next? We had no money for rent, no money to buy seed to plant nor any land to put it in. Many people were taking ships to America, but we had no money for that, so we had no choice but to start begging so we could get to Dublin and take a ship to England. I don't know how we got there, but we did. The ship was overcrowded with starving Irish. I will not tell you what the journey was like. It is not for your ears. But I will tell you that it arrived in Liverpool with thirty corpses on board. There were more soup kitchens in Liverpool, but the place was getting crowded. We slept on the floor of a boarding house with two other families. The landlords were getting tired of all these starving Irish who could hardly pay the rent, and we heard that some of the Irish were being sent back to Ireland and left at the docks with nothing. We didn't want that to happen to us, so some of us decided to make our way to London and try to get work building the new railways, begging for food and fares, sometimes getting a lift on a cart. We managed to get a bit work along the way, working in the fields, or stone breaking, but the people didn't seem to like us being there, and it was worse when we got to London. There was little employment and the only place to live was in a room with a family of five. My sister, after all the hardships, has taken to her bed, and I fear she…'

He stood up.

'I must go and take this to her at once,' and he looked around to see which way he should go.

Isobel found that her face was wet with tears. She stood up and tried to speak, but nothing came out. Instead she caught Joe's arm.

'Let me walk with you,' she managed to say.

Joe said nothing, but nodded and they walked up St. Martin's Lane. As they neared the Seven Dials, Joe turned to her and said, 'you mustn't come any further Miss Brite. You must go home. Thank you for all you've done. I will never forget it.'

'Oh, Joe,' she said, 'it's nothing. I wish there was more. I'm so sorry Joe, for your family. I did not know, I mean I knew, but I did not realise how bad things were.'

Joe hung his head. 'That's the trouble, Miss. I don't think many people knew. Otherwise, they would have done more, wouldn't they?' He shook his head, 'I don't know, I don't know. There are no words...'

Isobel touched his arm.

'I hope your sister recovers, Joe. If you need any help, you can ask for me at the theatre where we met.'

'Oh, no, Miss. I couldn't do that. They'd throw me out anyways.'

Isobel suddenly remembered her purse, and took what she had out of it, pushing it into Joe's reluctant hands.

'Please, take it,' she said, 'I can afford it.'

Joe nodded, a tear falling down his cheek. Then he was gone, walking quickly up the street, the pie under his arm.

Isobel watched him for a few moments and then turned to the street to look for a cab.

For the next few nights Isobel found it difficult to sleep. Images of the rotting potatoes kept coming into her head, and even worse pictures of people and children looking like skeletons, lying down and dying in the fields.

She had never known her mother's family, but she could not help wondering now whether she had cousins over there in the same plight. But what could she do? She did not even know their names.

Every day she kept wondering about Joe and his sister. Would Bridget survive? Would Joe manage to find work? She had suffered sleepless nights before, but it had always been because of her own problems. She had never lost sleep for others before.

After three days, she had come to a decision. She could do nothing for her mother's family perhaps, but at least she knew someone that she could help. The next morning, she got up and dressed in her oldest and shabbiest clothes, and then went out and bought bread, ale, fruit and cheese, stowing them away under a cloth in a basket.

The place Joe was living was a little north of the Seven Dials, and she approached the area from Great Russell Street and then turned left into a maze of narrow lanes, courts and alleys.

The first thing that she noticed was the stench. All kinds of filth ran through the streets, and the air was thick with the smell of rotting fish and effluence, both human and animal. Around her were the sagging walls of tenement buildings, some, where the windows had no glass, with feeble attempts to keep out the cold with newspapers or rags. Children with nothing on their feet played in the streets amongst the filth, and women who were quite obviously prostitutes hung around on the corners talking to each other, no doubt waiting for the evening when they would venture out towards the streets where they would find trade. It was unlikely they would find anyone to pay them here. As she walked, trying to keep away from the worst of the dirt and holding up her skirts as much as she could, she was nearly knocked down by two men running out of one alleyway, but instead of apologising they called out abuse to her, and then proceeded to fight and brawl in the middle of the street, using the coarsest of language that shocked even Isobel's hardened ears. No-one else seemed shocked or dismayed by this. It was obviously something that happened all the time. A couple of the prostitutes joined in with the swearing, egging the men on.

She very nearly turned back, feeling at once out of place and fearful of her safety. She thought of how shocked her stepmother would be if she knew where she was, but this only served to make her grin and continue on her mission.

She approached an older woman in rags who was sitting on a stool on the doorstep of one of the tenements. Her hair, which was long and grey, was hanging round her shoulders and had obviously not seen a comb for many a day. Next to her were several sorry looking birds in cages.

'Looking for a bird, are you? They sing pretty they do.'

Isobel looked at the birds and felt that they would probably never sing again, but she said nothing.

'No, I'm sorry, but I wonder if you would be kind enough to tell me where Ivy Lane is?'

The woman spat on the ground, and Isobel just managed to pull her skirt out of the way.

'What's it worth?' she snarled.

Isobel had been prepared for this. She took a few pennies out of her pocket to give to her. The woman snatched them out of her hand, bit each coin, and spat once more. Then her eyes shifted to the basket Isobel was carrying. Isobel tore off a hunk of bread and gave it to her, and she immediately stuffed it into her mouth and swallowed it almost whole. Putting her pipe back in her mouth the woman made a small sideways nod with her head, which Isobel took to mean the direction she should go in.

After walking up and down Ivy Lane and asking more questions, Isobel finally found herself walking up a rickety staircase in a dark, damp and smelly building that echoed to the sounds of bawling children and barking dogs. Behind closed doors she heard the occasional hacking cough, couples arguing or women shouting at their children.

But behind all these sounds there was something else. Something that made Isobel stop on the stairs and listen. Someone was singing. A male voice, clear and harmonious, in a room just above her.

Isobel gasped and nearly dropped her basket, for it was a song she recognised; one her mother used to sing to her to help her to sleep. She had not heard it since she was about five, but there was no mistaking it. She knew it now as an

160

Irish lullaby, its lilting, haunting melody tugging at her heart, bringing a nostalgic tear to her eyes.

She followed the sound to the room the voice came from, and opened the door just a crack. She smiled, for, as she had suspected, it was Joe who was singing.

He was sitting next to a dirty, sagging mattress upon which lay a young woman covered in rags. The room was stuffy and cramped, but Isobel was moved by the sight of some flowers, now fading, in a jug by the make-shift bed, presumably an attempt by Joe to brighten things up for his sister.

Joe started at the sight of Isobel, stopped singing and jumped to his feet.

'Be Jesus! Miss Brite! You… you should not be here! How on earth…?!'

'I'm sorry I startled you Joe,' said Isobel, 'but I brought some things for your sister.'

She looked down on the pale, fragile looking woman, and kneeled down on the filthy bare floor. The woman's dark hair, which should have been long and thick, straggled untidily across the pillows, and her face, which was obviously once pretty, was drawn and sallow.

'How are you Bridget? I hope these few provisions might give you some strength back.'

Bridget smiled weakly. 'Joe told me about you. I am so glad to meet you, but you should not have come to this terrible place.'

'Indeed, I should!' said Isobel, 'or I cannot call myself a friend, and I hope we can be friends?'

'Oh, I would like that. Joe and I have no other friends here. You are so good!'

'Well, that's settled then,' said Isobel, looking back up at Joe, who was still staring at her as if she was a ghost, 'we are all friends. And Joe, I wish to speak to you.'

Out in the narrow hallway, she spoke to him frankly.

'Your sister will never be well again in this place. Joe,

you must get her away from here.'

'But how…?'

'I will help you. Excuse this question, Joe, but can you read and write and add up numbers?'

'A little. I used to do the accounts at home. But…'

'That is perfect. I live in a house large enough for three, plus my maid. You will come to me. Bridget will be my companion when she is well enough, and you will work for me, and help me keep my accounts. It is not charity, Joe. I am offering you employment. I have worked it all out. We can discuss the details later. Now, if I send a carriage to Great Russell Street at three o'clock tomorrow, do you think Bridget would be able to walk that far?'

Tears were in Joe's eyes as he replied.

'Oh, Miss Brite. I could never have dreamed… but, yes, yes, I think she will, if she knows… Oh, but how can we thank you?'

'By your sister getting well again Joe, and you doing a good job for me. That would make me happy and be thanks enough. Now, don't forget. Three o'clock tomorrow, and you will be taken straight to my house where I will meet you.'

As she started to go down the stairs, she stopped and turned back.

'And Joe, where did you learn to sing like that?'

'I never learned, Miss, I just copied my mother. She sang like an angel.'

'Yes, she must have done,' said Isobel, and turned away.

CHAPTER 15

Joe took to his new employment with enthusiasm, answering to callers, looking after Isobel's accounts and paying her bills. He had learned to do this at home for his parents, and he knew his figures and arithmetic well. However, his reading and writing were almost non-existent, so Isobel spent a couple of hours every day with him, teaching the basics, going over newspapers with him, going over any words he found difficult. She helped him with his writing, and within a few months he was able to open and reply to her correspondence. Meanwhile, Bridget slowly began to recover, her cheeks took on a little more colour and she began to look a little less emaciated. Her almost black hair recovered its natural curl, and her dark eyes began to shine.

On evenings when Isobel was not at the theatre, or out occasionally dining with colleagues, the three of them would sit together and talk about their lives. Joe liked to talk about Ireland, although sometimes this would make Bridget tearful, and then they would change the subject, and Isobel would tell them about her life and how much she loved London. Joe would say that London was all very good as long as you had money or good friends, and it became a little private joke between them. From then on, if anyone mentioned how wonderful London was, one of them would say 'with money and good friends', and they would laugh together.

Sometimes Isobel would ask Joe to sing to them and when he did, usually a gentle Irish ballad, she would feel goose bumps on her arms and tears would often spring to her eyes.

Helping Joe with his literacy, and being continually in work, starring in a play at Drury Lane and usually at the same time learning a new part for the next week and rehearsing during the day, Isobel found herself continually busy. At night she fell gratefully into her bed and slept soundly until the morning, and she had no time to think about anything other than her work and her friendship with Joe and Bridget. She was tired much of the time, but she felt happy and content.

One morning she was listening to Joe singing as he was sorting out the morning's post in the rooms below. It struck her how much stronger his voice was now that he was happier and healthier. A new thought struck her.

'Joe,' she said, as they sat down to breakfast, 'you love singing, don't you?'

'Oh, indeed I do, Miss. When I sing it's like the whole world stands still, and I feel at one with everything. It can be sad, you know? But even when it's sad, it feels good. Aww, I can't explain it…'

'Oh, but I know exactly what you mean,' she said, 'that is how I feel when I am on stage. I can be playing a tragic death scene with the whole audience in tears, but it feels wonderful!'

'Isn't that the truth, though?' said Joe, laughing.

'Joe, have you ever thought of singing in public, for an audience?'

Joe stared at her.

'What, me Miss? Oh no, no, I've never thought of that. I'm not sure I could.'

'Wouldn't you like to convey what you feel when you are singing to an audience? To have them feel what you feel? A song can say so much more than mere words, and it can make people cry, or make them laugh and feel happy. Wouldn't you like to be able to do that?'

'Well, to be sure, that does sound good. But I don't know. Do you think my singing is good enough to be up on a stage an' all?'

'Yes, I do. And don't argue with me Joe, because I know what I am talking about. I have been in the theatre now for nearly ten years and I had to learn to sing and do it well enough to affect an audience, but you are a natural. With a little bit of training to build your confidence and help you with breathing and pacing I think you would do very well very quickly.'

'But how would that happen, Miss Brite? Where would I go?'

'I think I can take care of that Joe. I have some friends who run an inn in Stratford upon Avon in Warwickshire. They employ singers and entertainers. They would, I am sure, be happy to give you some tuition and give you some experience in front of an audience. What do you think?'

Joe looked crestfallen.

'To go away from here? From Bridget? From you?' He blushed suddenly.

Bridget had been watching them both very closely and noticed Joe's discomfort. She put her hand on Joe's and said, 'It might be an exciting opportunity Joe, and perhaps I could come with you.'

Isobel had also noticed the words Joe had used and found herself staring very hard at her breakfast plate. For the first time since meeting Joe she realised that she would miss him if he was not here.

She had always thought Joe to be quite handsome, in a very Irish, rugged way, but she had never at any time thought of him romantically. He was a friend; someone that she had wanted to help. Since Frank, she had not had any intention of forming any attachments. She never wanted to be that vulnerable again. Which was why she kept herself to herself at the theatre and turned down the offers she got at the stage door.

Yet, with Joe's two words, 'From you?', revealing a possible fondness that she had not expected, she began to question herself. Joe was easy to be with. He was intelligent and clever. He made her laugh. Without him here the house would seem empty.

But she also recognised with a sudden increase in her pulse that she cared for him. Cared for him enough to send him away for the sake of his own career. A career that she knew, with the right training, that he could be successful in.

She steadied herself.

'I am sure Bridget could go with you, Joe. And you will like Stratford. It's much quieter than London, with the River Avon running by, and the countryside there is very pleasant. You might feel more at home there than in the city. And I have some free time coming up in a few weeks. The opera is on at the theatre, and I do not have a part. I could come and stay for a while.'

Joe kept his eyes lowered.

'If you think they would have me.'

'I will write to them today. I am quite certain they will be happy to take you on.'

A few months later, Joe and Bridget had settled in Stratford, and Isobel was glad to be leaving London to join them. The recent outbreak of cholera was frightening and had already claimed thousands of lives. She missed Joe and Bridget being around the house, and she was tired. She was looking forward to taking a break from work and spending time with her old friends.

Henry met Isobel at Leamington Station in a brougham. Isobel was overjoyed to meet her friend from the old circuit days, which seemed so long ago now. Henry explained that Caroline had stayed at home because their new baby, Harriet, was having teething problems and she did not want to leave her with the nurse. After the tragedy that had happened to her niece at Northampton when Frances' daughter had been accidentally poisoned for the same condition, she had always been frightened to leave anyone in charge of her children.

'So,' said Henry, once they had made themselves as

comfortable as possible in the small carriage, 'I expect you would like to know how your protégé is getting on?'

'Indeed, I would,' she replied, 'I hope that he has proved himself as worthy as I guessed he would be.'

Henry sat back and viewed Isobel through half closed lids, a small grin playing around his mouth.

'I would never have known,' he said at last, 'when you joined us, wide-eyed on that chill morning in Daventry – what is it now - ten, eleven years ago? - not only what a talented actress you would become, but what an eye for talent you would have. Joe has proved himself more than worthy, my dear, he has become almost indispensable. People of the town come to the Golden Lion just to hear him sing. My only criticism is that while he is singing, the audience is so enthralled that no-one buys any ale during the performance!'

Isobel laughed and clapped her hands.

'There! Didn't I tell you? Does he not have a lovely voice? And his delivery! It can make you cry, or laugh or want to dance. He is able to hit exactly the right tone, the right ambience, is he not?'

Henry continued to watch Isobel, noticing how flushed her face was and how bright her eyes as she talked about Joe.

Ho, ho! he thought, *so that way lies the game.* Out loud he said, 'And I understand from your letters that you rescued him from the slums? Tell me, what is his story? He has told us very little.'

So, Isobel told Henry everything that she had not had time to put in a letter: the famine, his escape from Ireland, the journey through England ending in the slums of London, and then how they had met.

Henry stared out of the carriage window as she talked, nodding, frowning and then shaking his head at times. When she had finished he said,

'This famine in Ireland brings shame on our nation. The

lack of aid is a national disgrace.' He turned to Isobel. 'It was brave and good of you to do what you did. You have matured and grown into a decent and admirable young woman, Izzie. I am sure that your father would have been immensely proud of you. As am I.'

Isobel flushed and held back a sudden tearfulness. Looking out of the window she saw that they were just about to go over Clopton Bridge.

'Oh, look,' she said, 'the dear old Avon! How pretty it looks in the sunshine.'

The river, with its swans gliding elegantly upstream, wound peacefully up to where the Holy Trinity Church stood proudly, the burial place of her dear Shakespeare. The town was important to her; the birth and death place of the man who had written the very plays that had brought her fame and fortune.

'How apt that you should be here, Henry,' she said, 'the birthplace of our dear bard. Just think of all the words we have spoken that came from his pen.'

'Yes indeed,' said Henry, 'and so many of us owe so much to him. Where would Macready, Kemble or any of us be now?' he chuckled, and then said, 'you will be interested to know that I have a little project here in Stratford concerning old Will, but more of that later. Here we are!'

They had arrived in Bridge Street outside the Golden Lion Inn, with its large four-gabled frontage, and the brougham entered through the arch at the side and into the yard.

Caroline came out holding her new baby, all warmth and smiles, and behind her grinned Joe, with his arm around his sister. What a happy meeting it was, and Isobel felt blessed to be surrounded with some of the people she loved most in the world.

With the new baby, there were now five children in the Hartley household, Frances, Henry Charles, Clara, year-old James and the infant Harriet. Caroline's sister Sophia was also there, working as a barmaid. There was a cool, polite greeting between her and Isobel, and a slight awkwardness, but mostly Isobel felt very happy to be here, on holiday in Stratford, and amongst her friends.

With all the people to meet, and the hustle and bustle of the hotel life, it was a while before Isobel had a quiet moment, and found herself alone with Joe in the front bar. Bridget was helping Caroline with the baby, Henry had gone to deal with new visitors and Sophia was at the bar.

Isobel suddenly felt shy, not a feeling that she was familiar with, and it made her feel self conscious and awkward.

'So, Joe…'

'Well, Miss Brite…'

They both spoke at once, and then laughed.

'How are you getting on, Joe? Henry tells me very good things about you. Are you enjoying it here?'

'Oh, indeed I am, Miss Brite. You know, I thought I would be too scared to sing in front of an audience, but when it came to it I found I rather liked it after all. And, I never thought that I could be paid for singing, for something I enjoy so much. It doesn't seem quite right. It's not like work, you know? Not like work on the farm…'

'I know, Joe. I know exactly what you mean. I love acting so much I sometimes forget that I get paid as well! I would almost do it without the money… well, perhaps not quite,' she smiled, 'but don't worry about it. You deserve it Joe. You have a rare talent, and it is only right that people should pay for the privilege of hearing you. I am looking forward to hearing you sing tonight.'

'I will be all the more nervous, knowing you are there.'

Isobel laughed, 'And all the times you have sung in my parlour without a care, Joe!'

'Ah, but that's different. I was just singing then. It

wasn't for show. Now, I am aware of every time I go a little bit flat, or say the wrong word...'

'Oh, but Joe, that's just part of the performer's life. We are always aiming for perfection. But, here's my advice. Don't try to be too perfect. It's the feeling that counts. If your voice cracks, or you say the wrong words, it doesn't matter as long as you feel the song, and the audience feels it too. That's the whole point of artistry. It is not to be perfect, but to be true.'

Joe thought about this, repeating the words, 'not perfect, but true.'

'Why, Miss Brite, that's beautiful. You are so right. It's the feeling it gives you that's the important thing, is it not? You have to sing well, of course, and hold a tune, but it's that catch in the voice, or a slight change in the timing, it kind of makes it... oh I don't know...'

'Human?' said Isobel, grinning as she watched Joe's shining eyes, talking about what he loved most.

'But that's it though! It is something that connects us all, that something different, something human, as you say, Miss Brite, that really makes a song.'

'Joe!', said Isobel suddenly, 'I've just had an idea. Would you like to sing a duet with me? Later this week? We could rehearse it the next few days and then sing on the Friday night. Oh, Joe, please let's do it!'

'There's nothing I would like better' said Joe, solemnly.

That night, Isobel watched as Joe sang some popular songs and Irish ballads. It was true, she thought, as she watched the enthralled faces of the audience, he had the ability to make an audience laugh and cry.

In particular, knowing Joe's history, she felt the tears springing to her own eyes as he sang 'The Cliffs of Doneen'. Only she knew what the words of the last verse meant to him:

Fare thee well to Doneen,
fare thee well for a while
And to all the kind people
I'm leaving behind
To the streams and the meadows
where late I have been
And the high rocky slopes
round the cliffs of Doneen.

As he sang she thought of all the Irish folk who were now forced to leave their homeland for ever, many seeking new lives in America. How heartbreaking it would be to leave the place you loved for somewhere so unknown and far away.

Then Joe cheered everyone up with a comic song, leaving them laughing, cheering and clapping.

After going through Isobel's own repertoire of songs, she and Joe finally decided on 'I Dreamt I Dwelled in Marble Halls' as their duet song. It was one she knew well, with lyrics by her employer, Alfred Bunn, for the operetta *The Bohemian Girl*, and the verses were easily interchangeable for a male and female singer, with Joe singing the first two verses, and Isobel the last two, and both singing the chorus.

It was so enjoyable for Isobel to work with Joe, with Henry playing the piano for them. The three of them worked well together, and while they took the song seriously, they had many laughs.

Isobel had not felt so happy since she had first started her theatrical days. Her life in London was enjoyable, but as a star of the theatre her life was not always her own, and even though she had many people around her, she had not made any deep relationships. That was her choice, but here in Stratford, free to do as she pleased, she realised how tightly managed her life in London was; how little time she could call her own, and in many ways, how lonely she was. She would never complain; she knew too well how lucky she was, but at times, being the star player of a large theatre was a little like being on a treadmill, and if you fell off, you would sink without trace.

Later, Henry told her of the little project he had mentioned earlier. He, along with Mr Morgan of the Jackman Company, had bought some shares in a little theatre on Chapel Street, and was becoming instrumental in putting on Shakespeare plays there. Not only that, but he had recently been elected town councillor. Having given up his London dream, he had found Stratford a happy place to settle, and was enjoying the new freedom of living in one place and able to develop friendships and a new and busy social and community life.

On Isobel's third night in Stratford, she was introduced to the audience in the entertainment room as 'the guest star from London' and received with loud cheers. But as Joe started to sing the first verse with his rich tenor voice, the audience, usually boisterous and noisy, began to quieten down.

I dreamt that I dwelt in marble halls,
With vassals and serfs at my side
And of all who assembled within those walls,
That I was the hope and the pride

I had riches too great to count, could boast
Of a high ancestral name;
But I also dreamt, which pleased me most,
That you lov'd me still the same…

That you lov'd me, you lov'd me still the same,
That you lov'd me, you lov'd me still the same.

I dreamt that suitors sought my hand;
  That knights upon bended knee,
And with vows no maiden heart could withstand,
  They pledg'd their faith to me;

And I dreamt that one of that noble host
  Came forth my hand to claim.
But I also dreamt, which charmed me most,
  That you lov'd me still the same…

          That you lov'd me, you lov'd me still the
same,
          That you lov'd me, you lov'd me still the
same.

As she and Joe sang the final chorus together, standing towards the audience but looking at each other face to face, there was complete silence. As they finished there was a moment's silence, and then they broke out into a loud ovation which lasted for several minutes. Isobel looked at Joe, feeling that she could burst with happiness right there, and Joe looked overwhelmed with what was happening both on stage and between them.

It was while Isobel and Joe were being congratulated afterwards, with Henry and Caroline hugging them both, and everyone agreeing that Joe had a great career ahead of him, that Caroline suddenly clapped her hand over her mouth and said,

'Oh, Isobel, I completely forgot! What with the baby teething and you so busy, I meant to tell you that a letter came for you from London today. I am so sorry! I hope it was not urgent!'

'From London? Oh, not to worry. It is probably from Bunn, telling me who is to be my new leading man in the coming season. It is not urgent. I will open it tomorrow.'

She was enjoying herself too much to want to think

about her work in London. Tonight, she and Joe were stars in Stratford. Tonight, she was among friends, happy with her life. It was a night to laugh, talk and celebrate, not to read letters of business.

CHAPTER 16

The next morning Isobel woke feeling happy and refreshed. She stretched and yawned, remembering the success of the night before, her duet with Joe and the happy discussions that went on late into the evening. Henry had opened several bottles of champagne and everyone had become extremely jolly.

The maid knocked on her door, coming in with hot water for washing.

'Is there anything else you need, Miss?' she asked.

'No thank you Mary… Oh, could you pass me that letter on the dresser there. Thank you. That will be all.'

The maid bobbed a quick curtsey and left the room.

Isobel unsealed the letter that had come from London yesterday and started to read.

In the next moment, she sat bolt upright, her hand to her mouth.

'No!' she said, 'No, it can't be! Mary! Mary!'

The maid came running back in.

'Are you all right Miss?'

'Yes. No. I need to get up. Help me with my dress will you?'

While Mary brushed down her day dress Isobel splashed her face with water, then, while Mary laced up her stays, she picked up the letter again to make sure she had read it correctly.

Theatre Royal, Drury Lane
London

My dear Miss Brite

I am delighted to write to you with the news of the newly contracted actor who will be playing opposite you in our next production of Antony and Cleopatra. *His name is Frank Douglas, and I understand from him that you have played together before, which is excellent news, as he tells*

me that you worked together very well. Mr Douglas has
spent several years in America where I believe he made a
good name for himself, and he now wishes to return to his
native soil and build a new career here.

How happy we will all be to have you back at the Lane
very soon.

Yours affectionately
Bunn

'Oh, my dear!' said Caroline, when Isobel showed her
and Henry the letter, 'I had no idea that he had returned
from America.'

'You knew about that?' asked Isobel.

Henry and Caroline exchanged glances.

'We read a review in the foreign pages,' said Henry.
'Apparently, his Iago was extremely well received, and he
has become quite a star. We did not tell you anything
because we hoped he would choose to stay in America and
make his home there, and we did not want to upset you by
mentioning his name. We thought it best to let sleeping
dogs lie.'

'What am I going to do?' said Isobel, staring into the
middle distance. They were sitting in Henry and
Caroline's private rooms with a pot of coffee and a basket
of breakfast rolls. Isobel had not touched her coffee nor
eaten anything.

She stood up and started pacing the room.

'I cannot do it. I will have to quit. I will write to Bunn
immediately. I will tell him I am ill. Oh but…' she
stood, her hand on her head. Bunn might want to take
Frank on for a long contract; what would happen to her
then, if she would not go back? 'Oh, he will be the ruin of
me!'

'Isobel, dear,' said Caroline, taking her by the arm and
leading her back to her chair, 'please try and stay calm.
Look, your coffee has gone cold. I will order some more.

Mary!'

Isobel stood up again.

'Oh, the audacity of the man! I can just imagine him telling Bunn how well we worked together. How he would enjoy that! I can imagine the smirk on his face. How could he do this to me? He must know how discomforting this would be for me; how could he be so selfish!'

'Hm,' muttered Henry, 'the man has never been well known for his consideration of others, that is true. But Isobel, you have to admit that an actor cannot allow personal affairs to interfere with work. You know that. My God, I never thought I would ever hear myself defending the man, but this is business. He has returned from America, hoping for the same success here. He cannot afford to turn up his nose at any work that comes his way, whatever the circumstances.'

Isobel sat down again and took a cup of coffee from Caroline without really noticing what she was doing, putting it down again without taking a sip.

'I cannot work with him. I simply cannot!' She put her head in her hands for a few moments, her palms covering her eyes to shut out the light, while Caroline and Henry sat looking at each other, and Joe sat silent at the further end of the breakfast table, wondering what was going on.

Isobel opened her eyes, her chin up.

'I will write to Bunn. I will refuse to work with him. I will tell him, it's either him or me. He will have to choose. After all, I have a following, he cannot afford to lose me; surely he would choose to keep me!'

Henry shook his head.

'A risky move, to call his bluff. Managers are not fond of their stars making demands and giving ultimatums. He may be looking for fresh blood; a star from America is a big attraction. Let us be honest, Bunn needs all the attractions he can get. It is well known it is hard work to keep the Lane afloat. And besides, according to the letter, he is already contracted. It would be too late to change anything now.'

'Oh!' screamed Isobel, 'this is too, too bad! Is there nothing I can do?'

Caroline stroked Isobel's hand.

'Isobel, my dear, perhaps you need to just give yourself a little time. Don't make any hasty decisions. You have another day here with us to think it all over, and we will be here to help in any way we can. You know, perhaps it won't be as bad as you think. Frank had already, well, mellowed a little when he was with our company. I know it would be difficult at first, but perhaps in time it would be less awkward and you could learn to be friends.'

Isobel could not see how she could possibly be in the same company as Frank without being continually upset and agitated, but she agreed that she needed to take a day to allow the news to settle.

'My dear Joe,' said Isobel two days later, as she stood in the courtyard, while Henry waited in the brougham, 'I am sorry I have not been myself the last two days, but I hope we will meet again soon, and perhaps we can sing together again.'

She shivered a little. The morning was chilly, with a stiff little breeze that heralded the coming of autumn. This week of joy and lightness seemed to have vanished along with the summer.

'That's quite all right, Miss Brite,' said Joe, falling back into formal address without quite knowing why, 'I will write, and you can too, if you wish. I know you have something that troubles you, and I… I wish you all the best, I really do. I hope you work it out, whatever it is. I will get on very well here with Mr Hartley and his good wife. I have meant to say how thankful I am to you for all you have done, but somehow it's difficult to find the

178

words.'

'There is no need, Joe. It is good for me to see you and Bridget so happy, and to know I had some part in that. I know you will always miss your family, but you must look to the future now, and perhaps look to London again when you are ready.'

They both were silent for a few moments, looking at the ground, not sure what else to say.

'Goodbye Joe,' said Isobel eventually, and he handed her up into the carriage and waved her away. Henry started up the horses and the sound of their hooves echoed around the courtyard as the brougham disappeared out under the archway and into Bridge Street beyond.

Joe stood looking at the vacant archway for some time, the image of Isobel waving from the carriage window still engrained on his mind's eye and wondering why he felt such a hopeless sense of loss.

'Well, my dear, we meet again!' said Frank, bowing in a slightly exaggerated fashion when Isobel appeared in the rooms used for rehearsals.

Isobel felt instantly both outraged at his familiar address, and at the same time sensed a jab of the same old excitement she used to feel at the opportunity to exchange verbal spars and jibes with this man. Of all the emotions she had expected to feel, she had not expected that.

'I am Miss Brite to you,' she said, haughtily, 'and will remain so for as long as we have to work together.'

Frank seemed momentarily checked by this cold repost, but the old twinkle was soon back in his eye, and he bowed again.

'As you wish, Miss Brite, but you may always call me Frank. I can never forget that we were once close.'

Isobel looked around to make sure they could not be overheard by the other members of the cast now entering the room.

'You must not address me like this again, Mr Douglas', she whispered, 'after all, you are a married man.'

Frank's face dropped all of its cheerfulness and he looked at her for a moment before leaning in and speaking in a very low voice, 'I thought you may have heard, but obviously you are uninformed. My wife and child died of cholera a year ago. I barely survived myself.'

Isobel looked back at him, unable to know what to say or how to feel, but before she could gather her thoughts together, Alfred Bunn had entered the room and was gathering the cast together so he could give them his seasonal address.

Isobel barely heard anything that Bunn said, the shock of Frank's news going round in her head and making her feel quite dizzy with contrasting emotions.

Frank, meanwhile, had moved away to the other side of the room and did not look at Isobel again until the time came for them to read their parts together.

It was not until much later in the day, when the company had gathered in the Nell of Old Drury for ale and pies, that Isobel had a chance to speak to Frank as he was sitting in a corner of the upstairs room by himself.

'Fr... Mr. Douglas,' said Isobel, sitting on the same settle, but not too close to him, 'I am at a loss to know what to say. I can only express how very sorry I am about your terrible loss.'

Frank did not look at her but stared for a long time at his tankard of ale.

'Thank you, Miss Brite,' he said at last, his voice low and soft.

Isobel searched for something else to say.

'I, I can only apologise for my discourteous reception this morning. I really did not know...'

'It is quite all right, Miss Brite,' said Frank, raising his head to look at her again, 'you had every right to speak to me as you did, and there was really no reason you would have known about…'

'No.'

There was a long silence. Frank stared at his ale again. Isobel did not know whether to leave or stay. After a while, she started to move, but Frank spoke suddenly.

'You know, she reminded me a little of you.'

'Wh… who?'

'My little girl. She was full of spirit, full of life. Always able to get around me in some way, no matter how naughty she had been.'

Isobel found herself staring at Frank's ale tankard along with him, almost holding her breath.

'What was her name?'

'She was christened Elizabeth. I called her Lizzie.'

There was another silence.

'She was seven years old when she…'

'I'm so sorry, Frank,' said Isobel, a little hoarsely.

'My wife died soon after. She lost the will to try and live. I very nearly followed them… but I managed to survive. Perhaps… perhaps it was the thought of coming back to England…'

Isobel spoke before he could say more.

'I am very glad that you are well again. I… I hope you find the success here that you did in America.'

Frank looked at her for a few moments.

'You certainly have made a great career for yourself, Miss Brite. Your fame crosses the Atlantic and was made known to me via the theatrical grapevine. I always knew you would do well. Is it not strange that here we sit, nearly eight years on, you a star in England, and I a star in America. How much water has flowed under the bridge since we last met.'

Isobel shifted uncomfortably. How she wished he would not refer back to the days when they were with the Jackman company. She was a fool then; it was embarrassing to be reminded of her own naivety and gullibility. She stood up before he could see her blush.

'Excuse me, Mr Douglas. I must go. I have an errand to make before we commence with rehearsals.'

Frank stood as well.

'May I just say, Miss Brite, that when I heard that I was to be working with you…'

'Please do not say it,' said Isobel. Then she stuck her chin up and turned to face him fully. 'If, if you must know the truth, I was dismayed when I heard that you were to be the new lead. I very nearly quit. But, we are professionals, are we not? We must learn to put the past behind us and get along as best we can. I hope that we can learn to work together without the need to look back. I do not intend to have any further private discussion with you; I merely came to give you my condolences.'

'Is there someone else?' said Frank, suddenly.

Isobel looked at him with horror. This was the kind of conversation that she had wanted to avoid. Yet, his question made her think suddenly of Joe. Kind, sweet, soft-hearted Joe. She missed him. She missed his singing in the morning, and the conversations they had together. She missed his quiet presence.

'Since you ask, Mr Douglas,' she said softly, 'there is a person whom I am fond of, but…'

'I see', he said, and she could see a flush of colour in his cheeks.

'Now I must go', she said, 'and we are not to have any further conversation of this nature. From now on our relationship is to be purely professional. Good day. I will look forward to working with you this afternoon.'

Frank bowed his head in response as she turned and left him.

Isobel had no errand to make, and when she left the pub, she had twenty minutes before she was due back in the rehearsal room. She was glad, though, of the chance to take some air, and she walked over to Covent Garden market and bought some apples, still flushed and disturbed by her conversation with Frank. She was cross with herself for allowing the conversation to go so far as it did. She had merely intended to express her sympathy over the loss of his wife and child. Now she felt flustered and unsure of herself. Why did he always have a way of making her feel so… so… Oh, he really was impossible. Even the grieving, more mellow Frank that she had witnessed today somehow had the ability to stir up her emotions in ways that were just not appropriate.

She went over their conversation in her head as she made her way through the noisy throng of Covent Garden. He had made her think about Joe, and now, again, the thought of him calmed her. Did she really have feelings for him? It was true that she did miss him. Was it possible that he felt the same?

'I will write to him,' she thought. 'As soon as I get back home, I will write to him. A nice, friendly letter full of everyday things. And then he will write to me, and perhaps I might see then how things are between us.'

She returned to the theatre, her mind clearer, and her heart more settled.

However, it was a few weeks before she found the time to write to Joe.

London
September 1848

Dear Joe
How long ago it seems since I was in Stratford, and having such a jolly time with you all. Was it really only a month ago? As soon as I arrived back in London, my life took on its usual busy-ness and I have hardly had time to think for myself, being so overwhelmed with learning new

183

parts.

It might amuse you to know that the theatre is to be teeming with <u>horses</u> at Christmas – as Mr. Bunn has booked Franconi's Equestrian Troupe. The papers have announced them to be appearing 'in full and effective force', so the old circus arena will be re-fitted and the whole theatre will be full of dirt and interesting aromas. Do you think the horses have the same sort of egos of some of our great actors, and will be demanding their own dressing rooms and private hay stalls?

Well – so much for legitimate drama! But I suppose I knew what it would be like when I chose to work for Bunn. The spectacle brings in much needed money, and perhaps Drury Lane would not survive without such amusements, for the Management are continually complaining about empty seats and low returns. I should probably be grateful to the horses for keeping me in work. My word, what a strange business this is!

The dreaded cholera is still rampant in London, and we are warned not to go near to the worst areas – one of which (you will not be surprised to learn) is the terrible place where I found you and Bridget. It seems such a long time ago does it not? I would advise you all to stay away from the city until things get better. I travel everywhere in a closed cab, and rarely enjoy a stroll as I used to, though I have to admit to visiting Covent Garden and buying some apples just the other day. One has to get out occasionally! But these are fearful times indeed, and it is no wonder that the theatre has no money and is booking spectacular events to bring in the punters.

The play has been moderately well received, but it is true the theatre does not feel quite the same at present. In such a huge theatre, you can almost feel the empty seats, like an echo out in the darkness.

Isobel paused, and looked out of the window. She had

meant her letter to be fun and trivial, with little anecdotes of her life in London, but instead the little fears that she held within her every day, and tried her best to quash down, were coming out of their own accord through the nib of her pen. It was true that audience numbers were down. It was true that the fear of cholera was everywhere. She had been aware of these things for some time, but in her usual optimistic manner had fobbed them off with such thoughts as 'Oh, things are bound to get better soon. I will be all right. I have always survived, and so I always will.'

But what if - Isobel allowed herself for the first time to look over the edge – what if they did not get better? What if she suddenly had no work? The theatre was a notoriously unstable and fickle business. She may be popular and adored, but what of that? She had seen greater stars than her suddenly dropped from public favour – for what reason? Age, a bad review, a younger, brighter rival, or perhaps even a change of what was fashionable in the theatre, leaving any actor or manager behind if they were unable or unwilling to move with the times. Bunn had gone through the bankruptcy courts before, and things looked to be going the same way again. Just recently, he had tried to put on a serialised play, which took place over two nights. But when the public realised they were expected to pay for both nights in the theatre, they had taken offence, and riots had ensued.

Had she become complacent? She knew, with a stab of fear, this was a dangerous word in her world. Too long had she been living a charmed life without giving a thought to how she could keep it so, or how long it might last. It was too easy to get lost in the joy of her work, and forget that she had to be a business woman too.

The answer for most single women was of course marriage. But marriage to money and status. She had no such option. The men she knew (and she could not help a fleeting thought of both Joe and Frank here) were both in the same unstable business, and those she knew with money were only the stage door hangers-on who knew nothing about her, and would surely expect either an 'arrangement' (some of them were already married), or, in the hypocrisy of the age that viewed actresses as no more than whores in respectable society, would expect her to leave her profession to become a full time wife and mother.

Isobel shuddered. Perhaps it was time to take action. It may be time to write some letters to other theatre managers, just as a kind of insurance. She liked Drury Lane, but most actors moved around and did not stay put in one place for too long. Perhaps it was time to move on, and certainly the presence of Frank was stirring up some uncomfortable and confusing feelings. Despite her determination to stay detached, she could not get used to working with him again as it stirred up so many memories of the past. She dipped her pen in the inkwell and went back to her letter.

Forgive me if I seem a little gloomy. I am thinking of late that it may be time for me to move on, to try for another contract with a different manager. I know that I should see myself as fortunate indeed to even have such choice. My career has been a successful one so far, and not many in our profession can even hope to choose their own path.

I find it so easy to express my thoughts to you, dear friend Joe. I know that you will always understand. I wish very often that you and our dear friends the Hartleys could be here in London. I have my sister here, and I visit her and her family often, but I have very few theatrical friends. My fellow thespians at the Theatre Royal are a pompous crowd, and I have to say I do not spend much time with them outside of our work. They no doubt think me cold and unfriendly; well, so be it. The people that matter know otherwise.

I must sign off now, Joe. I have some business letters to write. Please send my deepest love and kind regards to Henry and Caroline.

Yours
Isobel

CHAPTER 17

Isobel was avoiding going anywhere near the River. Since the new sewage works had started to pour everything into the Thames, the smell nearby had become almost unbearable. She felt sorry for anyone who had to live or work by it, but supposed they must become used to it. Even so, with the warnings on pamphlets spread around the city that these foul smells carried the cholera it seemed sensible to stay as far away as possible unless absolutely necessary. Rumours that drinking water may be contaminated led Isobel to drink only beer when she was thirsty. Some people dismissed this notion, saying that it was a well-known fact that disease was carried by miasma, and you were better off avoiding bad smells than any water. But Isobel noticed that those who expressed this view were not great water drinkers themselves.

On a cold day in January she was on her way to meet the inimitable Madame Vestris, who was currently the joint manager with her husband of the Lyceum Theatre, down towards the Strand. As she crossed Wellington Street she threw a coin to the crossing-sweeper, a tiny ragged boy who looked unlikely to see his next birthday, who swept away the dirt and dung as she made her way carefully across the filthy street, lifting her petticoats clear of the mud. There was no doubt that London was becoming dirtier as every year went by. On cold and dreary days like this she sometimes wondered how she had ever been so excited by the city when she had first arrived here.

She reached the other side of the street just as a hackney carriage swept by, spraying a fan of mud towards her and despite her effort to sweep her skirts out of the way, the bottom of her gown was spattered with dirt.

Isobel sighed in frustration, and continued towards the theatre. It had seemed such a short journey from Drury Lane to the Lyceum, and ridiculous to do anything but walk, but she was beginning to think she should have taken a cab even so.

Entering the theatre by the stage door, she was struck by how clean and well maintained everything was back stage, cleanliness very often being focused on the front of house in many theatres, and back stage areas left to deteriorate until the paint was peeling off the walls and dirt accumulated in corners. But here, it seemed, the people who used the areas behind the scenes were as well cared for as the public who visited at the front. She had heard that Madame Vestris, and her husband, Charles Mathews, had a very good reputation for looking after their employees and keeping the environment they worked in as pleasant as possible. It would seem that these stories were true.

Upon meeting Madame Vestris, Isobel was at once struck by her extraordinary beauty, despite the fact that she was in her early fifties. Her eyes were large, dark and expressive, her mouth a pretty cupid's bow, and her dark, full Italian hair in an abundance of ringlets which framed her face. And when she spoke, her voice was deep and rich, reminding Isobel that Madame had once been infamous for being the first actress to play men's roles.

'Ah, Miss Brite,' she exclaimed, immediately standing and coming towards her with a hand held out, 'how delighted I am to meet you at last! Oh, but look at your poor gown, *peccato!* Ai! One cannot walk anywhere in London today. Sit down, my dear, please.'

As Madame sat, she swept up a rather ancient looking spaniel that had been sitting underneath the table and sat him on her knee.

'Oh,' said Isobel, 'how adorable! May I stroke his ears?'

'Oh yes, that is his favourite thing in all the world!'

After a small pause, while both women petted the little dog, who finally, satisfied with much ear stroking and scratching, curled up on his mistress's lap, heaving a great sigh and eyeing Isobel with large, wise eyes before dropping off to a contented slumber.

'So,' said Madame Vestris, getting down to business as quickly as possible, 'Bunn is heading for bankruptcy again, and you are looking for a new employer, no? I saw that most ridiculous French serial play. No wonder there were riots; expecting people to pay for two nights indeed! And what was he thinking with that dreadful circus?'

'I believe it is called Desperation, Madame,' said Isobel with a sardonic grin. She was liking this woman very much.

'Oh, my dear, please call me Elizabeth, and I shall call you Isabella, no? Such a pretty name. And indeed, you should not be wasted under Bunn's foolishness. I foresee the bankruptcy courts for Bunn, yet again. All the same, we are all having to cut our cloth, as the saying goes. The audiences prefer spectacle and comedy to the heavier drama these days, so I hope you will not be too disappointed, but I think we have something better to offer than Bunn's outrageous follies. It is a shame, because you are a very good actress indeed, and deserve the classic parts. I saw you – I think it was a year ago perhaps – you have such a great presence on stage, very commanding; and yet, you have a stillness sometimes which pulls the audience in. Very clever, very clever. You learned your craft in the circuits, is that not right?'

'Why, yes, it is,' said Isobel, impressed by her knowledge, 'I was taught by some very good actors in that company, and of course my dear friend Henry Hartley...'

'Ah, Hartley... Yes, I think I saw him once. He came to see me. A good comedian. But, you know, times were harder then, and I could not take him on. A shame. Where is he now?'

'He runs an inn in Stratford upon Avon.'

'Ah, well. That is the theatre for you. Talent is no

measure of success as we all know. It is a fickle business. But you…' she leaned forward, 'you are a survivor, are you not? Like me? I see myself in you. You have had hard times, but you always see the way forward, no? I like that. You can also adapt and play the comic role. Have you ever thought of going into management?'

Isobel raised her eyebrows. The question was a sudden one, and completely unexpected. 'Why, no. It seems such a perilous career.'

'Hm. No more than that of an actress. Of course, you are still very young but what about when you are older and the work declines? You could do worse.'

Then she cocked her head a little as she stroked the dog's head, and smiled a knowing little smile and said,

'And what it is like to work with the great Frank Douglas?'

With dismay, Isobel felt a blush rise on her cheeks. Why was she asking her this?

'He is a very good actor. We have worked together before.'

'Ah yes, so I believe.'

'How did you know?'

'Oh, he told me so himself. You are not the only person looking to leave Bunn's sinking ship!'

Isobel inwardly cursed. How typical of Frank to be already ahead of her. How would she ever get rid of him? And how would it look if he took a contract at the Lyceum, and she followed suit? Would it not look as though she had followed him there? Oh, wouldn't he just enjoy that!

Aware that Madame Vestris was watching her closely, she quickly dissembled, smiling and nodding.

'Oh, he will be a credit to your establishment. I first saw him playing Hamlet. I have never seen a better Hamlet since,' she said, truthfully, 'I believe he was very popular in America.'

Madame cocked her head.

'Hmm, I wonder why he returned. He is very fond of you, no?'

Isobel felt herself blush again, and realised that there would be no fooling this woman. If she was to be a possible ally and future employer or colleague, then she must place her trust in her and treat her as a friend.

'Well, Madame... I mean Elizabeth, I will be honest with you. It is true that Frank and I once had an attachment of sorts. But...'

'...he was forced to marry another?'

Isobel looked at her in surprise.

'My dear, you should know by now that in this business of ours it is impossible to keep anything secret. People, both inside and outside the theatre, love a scandal and will take any little hint of any interesting "friendship" and discuss it in any way they can.'

'I can assure you that there was nothing scandalous about our relationship,' said Isobel, remembering with another blush that embarrassing evening in the Unicorn Inn.

'I am sure that is true, but most people will believe whatever they wish to believe. But perhaps that is the price we pay for our freedom, no? Yet, it surprises me that with your looks you have not yet married. You must not be short of offers.'

'I keep myself to myself.'

Madame nodded.

'You are probably very wise. And yet, I myself eventually succumbed to the delights of marriage again; but it is a very practical partnership too. We work well together. My husband treats me as an equal, and I would not have married under any other arrangement. You could do a lot worse than Frank Douglas.'

'Oh but... he has not...'

'No. But I think he will. But make sure, when he does,

that any arrangement is on your own terms. We women of the theatre share a freedom that is unheard of in the rest of society; you do not want to lose that. But if you can marry well, then such a partnership can be of great mutual benefit. Support when times are hard, twice the income when they are going well, and if one of you is not working, then at least you may still have income if the other is.'

Isobel thought about this for a moment and admitted to herself that it would certainly be pleasant to have someone there when things got tough. She was always the one who had to work out her own problems, to decide on the next course of action. While she knew she enjoyed a certain level of independence, it was also at times exhausting. How nice it would be to have someone by her side to confer with; to commiserate with her after a hard day, and to share some of the mundane, day-to-day decisions that had to be made. Of course, for a while, she had had Joe who had filled that place as an employee, but her house did feel empty since he had gone.

'But you did not come here today to talk about marriage! My dear Isabella, if your contract with Bunn is coming to an end next month, then I would be delighted to take you here for a season. I have seen you act, I need no further proof that you would please our audiences immensely. Remember, though, this is a much smaller theatre than that you have been used to, but I know you will be able to accommodate. After all, you started in very small theatres indeed!'

A few days later Isobel received a letter from Joe:

Stratford

My dear Isobel
My sincere apologies for my not writing sooner. I always try to answer your letters as soon as I can, but my

193

sentences and spelling are still not good, and I do not want to send you pages of terrible mistakes and scrubbings out, so our friend Caroline still helps me to write my letters – but what with all the Christmas festivities and so many songs to memorise and rehearse last month, it has been very slow progress indeed!

I am very worried for your health when we hear all the news about how the cholera is growing worse in London. Please, dear friend, be careful!

I would dearly love to come to London. I do not mean for just a visit, but to work. I so love to sing. It seems incredible to me that I can be paid for doing something that is such a joy – but I have had long talks with Mr. Hartley, who is very knowledgeable about these things, as I am sure you know, and he tells me London would not do for me right now. The inns and taverns in London that have singing are very different to what I am used to. The type of song I sing is more rustic and genteel, and the type of songs they like in London are a little 'rough' and not at all my style.

So, I have decided for the moment to stay in Stratford, and perhaps develop some new work that might be more suited to the London audiences. The Hartleys say I should keep to what suits me, but I cannot rely on their good natures for ever, and I do want to earn a proper living. London, as Mr. Hartley is always saying, is the place to be if you are an entertainer (with money and good friends of course!!), so I must set my sights there and try to do what pleases.

I also miss our friendship, and I hope it will not be very long before we can be in each other's company again.

The Hartleys send their love to you, as does my dear sister, who is now in robust health, and sends you many hugs and kisses!

With many kind regards
Your friend

Isobel could not help smiling a slightly wry grin when she thought of Joe singing in one of the musical taverns of London. Those places were loud, and the type of popular songs sung were bawdy and crude. This was not Joe's style at all, and she could not imagine him singing such songs. The thought of innocent, sensitive and shy Joe trying to develop into such 'popular' singing so that he could get work in such places almost brought the tears to her eyes.

She put down his letter and sighed, suddenly feeling very sad. She thought of those months when he and Bridget were living at her house and how happy they all were, and of course it was wonderful that the Hartleys were able to give him work, but oh she did miss him. The house always seemed so empty and quiet these days. And now the chances of seeing him at all seemed very slim. He could not possibly work in London, and she was committed to her work here. It seemed that the world was driving them apart.

She had another surprise when Frank came to her dressing room one day and told her that he was leaving Drury Lane to go and work at the Olympic Theatre.

Isobel stared at him in amazement.

'But Frank, I thought you had signed a contract for the Lyceum!'

'Not so, Miss Brite. It is true that I went to see Madame Vestris, but in the end, I decided to decline her kind offer.'

'But why? I hear so many good things about her management, and the money is good…'

'Oh, indeed. And I think it is a good move for you. This place,' he waved his hand to indicate the building around them, 'is sunk for the moment. It will only drag you down with it. But, well, it has been made quite clear to me that you are not happy working with me…'

'Oh… but…'

'No, I am sure you will be happier if I am removed from your daily sight. I have been offered a short contract at the Olympic, and after that, well, we will see how it goes.'

Isobel was in a state of confusion. She had been certain that Frank would thoroughly enjoy annoying her by joining her at the Lyceum. This was so unexpected she did not know what to say, or even how to feel. She tried to think of more practical matters.

'But the Olympic? Surely their returns have not been good lately; are you sure this is a wise move?'

'It is but for a short period. It gives me space to think about my next move. Perhaps I might even return to America…'

'Oh,' said Isobel, unable to think of anything else to say. This was unexpected.

She was aware that Frank was looking at her through narrowed eyes.

He sat down on a chair and picked up a little hair piece from her dressing table, turning it over in his hands.

'I might do better in America. They liked me there. There seems little for me here. Unless…'

Isobel looked at the floor. Then brushed some imaginary dust off her shoe.

'Unless?'

'Unless there was something to keep me here.'

Isobel continued to look at her shoe, pointing her toe and looking at the sides.

'Isobel?'

'Oh, I am sorry, Frank; I was just wondering whether these shoes are good with this gown, or whether I should wear the red…'

'You really are incorrigible!' said Frank, not able to suppress a grin, 'you know damn well which shoes go with which gown!'

'Really, Mr. Douglas, please do not swear in here or I will have to ask you to leave.'

'As if you cared,' he said, 'I know you have heard worse, and said worse; you are just playing with me. I know you too well, Isobel.'

'Do you, Frank?' she said, looking at him fully in the eyes now. 'Do you really?'

Frank stood up impatiently.

'Enough of this,' he said, 'I shall ask you outright. Do I have any hope? Is there a possibility that you might make it worth my while to stay in London?'

Isobel sat in her chair and looked at her hands. It was true that she still found his presence exciting. She still enjoyed the sparring matches between them, and his presence always made her feel alive, even when he infuriated her. And, he was now free. But, her past experience, the heartbreak and feeling of desertion after he had left to marry another woman, albeit out of necessity, left her with a foreboding of danger. She wanted to trust him, but she questioned his trustworthiness.

As if he read her thoughts, he said,

'I assure you there is no possibility of the same thing happening as before. My days of, shall we say, "amorous adventures", appear to be over. It seems that there is only one lady who interests me, but if I no longer interest her, then I will return to America, my tail between my legs, never to return to the shores of old England.'

Isobel could not help rolling her eyes at his over-dramatic statement, but as her face was still turned down, she knew he could not see her. And despite his theatrical prose, she knew he was speaking the truth. She experienced a little frisson of pleasure, knowing that he still had these feelings for her, and that the attempts at flirtation over the last few months had only covered a more deeper feeling. Why hesitate? It had become clear to her that she still had feelings for him.

Still, she wavered from committing herself. She was unsure that her feelings for him were the same as they had been… could it really be ten years ago? She was naïve then, no more than a girl, falling in love with the first man who had paid attention to her. She was a mature woman now. She had turned thirty last August. In the eyes of some, too old to expect romance and marriage. They had both matured. And Frank had mellowed; there was no doubt about it.

She remembered the words of Madame Vestris, that she could do a lot worse than Frank Douglas; and it could be a very practical arrangement, as well as good companionship. It could be her last chance for marriage.

And yet…

She spoke, still looking demurely down at her hands.

'I cannot answer your question right now Frank. I am not the impulsive young lady you once knew…'

'We are both older and…'

She looked up at him.

'Wiser? Yes. We are. That is why I must have time to consider what you have said.'

There was a pause. Frank then nodded, stood up, put his top hat on his head and picked up his walking cane.

'Very well. My contract at the Olympic lasts until the summer. But I will need to know before the end of March so that I can make arrangements for my departure, if that is to be necessary. You know where to find me. If I do not hear from you before the 31st, then I will know my answer.'

He looked at her for a few moments, then said,

'The years have been good to you, Isobel. You are still the most beautiful woman I know.'

With that, he lifted his hat, bowed, and left the room.

Isobel looked at the closed door for a long time, then, taking a short glance at herself in the mirror, she stood and prepared herself to go home.

When Isobel transferred to the Lyceum Theatre, she found the reports of Vestris' good management to be very true. The greenroom was decorated like a lady's drawing room, with chandeliers and comfortable arm chairs; and on opening night, tea and coffee was served there for the refreshment of players and guests.

But, like Drury Lane, the houses were not full. The Vestris management focused on light drama and comedy to bring in the audiences, and were doing better than some, but even so, they were struggling, like many theatres, to make good profits.

The play currently on when Isobel joined the company was *Hold Your Tongue* by James Robertson Planche, with Madame Vestris and her husband starring in the main roles. Isobel watched the play with enormous pleasure, recognising Madame's talent as the lively lady of fashion. Isobel's first part was in another of Planche's comedies, *The Seven Champions of Christendom*, a kind of fairy-tale with political references. She did not enjoy these kinds of parts as much as the more classic Shakespearian roles, but if this was the way that theatre was going, then she must run with the tide. She enjoyed rehearsals here; the Matthews and Vestris management maintained a well organised, but relaxed rehearsal system, with the actors being very well looked after, worked hard, but not to exhaustion, and all comforts and needs catered for. It was a joy to work for this husband and wife team, and quite different to the almost Spartan and full-on work ethics of the managers she had been used to, both in London and the provinces.

In her spare moments, she thought of Frank and his offer often. She missed him; she missed his sharp wit and their conversations full of lightly barbed comments and teasing. But she still could not make up her mind. Ten years ago, she had believed that her attraction to him, and their easy, playful way of being together was love. But was it? Did she really love Frank, or would this merely be a marriage of convenience, albeit with added benefits? Sometimes she thought she really should marry him; it would be such fun to be with him all the time, enjoying the kind of daily badinage that they had always enjoyed, and then at other times, she thought that perhaps she would not like that all the time. She liked her quiet life away from the theatre, where she had the chance to breathe and be herself.

Pondering on this as she alighted from her cab one evening after rehearsals, she was surprised to see a figure sitting on the area steps of her house. Thinking at first it might be a vagrant, she approached cautiously, but as he turned round, she exclaimed with joy:

'Joe? Why, Joe! But how lovely to see you! What on earth are you doing here in London?'

Joe's face lit up in a broad smile at her reaction, and he returned with a light bow.

'I have been investigating my options,' he said, sweeping off his hat and turning it round in his hands.

'Come in, Joe. I will get some tea, or would you prefer something a little stronger? Brandy, or wine? Martha!' she called to her maid, 'Martha! We have a visitor! Have you eaten, Joe?'

'No, not since about three, but...'

'Martha! Get the ham from the pantry, and a flagon of wine! Joe, you must be cold. Do come and sit by the fire.'

Having settled them both in the parlour with some cold ham and a loaf of bread, and poured them both a glass of wine, Isobel again asked Joe what brought him to London.

'Well, I thought it might be a good idea to come and see for myself what kind of opportunities there might be for a singer like me.'

'And what did you find?'

Joe looked sadly into the fire.

'You and Henry were right. The places I have seen are not the kind of places that would enjoy my style, and I don't really think that, well, the kind of songs… I'm not sure if…'

Isobel grinned.

'You mean, you don't think that you wish to start singing bawdy songs, is that it?'

Joe laughed with relief.

'It's not that I'm some kind of prude, or perhaps, well, I might even enjoy the occasional witty…'

'…or not so witty…'

'…song, yes,' he said, laughing again, 'but it's just not something I could see myself doing.'

'No,' said Isobel, 'it is not something I could see you doing either.' As she said this, she thought that it was certainly something she could see Frank doing, and had at times seen him break into the occasional suggestive, or even obscene, verse when he had had several more tankards of ale than was advisable. She had laughed at them herself; as a theatre veteran of ten years, she had learned not to be priggish, but still, she sometimes wished Frank would be more… what? What was it that was missing?

'Anyway,' Joe was continuing, 'I could not come to London and miss an opportunity to see my friend.'

'You should have written, Joe, I would have made sure I could have been here sooner, and had something prepared for you. And why did you not ring so that Martha could have let you in?'

'Oh, but I did. She told me you were not here. I did not want to put you to any trouble. Your life is so busy, and I thought it might be awkward if you did not arrive soon, so I thought it best to wait for you on the steps. I did not write because I was not sure how much time I would have, and whether my letter would arrive in time. It was rather a last-minute thing.'

Isobel smiled. It was so like Joe to consider someone else before himself.

'So, what will you do next?' she asked.

Joe stared into the fire.

'I suppose I must stay in Stratford for the time being. What I earn from singing, and I sometimes work behind the bar for the Hartleys, is enough for me to get by. But…'

He continued to look at the fire.

'But…?' Isobel questioned.

Joe looked uncomfortable. Isobel felt that there was something he dearly wanted to say, but was unable to say it.

'I, well… you see, if only I was in a position… but it does not seem possible. If only I was able to offer more, but it just cannot work. It will not work.' He seemed to be talking more to himself now.

'Joe? What won't work?'

Joe looked at her, and then seemed suddenly embarrassed. He got up abruptly and bowed rather stiffly.

'It's getting late. Thank you so much for your kind hospitality. I really must go now.'

'But Joe, won't you stay? You surely are not travelling back this evening?'

Joe's eyes opened wide.

'Stay here? Oh no! That would not do at all! No, I, thank you, but I am booked in at an inn nearby. I shall be travelling back on the train in the morning.'

Isobel felt crestfallen. She was so enjoying Joe's company, and this visit felt far too brief.

'When will I see you again, Joe?' she asked.

Joe looked at the ground and shook his head.

'It seems that we are not meant to…'

He paused, and then looked at her.

'You see, you are Isobel Brite: a bright star; your career is here in London, and you are self-sufficient. I am Joe Denny from County Mayo. I earn enough to get by. I

cannot earn a living in London – not the sort of living…
it's impossible. Now, I have said too much. I really must
go. Miss Brite, it has been a delight to see you again. I
hope we will perhaps meet again soon. Thank you for the
ham.'

And, fumbling with his cap, and almost tripping over the
rug in the hall, he took his coat and left, turning to wave
goodbye at the bottom of the steps, while Isobel waved
back in some confusion.

CHAPTER 18

Over the next few days Isobel turned over in her head Joe's abrupt appearance and odd behaviour. She did not want to make assumptions, and she tried very hard to find some other explanation, but it really did seem as if he had been almost about to make a proposal of marriage, but had stopped himself several times. Isobel was wary. She had believed twice before she was about to receive a proposal, and had been bitterly disappointed. But this was so different, and poor Joe seemed so discomforted and awkward.

So, lying in bed one night, unable to sleep, she asked herself the question; if he had proposed, would she have said yes?

Being married to Joe would be so different to marriage to Frank. What would it be like? Quieter, perhaps. Peaceful. Mutually supportive. Caring. Whereas marriage to Frank would be? Exciting, fun. What else…?

She turned over and inwardly berated herself. What on earth was she thinking? Neither man had even mentioned the word 'marriage', and here she was trying to decide between the two as if she had had two clear proposals. Frank's words had been, 'dare I hope…?', which, coming from Frank could mean anything in all honesty; whereas Joe had seemed to want to say something, and then talked himself out of it. It could have been anything. She could not think what it was he was trying to say, but really, she should not assume it was a proposal of marriage. Could she?

And if it had been, she thought, as she turned over again, why had he talked himself out of it? Well, she knew the answer to that. It was as clear as day. He felt he had nothing to offer her. He had virtually said so. All that mumbling about not earning enough; her being self-sufficient, and him being merely Joe Denny from Ireland.

None of that mattered to Isobel. But it was true that, should there be any question of marriage, their situation was not an easy one. Her career was in London, and if Joe lived in London he would not be able to work at the thing he loved. Sure, he could go back to being a navvy or a labourer, but how would that feel for him when she was earning enough to keep them both comfortable? The alternative, for her to move to Stratford, was impractical. They would both lose her earnings, and she would lose her career, which was not something she could contemplate, and he knew that. Dear Joe. He would never put her in a position where she would have to even consider sacrificing the life she had.

In the days that followed, constantly aware of Frank's deadline, she went through every day turning things over in her mind. Why could she not make a clear decision? It was not as if Joe had actually proposed, so there was really no decision to make between one or the other. The one was a request for some sort of decision, and made perfect practical sense, the other was nothing at all; no proposal and a situation that would work for neither.

Yet, still she prevaricated. Just as she thought she might accept whatever it was that Frank was offering, she would see Joe's sad face staring into the fire. But when she started to think that she would not take Frank on, she saw that she would be throwing away a life of fun and a workable, practical arrangement that could also be lucrative. As well as getting on well together, she and Frank worked well together. Perhaps, in future, they could even go into management together, as Madame Vestris had suggested.

But then, she would be throwing away any chance she might ever have with Joe. Perhaps there might come a time in the future when things could be more easily arranged. Perhaps he could find some sort of work in London while he practised singing and could perhaps find something that suited his style that might bring him an income.

The more she thought of it, the more she realised how strong her affections were for Joe. The more she felt she could marry Frank, the more the thought of Joe pulled her back.

Could she not find some way of making it work? Perhaps she could continue searching on his behalf, trying to find a place for him in London that would suit him. Yes, that was a good idea.

But it would mean letting Frank go for good without any guarantee that things would work with Joe.

Well, she had lived without Frank in her life for ten years, and for most of those years she had been happy. It was possible for her to be happy without him again. Hadn't she managed herself well enough on her own? Perhaps it would be fun to see if she could promote Joe's career as well, and see what might happen. Perhaps she could begin to make some enquiries…

A few days later, she was sitting in the Lyceum greenroom, pondering these thoughts over a pot of coffee. It was the 29th of March, and she would have to speak to Frank tonight, or tomorrow. She had to make up her mind. She was not due to perform that night, but had been busy in rehearsals all day, and was just taking some refreshment before contemplating walking over to the Olympic to see Frank and tell him… what? It really looked as though she was going to turn down his offer. She hoped he did not take it too badly…

She got up, wrapped her cape around her shoulders and went to the stage door, stepping out onto Exeter Street. As she turned into Wellington Street, she noticed a red glow in the sky towards Drury Lane, and people in the street were stopping to look.

Alarmed, she asked someone what was happening.

'It's a fire, Miss. The Olympic's on fire.'

Isobel turned sharply to him.

'Did you say the Olympic?'

'Yes, Miss. I passed there just a few moments ago. Flames were shooting through the roof. It was a terrible sight!'

Isobel did not wait to hear more. She picked up her skirts and ran across Catherine Street and then turned the corner into White Hart Street, running towards Drury Lane as fast as she could go.

When she reached Drury Lane, she could hardly get down the street for the crowds of people who had gathered to watch. It was a scene of utter chaos. Several buildings around the theatre had also caught fire, and the poor unfortunates who were trying to get their furniture out into the street found themselves and their belongings being trodden on by people thronging to get a better view of the flames. Fire engines were trying to make their way down the crowded street, while police officers were trying to control the crowd and drive them back to allow the machines through.

The noise was deafening. Behind the shouts of the police, the frantic bells of the fire engines and the murmerings of the crowd, came the loud, sickening crackling of the flames, and now and then the awful sound of crashing timber as parts of the theatre crashed to the ground. Isobel could feel the heat of the flames from where she stood, and everywhere there was the terrible smell of burning wood and upholstery.

'Move along there!' shouted a policeman right behind her, 'Make way! Make way!'

'Oh please!' shouted Isobel, 'can you tell me, is anyone still in the theatre, do you know?'

'I can't tell you Miss. Move back, now! Let the fire engines come through!'

It was hopeless to try and get anywhere near the theatre

now. The crowd was slowly being moved back, and the front of the building on Wych Street was increasingly looking as though it might fall into the road at any moment. It was too dangerous to get nearer, even if she could.

She looked around to see if she could see anyone from the theatre, but they were unlikely to be here. Perhaps, if she could get around towards Newcastle Street, and the stage door on the alley way, she might find someone who knew Frank, who could tell her where he was.

Pushing her way through the crowds again, she ran down the narrow part of Drury Lane to the Strand, turning left, past St. Mary's Church, and left again into Newcastle Street, where more crowds were watching the conflagration. The clanging bells from the fire engines pierced through the shouts from the officers and the people, and still the fire was raging and crackling above her. She could see terrible, long tongues of flame rising from the roof of the theatre, and she could taste the acrid smoke at the back of her throat.

Squeezing through the crowds as best she could, she finally managed to move up Newcastle Street to the narrow alley where the stage door was, and found some people standing around some salvaged theatrical props and furniture, looking dazed as they stared up at the burning building from a safe distance.

'Are you from the theatre? Do you know Frank Douglas?' she gasped, grabbing the sleeve of one man who looked like he might be a stage hand.

The man looked at her with some concern.

'Mr Douglas? Are you a friend, Miss?'

'Yes, I am.'

'I saw them carry him off on a stretcher. The actors were dressing when the fire broke out. I believe he tried to help, and… Hey, Jack! Where did they take Mr Douglas?'

'Mr Douglas?' said Jack, another stage worker, 'I think they took 'im to Bart's.'

'Bart's?' said Isobel, feeling sick to the stomach, 'you mean, St. Bart's, the hospital?'

'Yes, Miss. He tried to help, see? Should of just run like all the others, but would play the damned hero, if you'll pardon my language.'

'But… what… I mean, is he…? What kind of…'

'Stand back, Miss! Look out!'

A large section of wall was crumbling to the ground just one hundred yards or so away, but the heat and dust it created was such that the crowd that had gathered at the back end of the theatre had to move back further into Newcastle Street. In the ensuing chaos and confusion, Isobel lost sight of the two men she had been talking to, and no doubt they were busy keeping people back and making sure the props they had rescued were safe.

St. Bart's Hospital was over near Smithfields Market. Running back to the Strand, she started running to the east, while looking out for a cab. She eventually managed to hail one, and sat, panting, as the carriage tried to make its way through the busy Fleet Street evening traffic. After what seemed like a lifetime, the cab at last turned left, past the Old Bailey and the Courts towards Newgate, then to be held up by the build-up of traffic coming from Holborn. She paid the driver, and got out, to run the rest of the way up Giltspur Street.

As she neared the grand edifice of St. Bartholomew's Hospital, she only now wondered whether she would be allowed in at this time of day. All she had thought about until now was getting to the hospital, but it was now almost dark. In all the chaos of the fire, she had forgotten that it was late.

Her fears were founded as she approached the entrance, to be told that no visitors were allowed in. Trying to find out more about Frank, she kept asking about Mr Douglas who had been admitted with burns. Everyone in the hospital seemed too busy to take much notice of her, but eventually she was able to find out that a Mr. Douglas had been admitted about an hour ago and was receiving treatment. The only other thing she could do was find out the times of visiting the following day.

Wearily defeated, but at least knowing that Frank was still alive, she left the hospital and made her way back home by cab. Exhausted, she threw herself into bed, but slept very fitfully and without refreshment.

She returned the following day, only to be told that Frank was still under treatment for burns, as well as inhalation of smoke, and would not be able to have visitors for several days. He was still at risk of infection, and his injuries were too severe. She returned every day with a basket of ham and cheese, until they allowed her to see him.

She found Frank in a small room. He was sitting up in bed. His head, and much of his face, was covered in bandages. When she entered the room, the one eye she could see rounded in surprise.

'Isobel?'

'Frank!' she said, moving to the bed and sitting down, 'I am so glad you are alive! How are you?'

'How am I? Why, as you can see, I am finished.'

Isobel was alarmed. 'Finished? What do you mean, Frank?'

He scowled at her with his one eye.

'Have you not eyes? Did they not tell you? Half of my face is gone. And with it my career. No-one will employ me to appear on stage like this. The next stop from here will be the workhouse, no doubt. And why have you come? To let me know the answer to my question? Let me guess: after considering the proposition from all angles, you have come to let me know that you are declining my kind offer, or words to that effect. No career, and no wife. One single mistake. I should have left that theatre when the alarm went up, but no. And do you know why I tried to be a hero? I thought that if I helped to save the theatre, or even a life, then you might think the better of me. Now, look at me. Ha! So much for the handsome hero of the piece! Do you know what this will do to my face? All they can do is apply silver nitrate. Silver nitrate! There! One moment of madness, and my life is over. I would have done better to have thrown myself into the flames there and then…'

'Frank! Please…! Don't speak like this…'

He stopped, and looking down, said quietly,

'Why are you here, Isobel?'

Isobel took a deep breath. She expected Frank to be glad to see her, but now she was here, and understood the full extent of his injuries, she saw that his survival of the fire was not the end of the catastrophe for him, but the beginning of a new one, the catastrophe of a once handsome actor, now unable to work because of disfigurement. He was right. Life for him from now on would be very difficult. There would be few options available for him except the workhouse or to find a different kind of work, and she could not imagine Frank as a labourer. She had been glad that he was alive, but of course, he would be devastated by what had happened, to see his career suddenly come to an end in such a way.

She had to answer his question.

'I was coming to see you at the theatre on that day, after rehearsals, and when I came out of the Lyceum, the sky was all ablaze, and somebody told me the Olympic was on fire. Frank, I ran all the way, and I could not get near to find out where you were. One of the stage hands told me you'd been taken here, and I set out immediately to the hospital only to find that it was too late for visiting. All that I could find out was that you were alive and being treated. I returned every day, and this is the first time they have allowed me to see you. I brought you some food. I did not know the extent of your injuries until this moment.'

Frank looked at the basket that Isobel held on her lap, lifting the cloth to give a cursory glance at what it contained. He dropped it back without comment.

'I see,' he said, 'and what were you coming to tell me, when you were coming to see me on that day?'

Isobel looked down, trying to work out what she should say. She had almost forgotten what her purpose had been when she stepped out of the theatre that night. Now, of course, Frank wanted to know the answer to his question. But how could she tell him now that she had decided to decline his proposal? Surely this was not the right moment. It seemed too harsh, too cruel. And not only that, but he would suspect that she may have been about to accept, only to change her mind now she knew what his injuries were.

Besides, had she really, completely made up her mind? She had only decided on one course of action after much deliberation. The decision she had made had still some uncertainty to it. But since the events of that fateful evening, had something changed? How quick she had been to run to the theatre, to find out what had happened to Frank, and to get to where he was as quickly as she could. She obviously was still very fond of him, she realised now. How could she turn him down when he was now in need? Could she not manage for both of them? She then remembered Madame Vestris' words about theatrical management. There was no need for Frank to leave the theatre; he could just change direction; with her help, they could become managers...

'Isobel,' said Frank softly, 'you may as well tell me. I won't be angry. I understand that you could not possibly want to marry a man with this...' he pointed to his face.

How Frank looked was not important to Isobel right

now. Her mind was full of possibilities for the future; they were both ambitious and they would make a good partnership. She could see them working together. It might take a while to succeed, but together they could do it…

'Oh, but that's where you're wrong, Frank,' she said, smiling for the first time in days, 'you see, my answer is Yes, I will marry you.'

He stared at her for a moment, and then frowned.

'I do not want your pity, Isobel.'

'I am not offering pity, Frank.'

'Are you sure? When these bandages come off, it will not be a pretty sight.'

'I am sure. I will not be marrying you for your face, Frank.'

For the first time, he smiled with a little laugh, and then winced as the facial movement stretched the side of his face beneath the bandages. Isobel patted his hand.

'Well,' he said, 'this must be the strangest engagement ever. I am not even allowed to smile.'

'I will smile for you,' she said.

PART III

1851 - 1853

But I have that within which passes show,

These but the trappings and the suits of woe

William Shakespeare, *Hamlet*, Act 1, Scene 2

CHAPTER 19

Isobel linked arms with her old friend, Caroline, as they stepped inside the great Crystal Palace, trying not to lose sight of Henry in the crowds.

'Oh, look!' said Caroline, squeezing Isobel's arms and pointing upwards. Following her gaze, Isobel marvelled as she saw great trees growing beneath the rounded glass roof. In front of them, Henry waved, shouting, 'Follow me!'

'I am sure he will guide us towards the steam engines,' said Caroline, 'but I do hope he will allow us to linger at the silk and ribbon making machines!'

Isobel smiled as they made their way, along with the excited, noisy throng, through the Great Exhibition.

When Caroline had written to her to tell her they were coming to London to see the Exhibition and inviting her to join them, she had jumped at the chance to see her old friends again. It had been too long since she had last seen them, or indeed had a day out to enjoy herself, away from the difficulties of domestic life.

As they made their way through the extraordinary exhibitions and displays of British and world goods and artefacts, as well as the great machines used to produce all kinds of household and industrial items all over the world, Isobel allowed herself to be swallowed up in the atmosphere of the exhibition, the first of its kind, and an experience of a lifetime. She found herself rubbing shoulders with people who had obviously travelled to London from other countries: Chinese and Japanese, dark-skinned Asians and West Indians, as well as all the different classes, rich and poor alike, and parties of schoolchildren, all wandering round, staring in wonder at the exhibits and gazing up at the spectacular glass building, and the trees it covered. The scene around her was bewildering, with rich tapestries and canopies hanging from pillars, grand statues everywhere, and in the very centre of the building a huge fountain made of glass, where Isobel and the Hartleys sat down at a refreshment area, feeling exhausted and their heads buzzing with all the different sights they had seen so far.

After they had discussed some of the wonders they had seen: the great diamond, the elephant and its howdah, the rich coloured silks of the Far East, Caroline turned to Isobel and put her hand on hers.

'So, tell me dear Isobel, how are things with you? And how is Frank? Your letters are full of little Kathleen a and how she is thriving, which is lovely to hear, but you say very little about yourself.'

Isobel thought back over the last two years as she sipped the rather lukewarm coffee that they had been served.

After a quiet wedding attended by the Hartleys, the Duncans, her stepmother and half siblings, Isobel and Frank had settled at her house in Bloomsbury.   At first, everything seemed idyllic. Despite his disfigurement, Frank seemed happy to be with her and was very attentive and affectionate. Her income from the Lyceum was adequate for both, but when she very quickly became pregnant it was with mixed feelings for both of them. Delighted at the thought of having a child, they both were also daunted by the fact that Isobel would now have to give up work, at least for the time being, leaving them without an income and forced to live on both their savings.

Isobel had discussed the idea of theatrical management with Frank, who had been enthusiastic about the idea, and had looked into the practicalities of setting up their own company and leasing a theatre. He had met with lawyers and other managers, but the more he went out to mix with others, the more self-conscious he became about his looks. As a well-known actor in America, he had been very used to people staring and pointing at him on the street, but now he noticed this happening again, but for all the wrong reasons. And when he met with other business people, he saw through their friendliness, and saw pity and masked disgust in their eyes.

As months went by, Isobel noticed that Frank stayed at home more and more, and was less willing to discuss their plans for the future.

As their money dwindled, they were forced to leave the Bloomsbury house and take rooms in Clerkenwell, a little east of the Grays Inn Road, a far more modest area than where she had been before, but with Frank not being able to earn an income at least for the time being, it was necessary to be careful with their spending.

When she went into confinement, all her thoughts and energies were taken up with the preparations for childbirth. She had been quite terrified at the prospect of giving birth, knowing that it was a dangerous process, especially having a first child at such a late age. In the event, despite spending an agonising eight hours in labour, with a doctor and Cassandra in attendance, her daughter was born safely, and seeing the glint of red in the wispy hair on the baby's head, she immediately named her Kathleen, after her mother.

For the months after the birth, she thought of nothing except her daughter's wellbeing, and spending as much time as she possibly could with her. Unlike some women, who handed everything over to a wet nurse, Isobel wanted to experience motherhood properly. Besides, they needed to save every penny they could. Her sister, now an experienced mother, visited regularly to help with looking after the baby. Frank, also, seemed to cheer up after Kathleen's birth, and doted on his daughter.

But once Kathleen was six months old, Isobel began to think again about the immediate future, and their plans for management which seemed so far to have come to nothing. Without letting Frank know, she went to see their bank manager, and was alarmed to find out just how much they had eaten into their savings over the last year. They would have to take action soon, in some way, otherwise… well, Isobel did not want to think how bad things could get, but it was enough to know that they were not in a good position, and she knew just how easy it was for people in their profession to fall very fast into poverty. Remembering her stepmother's fears of the workhouse, and the slums of Seven Dials from where she had rescued Joe, fear began to grip her insides.

'Frank, dear,' she began one cold autumn evening as they sat by the fire after Kathleen was asleep in her cot, 'we must start thinking about our plans for the future, do you not think? Have you spoken to Mr. Higgs about forming a company yet? Or made enquiries about the theatres? If we do not do something soon, the money will run out, and we will not be able to…'

Frank was staring into the fire, the scarred side of his face in shadow. He always insisted on sitting on the left of Isobel so that that part of his face was away from her. He scowled as she spoke.

'What are you saying about the money? What do you mean it will run out soon? How would you know?'

'Well, I went to see Bates yesterday…'

'You did what? Without my knowledge?' He stared at her, and Isobel shrank at the fierce look in his eye. She had never before felt afraid of Frank, but since the accident he had not been himself. She constantly hoped that he would get better after a while, particularly after the birth of their daughter, but although he had shown an interest and enjoyment in the child, he had again sunk into low spirits, and was often uncommunicative and morose. He was not the fun person she used to know.

She smiled at him, trying to cheer him into their old way of talking.

'Well, my dear, you know how I love to be involved in

everything that goes on. It is my very nature, is it not? I felt I needed to know where we stand, so that we can plan…'

'You are my wife!' he shouted, 'you have no right to go to my bank manager, and look at my financial affairs! It is my money, and it is up to me how I use it.'

Isobel felt as though she had been slapped. Half of the money in Frank's account had been hers. While he was legally correct in that all that had been hers was now his, she had always thought that they both agreed in sharing their property, she had never thought that Frank would take this stance.

'But Frank,' she stuttered, 'if we are to go into management together, we must surely both…'

'Hang management!' he said, 'it was always a futile idea, Isobel. A fantasy and a dream. It will never happen. Do you really think that I am going to work behind the scenes, hiding myself, moving money and actors around, sitting in some poky little theatre office, while you are out front, parading yourself on stage, getting all the glory and the praise?'

He stared into the fire again, while Isobel stared, unbelievingly, at him, feeling as though her world was crumbling around her.

'Then what are we going to do?' she asked, quietly.

He stared into the fire for a long moment.

'*We* will not do anything,' he said, '*you* will go back to work. I told you a year ago, I am finished. You chose to marry me, Isobel, so you cannot blame me for our present situation.'

'But what about the baby? We cannot afford a nurse on just my wages…'

'Then she can go and stay with your sister. She has raised several children. One more would be no hardship.'

Isobel could barely believe what she was hearing. Yet, if she was honest with herself, she had known for a long time that all was not well. Frank had not been the same person since the accident, but in all the flurry of marriage and parenthood, she had ignored the signs that something was wrong. Now she saw that in that one moment, when she decided to marry Frank she had changed her world for good. Because… why? Because she had felt sorry for him? Because she thought they could work together? Because she thought he would continue to be the Frank she had always known; the one who made her laugh one moment, and infuriate her the next? Who made her feel alive and excited? But had she really married him because she loved him? If she loved him, she might now be able to help him, to get him through this period of bitterness and hopelessness. Yet, all she felt right now was a feeling that she had to get away, to get out of this house that felt heavy with Frank's silent moods.

So, she had agreed to his suggestion. She had begun to look for work, and had arranged with Cassie that as soon as she started work again, that Kathleen would stay with her. It broke her heart, but she was determined that she was not going to be dragged into poverty by Frank's inertia, and she promised herself she would spend as much time as she could with her daughter once she was earning money again.

But finding work was not as easy as she thought it would be. The legitimate drama was at a low ebb. Theatres were pandering to the demands of audiences and putting on melodrama, farce and spectacle. Though Isobel longed to play Shakespeare again, she was quite willing to play these kinds of roles; but after a year away from the theatre, she found to her alarm, that managers preferred younger actresses to employ for these productions. Isobel was now thirty-three, a matron in theatrical terms.

She went to see Samuel Phelps at Sadlers Wells, who was producing Shakespeare against all odds, and Charles Kean at the Princess, who was focusing on the classics, but they both had their cast lists full. Macready had retired in February, and new stars were rising. A new era seemed to have begun without her. With a cold chill, Isobel began to realise that her time as a young star and romantic heroine was over. Leaving the theatre for twelve months was perhaps the worst thing she could have done. How short was the memory of the audiences. The thing she had most dreaded had happened. She had been forgotten.

How complacent and arrogant she had been, thinking that there would always be a place for her!

Weeks went by, and she felt more and more distressed about how she was going to provide for her family. So, when she received the letter from Caroline, asking if she would like to join them, at their expense, at the new Great Exhibition in Kensington in May, she jumped at a chance to spend an enjoyable day out with her old friends, to forget her problems, to relax and perhaps laugh a little.

So now, she was sitting here with Caroline and Henry, and Caroline was asking how things were, and she did not know how to respond. She did not want to lie to the two people who had been so kind to her through the years, and yet to tell them honestly how things were was a humiliating prospect.

'Well,' she said, 'I hope to return to work soon, if I can find a place...'

'And Frank?' asked Caroline, 'did you not say that he was considering management, that you both were?'

Isobel looked down.

'Oh... yes. I... he's not ready yet. Perhaps in time...'

But it was no good. The tears filled her eyes. She tried to continue but her voice came out in a squeak. She hastened to find a handkerchief in her pocket, and sat wiping her eyes, unable to continue. She attempted to apologise, but all that came out was a strange wail.

'Oh, my poor Isobel!' cried Caroline, throwing her arms around her, while Henry shook his head in sympathy and patted her hand. He and Caroline exchanged glances. They had both been uneasy about Isobel's marriage to Frank.

Over Isobel's head Caroline said to her husband:

'It is too noisy here. Shall we leave now and take a walk in the Gardens?'

Henry assented, muttering to himself,

'Damn Frank Douglas! I always knew he was trouble. Why, oh why could she not have married poor Joe?'

On a seat by the Serpentine the three of them sat looking out over the water, while Isobel told them of the last two years. It was busy with the overspill from the Exhibition, and people strolling along the path, feeding the ducks, but it was good to be in the open, away from the jostle of the indoor crowd.

'I knew it would not be easy at first, and that he would find it difficult, so I tried to be patient, and I thought that over time things would get better, and he would become his old self again, and that we would start a new working life together. But it has not turned out like that at all. He has got worse, not better, and now does not seem to want to work at all! And now, I am unable to find work myself, and I do not know what is to become of us! Oh dear, I have spoiled your day, and I feel so terrible!'

She again was overcome with tears and sat with her head in her hands, while Caroline supplied her with a clean handkerchief.

'My dear, you have not spoiled our day at all! We have had a lovely time at the Exhibition, but I was getting rather tired of the crowds, anyway, and it is nice to sit here; and we would not be very good friends to you if we were not prepared to listen to your troubles.'

Isobel finished wiping her eyes and looked out over the

223

calm waters of the Serpentine, where a swan was gliding by with a family of cygnets. She felt tired but more peaceful now that she had shared all the emotions and thoughts that had been inside her head without an outlet for so long.

'The first thing you should know,' said Henry, 'is that, no matter what happens; should you find yourself in desperate circumstances, of whatever nature, there is always a place for you with us.'

'Yes, indeed!' said Caroline, squeezing her hand.

Isobel felt a fresh rush of tears in response to their kindness.

'Oh, you are both so kind…'

'The second thing you should know', continued Henry, 'is that, while Frank may have changed, you have not. We know you very well, and we know that you are a fighter and a survivor. We have always admired your ability to pick yourself up when life gets difficult, and forge ahead, finding a new path for yourself. Your idea for management was possibly a good one, but unfortunately you have been held back because of a… a difficult marriage. You will find a way forward, dear friend. You always have done, and you always will. Be of good cheer. I am quite certain that things will get better in time.'

Isobel took a deep breath. Henry's words renewed the inner strength that she had often felt in the past, but had recently felt lacking.

He was right. The path ahead may be difficult, but she would find a way, even if she had to adjust her ambitions and plans for the future. She would have to start again. She had done it before. She was older now, that was true; not the youthful beauty that she had been, that had easily got her employment. But she had experience now; she was not the innocent child she had been then; she knew her business and how it worked. She would find a way. She had to, if not for her and Frank, but for the sake of her beloved daughter.

Frank awoke, struggling to pull himself out of the old dream, the one that haunted him more and more.

The cold, grey walls of the workhouse seemed to close in on him. No way out. The other children, their faces like devils' masks, taunted him.

Frank sat up, his skin prickling all over, and sweat trickling from his brow.

Why must he be forced to remember? Why must he be so taunted by these dreams? These memories?

The illegitimate child left unwanted on the steps of the workhouse, he had grown up without the love of a mother, father or siblings. Many of the children who lived there had at least one parent in the workhouse, and were allowed to see them for at least a small part of the day.

Living by his wits, he had quickly learned that his good looks, his soulful, large eyes, would easily attract the attention of the female servants, who would coo over him, and give him extra rations, by just the turn of his head or an appealing look. The other children hated him for it, and away from the eyes of the wardens, would bully him, with verbal taunts and other torments, such as invisibly shoving him to fall out of line, so he would get into trouble.

Growing up, his one saving grace, his one ability to gain positive attention, was his natural talent to entertain. To gain the appreciation of his fellow inmates, he would stand up and sing, or tell a joke, to make the others laugh. And as he grew into a young adult, and left the workhouse for work, he found those talents had a particular effect on the women he met.

Starting work as a boot boy in a local big house, he again found his need for attention was satisfied by entertaining his fellow workers.

A theatrical company passing through the village

showed him possibilities of a new life; where being the centre of attention could actually be a way to earn money and live a life of fun, and where there would be many chances to meet women.

Putting his past behind him, he learned to read and write, and mimicked the accents of fellow players, turning himself into a gentleman of charm. Never did he mention to anyone that he had been brought up in a workhouse, not even to Isobel. It was a part of his life he would put behind him and forget forever.

Until now. Deprived of his one means of gaining that attention that he craved since infanthood, the walls of the workhouse closed in on him again.

CHAPTER 20

Inside the Eagle Tavern it was noisy and stuffy. People were constantly moving between the concert room and the pleasure gardens outside to get some air, shouting to each other, or talking across the tables to each other. Waiters scurried this way and that, delivering glasses of brandy or rum with water, bottles of ale and stout, sherry for the ladies, and ginger beer, as well as small plates of snacks: sweet biscuits and pastries. Glasses clinked, bottles popped, and people laughed. Between the benches, people got up to dance as the orchestra played a popular jig, surrounded by splendid painted walls ornamented with gilt and plate glass.

As the orchestra ended the dance number, and people returned to their seats, a fight broke out in front of the stage. A man had been making eyes at another man's young lady, and the young lady's young man had not been able to contain himself any further and had punched the other young man in the eye.

It was while this little dispute was still being cleared up by attendant officers, and the young lady in question was sharing an hysterical account of the event with her friends, that Isobel walked out onto the area in front of the orchestra.

Nobody turned to look at her. Most of the audience were still trying to crane their necks to view the little drama going on before them, laughing and jeering as the two men were led away, the ladies following, the disputed one sniffing into a handkerchief, and her friends giggling behind their hands.

Isobel waited until the offending party was out of view. The noise, however, did not die down. There was no sudden hush at her appearance, and the general hubbub of the concert hall continued. Someone shouted: 'Get on with it then!', which resulted in some raucous laughter.

Isobel took a deep breath. She had become used to recognition by an audience in the theatres; a sudden hush as she entered the stage. This was not going to be easy.

Isobel signalled to the orchestra to begin.

She had rehearsed a song that she had once sung in the circuits, and hoped it would please the London audience.

It was a long time since she had sung in front of an audience, but while she had prepared her song, sitting rocking Kathleen's cradle, and performing it for Cassie and John, she felt that her singing voice had improved with age.

It had been a difficult decision to present herself to the managers of the new music halls. It felt like an enormous step backwards, like she was returning to the first, raw days of her career. Sometimes at night, she wept for grief at the loss of what had been her life: her independent, affluent life as a star of the London stage. Now, turning to the taverns; the new, rising music halls, she would earn less than a third of what she used to, and she was going to have to work very hard to earn just enough to keep her, her husband and child in food and rent money.

In a clear, commanding voice, the voice that was used to hitting the back of the vast Drury Lane auditorium, she began her song.

Tell me the tales that to me were so dear,
Long, long ago, Long, long ago...

The noise of the crowd continued. Some people continued to talk and laugh amongst themselves, some called to waiters, and some wandered off to take the air in the pleasure gardens. Here and there, a few people turned to watch and listen to Isobel.

She was glad that she had chosen a song that people knew, and would have heard in other taverns, and perhaps even sung at home around the piano. As her clear voice rang out across the crowded room, more people turned, and some started to sing along. She encouraged them, waving them along for the last verse, until most of the crowd were singing and swaying, and others had come in from the gardens to see what was going on and to join in. As she ended the song, she led them again in an encore, and they clapped and cheered as she left the stage. She was only employed to sing two songs, one now and another later on. She felt exhausted already. She had performed her first song successfully, but she had had to dig deep in herself to create the enthusiasm for herself and the audience, when all she really wanted to do was perform drama. This was not her favourite area of entertainment, but she had learned to sing and dance, as well as act, in her days at the Jackman Theatre Company, and it would have to serve her now, as she re-started her career and earned enough money to survive.

After coming off the stage, she went to sit outside in the pleasure gardens, joining Cassie and her husband, who had come out to see her sing and congratulated her on how she had charmed the rowdy audience. As they called the waiter to bring them refreshments, a voice behind Isobel boomed in her ear:

'Miss Brite! So, we meet again!'

She turned to find the now familiar face of Mr. Charles Dickens, though she found him quite changed from the last time they had met. He now wore a longish beard, and his face seemed pale and tired, his eyes not quite as lively as when they had met before. She remembered reading in the papers of his two bereavements earlier this year, his father and his daughter, and there was no doubt these deaths had had a strong effect on him. He was again accompanied by his friend, Forster.

'Why, Mr. Dickens! And I remember your friend, Mr. Forster too,' she said, as they all bowed, 'we are quite the same party as all those years ago, for here again is my sister and her husband! Except, that I am now Mrs. Douglas.'

After all the greetings and niceties had been dealt with, Dickens and Forster joined their party, and Isobel found herself in conversation with the great man.

'You have a good, strong voice, Mrs Douglas,' he said, 'but have you left the theatre stage for good? I have seen you act many times at Drury Lane, and surely that is where your real talent lies? And, is not your husband here to support you?'

Those large, expressive eyes of his looked straight at hers with this blunt enquiry, and she looked away.

'My husband does not go out very much, Mr. Dickens. Two years ago, he had a terrible accident that disfigured his face, and he does not like to be seen in public. As for my career, I left the theatre for two years when I had my daughter, and so far, it has been a little difficult to find work again.' She laughed a little, to try to trivialise the situation, and to prevent a rush of emotion that might at any time bring tears to her eyes.

'Hm,' he uttered, 'I am sorry to hear that. Your husband is Frank Douglas, the actor, is he not?'

'Yes.'

'Yes, I read about the event in the papers. A sad occurrence indeed, he was a good actor. But, you say he does not go out?'

'No, he is very conscious of his... the way his face is...'

'I see.' He frowned, and then spoke almost to himself. 'That is odd. I could have sworn... but no, I must have been mistaken...'

'What is it?'

'Miss Brite... forgive me, I mean, Mrs Douglas, I am out most nights at present. My new house near Tavistock Square is being refurbished, and it is impossible for me to stay there, so I come out, like an owl, every night. It helps me. I watch people, and everywhere I go I find characters with whom to fill the pages of my books. I do not tend to forget a face. Sometimes they haunt me in my dreams.' He paused, looking into the distance, and then spoke in a lower voice. 'Those wishing to remain in the shadows come out at night: the criminals, the women of the night, the crippled and the disfigured…'

Isobel turned sharply to him.

'What are you saying?'

'Forgive me, I do not wish to alarm you, and I am probably much mistaken. There are some taverns I visit that are not fit for ladies such as your good self. I go there, as I say, to find and observe, to fill my pages. The person I saw a fortnight ago in one of these places did look like your husband. I remember thinking so at the time. He had a terrible burn scar on the left side of his face.'

'You must be mistaken,' Isobel said quickly.

'Yes,' he said, smiling benignly, 'I must have been. Of course, if your husband does not go out, then you would know if he had deviated from that habit. Forgive me, I did not mean to alarm, I was merely thinking out loud. It was wrong of me to say anything. Please, let me order some wine and something to eat…'

While Dickens called the waiter, Isobel thought back to two weeks ago. She and Kathleen had been staying with Cassie for a few days as Kathleen was teething and wakeful at night, which in turn kept Frank awake, and then he would be bad tempered the next day. So, Isobel had found an excuse to go and see Cassie, leaving Frank alone in the house.

Could he have gone out on one of those nights? Surely not! Frank hated being seen in public. Yet, these taverns that Dickens spoke about were dark places, full of people from the lower side of life, those who were shunned by 'society', just as Frank felt he was shunned himself. Perhaps he could feel more accepted in a place like this, with other people who did not like to show their faces in the light of day…

Isobel shook her head. What was she thinking? She could not be suspecting Frank of visiting these places behind her back, perhaps even staying out all night…?

Again, Isobel's mind took her to a place she did not want to go, and she brought herself back, chastising herself for even thinking such a thing. She must not fall into the trap of suspicion; that could ruin a marriage. She must put these thoughts behind her. Why, just ten minutes ago she would not have contemplated such a thing, and it was only that Mr. Dickens had thought he had seen someone that looked a little like him, and he must have been mistaken. It must be a coincidence. A man with a scar, in a dark tavern. There must be many such people. Obviously, he was mistaken.

Dickens was pouring wine into her glass, and Cassie was laughing at something that Mr. Forster had said. Isobel joined in, not knowing what she was laughing at, but trying to bring herself back into the present, shrugging off the little fingers of doubt and fear that crept into her mind.

The days went by in an exhausting routine. Now Isobel was working, Kathleen was staying with Cassie much of the time, so Isobel got up early every morning, cleaned the house, for they no longer had a maid, and made food for Frank, and then walked to the Duncan's house on Red Lion Square to spend some time with her daughter. From there she walked back to Clerkenwell, sometimes getting a cab if she was running late, to go and sing at the Eagle. Returning home late, she would collapse into bed beside Frank, who was often already asleep.

The times spent with her daughter were the highlight of her days. Kathleen was an energetic, bright child, full of laughter and curiosity. Isobel loved playing games with her, teaching her pat-a-cake, and singing songs like 'This Little Pig' making her giggle by grunting like a pig and tickling her toes. Cassie, who had always been good at drawing, had presented a portrait of Kathleen to Isobel on her birthday, and Isobel treasured it, keeping it in a frame by the bed and picking it up often to look at whenever she missed her daughter.

But the shadow of Frank's melancholy continued to grow. It darkened Isobel's world as she realised that he showed very little interest in his own daughter. He barely showed interest in Isobel herself, and at night only took her in his arms occasionally, more to comfort himself than for any thought of her. When they were first married, their love-making had been exciting, passionate and ardent, and Frank had been loving and kind, eager for her to share the pleasures of the marital bed. But as his malady grew, as he realised that his presence in the world was no longer acceptable in the way it once had, he grew distant and detached. When he made love to her it was without joy; it was a duty to be performed, and he no longer took pains to give her pleasure.

It was several months after her meeting with Charles Dickens that she heard of a new venue that had just opened that year on the Surrey side of the river in Lambeth. It was built solely as a music hall, a new idea in the entertainment world. Isobel heard that it could hold around seven hundred people, and was purposely encouraging women to the audiences by introducing a ladies' night, where women could accompany a gentleman, in an attempt to make this kind of venue more respectable than the back-room song rooms which had mostly been only available to men, with the entertainments usually being of a bawdy and rowdy nature. The Eagle, where Isobel had been working, accepted a broader audience, but was really no more than a tavern with a stage; but now, Charles Morton, who owned the new Canterbury Hall, was attempting to make the performance of song a respectable entertainment in its own right, and was looking for singers to perform light music and ballads. The rumour was that he had already employed Sam Cowell, the great comic actor, whom Isobel had once seen perform at the Olympic, to sing, and that he was already pleasing the audiences and beginning to fill the seats at Morton's new venture.

On a night off, Isobel decided to take herself along to the Canterbury, and see for herself what kind of a place this was, and whether it might be worth her approaching Mr. Morton for employment. Telling Frank she would be working that night, she set off as usual, but took a cab as far as Westminster Bridge. Here, she alighted. It was late summer and despite it being early evening, the air was still warm and balmy, and she decided to walk across the Bridge.

Couples arm in arm, strolled across the bridge, admiring the view of the new Houses of Parliament, only recently opened again after their reconstruction, and leaning over the parapet to watch the boats pass through.

Isobel was used to walking in London on her own, though it was unusual for women to walk without a companion in the city streets unless they were a servant, a hawker or whore. A woman like her, with finer clothes than most lone female street walkers, would often elicit stares and looks of shocked curiosity, but it did not bother her. She had always been independent, and she shrugged off those disapproving stares. She enjoyed walking; she had done since the days of walking to and from the venues as part of a travelling theatre, and she loved to walk the streets of London. Of course, she was sensible, and kept away from notorious areas, and took cabs if she felt uneasy.

But tonight, she realised something was different. An evening stroll across the bridge should have been a pleasure, but as she saw young ladies, their arms on the arms of their husband or beaus, the younger ones perhaps laughing or smiling demurely, the older matrons sedately walking in silent companionship, Isobel felt for the first time ever that she was missing something. Standing looking over the great river, she looked at the finger of her left hand, and the gold wedding band with its ring of diamonds. She was a married woman. But where was her husband? Why was she not here with someone to rest her arm on, to laugh with and to admire the view with?

If anyone had told her, thirteen years ago, that one day she would be married to Frank Douglas, she would have thought that she could not possibly experience any greater pinnacle of happiness. She would have envisaged an evening like this to be full of laughter and delight. They would have gone to the Music Hall together, full of anticipation at this new style of venue, and have enjoyed the evening, whether the entertainment was good or bad, because they were in each other's company. They would have applauded the great performances, and giggled together at the bad ones. They would have shared a bottle of wine, and gone home in a cab, her head resting on his shoulder, mellow and peacefully happy.

And here she was, married to Frank, but on her own, walking through London as she had done as a single woman. A breeze, carried along the Thames, curled round her shoulders, making her shiver a little, and wrinkle her nose as the water's stink reached her. She pulled her shawl a little tighter.

For the first time since she had been married, she allowed herself to realise something. Up until now, she knew that there were problems; the problems she had admitted to Caroline and Henry, but she always saw them as surmountable. She and Frank were a good match, and any difficulties between them would be temporary.

But now, as she stared out across the cold, dark waters of the river, she admitted to herself that she was in an unhappy marriage. Frank showed no signs of recovering from his malaise, and she did not know what to do about it. They grew ever detached, and he saw his daughter less and less.

A single tear made its way down her cheek.

What had happened to her life? Just three years ago she had been happy and content, earning an independent income from work she loved, with no sense of needing extra companionship other than her friends and her sister's family. Perhaps she had been a little lonely at times, but she had never complained. She had been acutely aware of how lucky she was; what a charmed and unusual life she led as a woman in this world, and she had only seen that it would continue, as long as she kept her wits about her.

Well, perhaps that was it. She had lost her wits. Frank Douglas had come back into her life and she had, despite all her instincts, been once more drawn towards him.

She reached into her pocket for a handkerchief, wiped her eyes and blew her nose. It was no good feeling sorry for herself. She could hear her stepmother's voice saying, 'You have made your bed, you must lie in it'. She laughed wryly to herself. For once, her stepmother's words rang true. She had made her choice, and she had to live with it, and get on as best she could.

She turned and made her way to the other end of the bridge. She must, as she always had, concentrate on her career now. It had always been her saving grace, and it would be again.

She got strange looks from the doorman when she arrived at the Canterbury alone. Although it was ladies' night, it was normal for women to arrive on the arm of a man. A woman on her own was viewed as a probable prostitute. But before he could say, 'We want none of your sort in here!' she looked him in the eye and said, 'My name Isobel Brite, the actress, and I am here to see the manager. I would like to pay to enter and see the entertainments first.' The doorman bowed slightly, and said, 'Of course, Miss Brite.' She could not be sure whether he knew the name, or whether he was just being polite.

She paid her sixpenny entrance fee and made her way towards the crowded auditorium, hoping she would be able to find a discreet table for herself. She could hear a performance was already under way. Somebody was singing an Irish ballad.

She stopped still. The hair on the back of her neck bristled. Something made her heart beat faster.

She knew that voice.

She pushed her way through the crowd, and between the tables where food and drink were being served by waiters rushed off their feet. She forgot about finding a table, and only thought to find a space where she could see the stage clearly. A party in front of her obscured the view, and she moved to the side of the room, remaining in the shadows, and stood still, a smile broadening slowly across her face.

For there, singing in that beautiful, heartfelt voice that she knew so well, was Joe Denny.

CHAPTER 21

Isobel found a small table towards the side of the stage where she could watch Joe. A waiter appeared, and she ordered enough food and drink to keep her going for the evening, knowing that it was all included in her sixpenny entrance fee.

As she listened to Joe's voice, she felt a mixture of emotions, not all of which were good.

She had not seen Joe since that strange evening when he had turned up on her doorstep, and had seemed so awkward. She had thought that he had been leading up to some kind of proposal, but later on, after she had decided to marry Frank, she had dismissed this thought. She could not now, however, avoid a pang of guilt as she remembered that she had promised herself to look out for a venue for him, and had so quickly forgotten to do so in her plans for marriage. Not that she had needed to do so, obviously, as it seemed that he had found the perfect venue for himself. Remembering Joe's desire to sing in London, but at that time there being no respectable place for his talent, she realised that things had begun to change in his favour. This type of venue would be perfect for him, and she was so glad that he was able to find a place where he could express his talents.

But she also felt uneasy about her lack of contact with him. He had not attended her marriage, though she had invited him, excusing himself due to a cold, and apart from a little note to him afterwards, hoping he was feeling better, and a short note from him congratulating her on her marriage, they had not communicated at all. She remembered how often they used to write to each other before her marriage, how easy and friendly their letters were, and how she would feel so happy when she saw a letter with his name on the back.

She felt guilty that she had made no attempt to write to

him over the last two years. In her letters to Caroline and Henry she would enquire after him, and send her regards indirectly, but for some reason she always felt uncomfortable now about writing to him personally. Something held her back, as if her marriage had changed whom she could and could not communicate with.

I suppose I am not free to write to a single man in the way that I used to, she thought to herself, realising that she had never quite admitted this to herself before. *No, not free in many ways. I'm a married woman. In the eyes of the law, my life is not my own.*

After Joe finished singing, Isobel found her way to a door at the side of the stage, and again used her name with the doorman there. 'My name is Isobel Brite, the actress. I am a friend of Joe Denny.'

She was allowed through, and caught Joe as he came off the stage.

'Joe!' she called, gently.

He peered at her in the darkness of the wings, and then his eyes rounded in surprise as he recognised her.

'Why! If it isn't Iso… Miss Brite!'

He then caught himself, and looking slightly embarrassed, said, 'I mean Mrs Douglas, of course.'

He looked around and behind her, as if expecting someone else to be there.

'You are here alone?'

'Yes Joe, quite alone. I came to see what was happening here, and what kind of venue it was, and then you popped up on stage and I got the surprise of my life! I had to come and say hello. I am so glad for you, Joe, you are now singing in London, just as you wanted to. How is it going? Are they paying you well?'

Joe looked around, uncomfortable about discussing his employment within earshot of his employers or fellow entertainers.

'Shall we go out front? I am finished for the night, and we can watch Mr Cowell. Have you seen him sing 'The Ratcatcher's Daughter'? It's funny and sad at the same time, and he is very clever with his accents and movements. He has the audience in stitches.'

'I would love to Joe, and you will make me look like a respectable woman. I can't tell you the kind of looks I've been getting, coming here on my own. Lend me your arm, and we will look quite the respectable pair!'

Joe looked a little uncertain and awkward.

'Are you sure? With you being a married woman, and all…'

'Oh, nonsense! My husband never sees the light of day, and he could not possibly begrudge me an arm to lean on when I am out. Far better than being alone.' Feeling suddenly light-hearted and in the mood to tease, she leaned closer to him and whispered in his ear, 'do you know what people think when they see me alone…?'

Joe stopped her, shocked.

'Shhh! Do not say such things! Why, how can you bear to be thought of like that?'

Isobel laughed a little, and felt a little guilty at teasing Joe, who she could see was still his unsophisticated self and had not been changed by his career.

'I can see that this business has not yet knocked the edges off you Joe. But I have been in it long enough not to be upset by what other people think. Why half the audiences I have ever played to think of actresses as no more than…'

'Oh do stop, Miss Brite… Oh bother!… I mean Mrs Douglas!'

'I am sorry Joe. I am teasing you. You do tease so easily! Here, give me your arm. If anyone can make me look respectable, it is you…'

Joe looked at her, not knowing whether to take this as a compliment or a jibe at his innocence. But then he caught her eye, and they smiled at each other, and then burst into laughter, bringing looks of annoyance from the stage manager who was just about to go on stage to announce Mr Cowell's entrance. This made the pair giggle even more, and they hastily made an exit through the door back into the auditorium.

Isobel had not enjoyed herself so much for such a long time, and it seemed strange to her that just a few hours before she had been feeling in such despair and sadness about her life. Nothing had changed, of course, but she laughed so much that night, that all that had been worrying her beforehand seemed a little lighter; a little less important.

One thing that had been of particular significance to her that night was that after she and Joe had arrived back in the auditorium, some people had stood up to applaud Joe, and then somebody said, 'Why, isn't that Miss Isobel Brite, the actress?', and they had then applauded her, and she had bowed and smiled graciously, whilst trying to look as nonchalant as possible.

When she and Joe had sat down at a table, she had said to Joe,

'Did you see that? They love you, Joe. You are going to do well! And they remember me. I am not forgotten!'

'Of course not,' said Joe, 'how could anybody forget you?' and then he had turned away awkwardly, to watch the performer on the stage.

Sam Cowell had made them laugh so much that tears ran down her face again, but this time with sheer joy. She and Joe shared a bottle of wine and some pastries, and they talked of old times, of the Hartleys and of Stratford. She learned that Henry was thinking of going back into performance again, and was in discussion with old Henry Jackman about appearing as a guest singer at the occasional venue, and his plans to form a new

Shakespeare theatre in Stratford were going ahead nicely.

She told Joe about Kathleen, about her little ways, and how Cassie says she is growing into a stubborn and determined little lady, just like her mother.

Afterwards, they shared a cab and Joe insisted on accompanying her all the way back to Clerkenwell, where he waited in the cab until she was safely indoors, before making his way back to the meagre rooms he was staying in south of the river again, close to the Waterloo Road. To save money he stopped the cab at the Strand, and walked back across Waterloo Bridge, smiling and frowning to himself in turns along the way.

Life went on as usual after this. Isobel wrote to Charles Morton about possible work at the Canterbury, and he wrote back in very respectable terms, acknowledging her experience and talent, but informing her that at present there was no space for another singer for at least a few months, so she continued at the Eagle, where she had developed a small following amongst the regulars who came to cheer every time she appeared on the stage.

On 30th September she received a letter from Henry telling her the sad news that her old manager, Henry Jackman, had died in Northampton, during the company's season there. Despite the ongoing demise of the circuit theatre companies, Old Henry had managed to keep the Jackman Company going by shrewd management and sheer determination, but his death seemed like the end of an era. Isobel was very saddened by this news, and shed several tears, remembering her first meeting with Jackman when she had auditioned for him all that time ago in Daventry, when Frank had led her into that old barn, and she had been full of excitement and hope for the future.

She sat with the letter on her lap, staring out of the window, struck with such feelings of nostalgia for those old days of working with the Jackmans, that she could hardly move for a while. It seemed at once another lifetime ago, and yet at the same time, just yesterday, hearing Old Henry's voice shouting, 'it is not your prerogative to arrive on stage when you please and speak your lines as if you were still a shoemaker's daughter!'

Isobel laughed to herself, a little sadly, remembering why she had been so distracted that day, and then remembered that Frank should know about Jackman's death too, and perhaps it might even motivate him to come out of hiding and attend the funeral, which was to be in a few days on 3rd October.

The news certainly seemed to have an effect on Frank, and they sat up that night, talking about Old Henry and their time with the company. They shared anecdotes, and Frank even laughed when she told him about that rehearsal when she had been so distracted, and why, and the way old Henry used to go red in the face and to shout, 'This is a respectable company!' whenever one of his actor children or stars got themselves into any trouble. For a while, Isobel thought that perhaps this might be a turning point for Frank, that perhaps it might bring him out of his misery for a while, bring him back to the Frank she once knew when they worked together. But when she tentatively asked him whether he might like to attend the funeral with her, it was like dark clouds suddenly covering the sun. He grew morose and went back into himself, saying, 'You go if you must. No-one will wish to see me.' Then he went to bed, and hardly spoke to her for the next few days.

So, Isobel made the journey alone to Northampton, taking the train from Euston, and booking in where the Hartleys were staying; the very same inn they had stayed at the last time she had been there eight years ago, when Henry had warned her that the travelling theatre companies would soon be a thing of the past. In many ways he had been right, and most of the old provincial circuit theatres were no more, but the Jackman company had managed to survive until now, one of the last of its kind. Isobel was glad, however, that she had got out when she had. If she had stayed with them, it would have been almost impossible now to get work in London at her age, and with the way people like Bunn and others were relying on spectacle, opera and comedy. The timing had been perfect for her, and had allowed her several years of success and freedom. But now, she knew she was at another turning point.

How odd it was, and somehow significant, that she and the Hartleys found themselves in the same place as they had been on that day when she had decided to try for the London theatre. Now, another milestone had been reached; Old Henry was dead, and she and all the company were looking to the future and wondering what their lives would be now.

'Well,' said Henry Hartley, leaning back on the old pub's settle, a mug of beer in his hand, 'here we are again. And a very sad occasion this time; a very sad occasion. I did not always see eye to eye with my father-in-law, but I had a great deal of respect for him. He was an astute businessman when all is said and done, and he knew how to get the best out of the people who worked for him.'

Isobel nodded, patting Caroline's hand beside her, who was dressed in black, as befitting the daughter of the deceased, and looking tired and red-eyed.

'Had he been ill, Henry?' Isobel asked.

'I saw him just a few weeks ago. We had been discussing my appearance as a guest at some future venues, you know. He did not look well. I think the strain of work and keeping everything going was telling on him. But of course, he was not young. I think his health had been failing for some time.'

'He was sixty-six,' said Caroline, who herself, despite

her weary countenance, was looking far younger than her forty-three years. Henry, however, three years her junior, was beginning to show his age. Isobel thought of how lithe and youthful he had been when she had first known him in the late 1830s, able to bring audiences to tears with his lively comic jigs and songs. He was now portly, and Caroline had told her in letters how he suffered from aches and pains in his knees and hips.

How time changes us, she thought, soberly, wondering too whether her own countenance showed the passing years.

In London's East End, the Ten Bells Pub on Commercial Road was teaming with life. It was close to midnight, and the pub was full of local weavers and labourers, some of them already drunk and spoiling for a fight. Jewish immigrants huddled together in groups, keeping a wary eye on the more established groups of Cockney and Irish, who saw the immigrants as a threat to their jobs. Prostitutes weaved their way around the tables, looking for trade, hoping to land a trick who rented one of the small rooms upstairs, so they'd get a bed for the night, and keep them out of the grim, rat-infested slum rooms they shared with other prostitutes. In dark corners, men gambled over cards, or talked business not meant for anyone's ears but their own. The pub was dark, lit only by the occasional candle on tables, and one or two gas lamps.

Into this pub came a man who walked with his collar up, and his hat pulled down so that much of his face was hidden, though as he walked past a lamp it was possible to see that part of his face was scarred and disfigured by burning.

As he sat down in the darkest corner, one of the prostitutes turned around to look at him, interested in whether the newcomer might be a possible new trade. However, she smiled in recognition. She knew him. He would come into these places now and then, and was a cut above the usual clientele, being well spoken and quite handsome, if you only looked at one half of his face. He paid better too. She moved over to where he sat.

'Hello Frank! 'Aven't seen you around 'ere lately. You gonna buy me a little drink then?'

Frank grinned and winked at her, pulling her down to sit next to him. Nodding to the barman, he ordered two large gins.

The crowd attending Henry Jackman's funeral at St. Katherine's church in Northampton was a large one. His family alone, with various spouses and their children, was numerous, and many who had worked with him had come from far and wide to pay their respects. Caroline stood next to her mother, Frances, with her other sisters and brothers, while Isobel and Henry Hartley, and the other husbands and wives and friends stood a little way back from the graveside in respect of the close family.

After the burial ceremony, the crowd moved away slowly and quietly, in small groups. There was a strong air of change, which the crisp, breezy autumn air did nothing to dispel.

Afterwards there was a wake, and in keeping with Old Henry's Irish ancestry, it was a lively affair, and many of the company got up and sang and danced, in celebration of the life of this much-respected actor and manager, who would never be known in the history books, but who had made his own mark on the old theatre circuits; a man who represented an era now fading away, soon to be forgotten.

Many of the old company who had worked with Isobel, spoke to her, asking about London and how it was to work in the big theatres. Some asked about Frank, and wondered why he wasn't there today.

'Frank is a little unwell at present,' she said to anyone who asked, 'he was very sad to miss the funeral, and sends all his good wishes.'

But Henry and Caroline, watching her give this pre-planned reply, looked at each other, knowing that this was very unlikely to be the truth.

CHAPTER 22

December 1852
The Golden Lion, Stratford-upon-Avon

My Dear Isobel
Greetings from a very windy Stratford! Caroline and I are both joined in wishing you and Frank a <u>very happy</u> Christmas! Caroline has specifically asked me to tell you to stay safe in all this stormy weather, and not to walk under any wobbly chimney pots (she will read about one terrible accident in the newspapers, and then worry that the same will happen to all her friends and family – but, there! I have done my duty).

Now, to business. The Jackman Theatre Company have now become "Jackman and Morgan", with Henry junior partnering up with Mr Morgan whom you met at the funeral, who is Harriet Jackman's husband of three years. The plan is for them to forge stronger links with various theatres with longer contracts, to cater to changing public needs. From February they will be playing at the Shakespeare Theatre here in Stratford on Chapel Lane, (in which I have recently invested, as you know), for a period of six months, and yours truly will be joining them for the season. They will all stay at the Inn for that time. Caroline and Sophia are both very excited at the thought of being back in the bosom of their family once more, and I do rather think that a very jolly time will be had by all.

My purpose in writing, my dear Isobel, is therefore, not only to wish you the greetings of the season, but to invite you to join the merry throng for at least a part of that season. Young Henry has already agreed that you would be welcome to appear as a guest star, if you could arrange it, and he is writing to you separately. Perhaps you would like to sing here in the evenings as well?

I was hoping that our mutual friend, Joe Denny, might

*be able to join us for some of the season, but he has
written to tell me that he is committed at the Canterbury
for the next few months. That is our loss, and the
Canterbury's gain. Ah well… we have taught him too well
methinks! I hope he does well. His character is such that
I do not think he will ever become one of those
vainglorious stars that the world has far too much of, for
my taste.*

*Our regards to Frank. I hope he has returned to full
health.*

*Your friend,
  Henry Hartley*

*P.S. Caroline is sending you something warm under
separate cover, so let us know it has safely arrived. I
believe she has knitted it herself, and will urge you to wear
it against the chill. I do not think it will save you from
falling chimney pots, however!*

*P.P.S. Caroline has just leaned over to read my letter,
and I have just received a rap on the back of my head for
the last. Such is the life of a respected Town Councillor!*

Isobel read the letter with a mixture of emotions. Firstly,
she was delighted to be invited to perform as a guest star
with the newly reformed Jackman and Morgan Company,
and the thought of it gave her a great feeling of pleasure
and excitement. How marvellous it would be to play a
Shakespeare role again with her old colleagues, but this
time as the guest star from London. She did not want to
be one of those 'vainglorious' actors, as Henry had put it,
but even so, there was something rather pleasurable about
returning as a successful London actress.

But, then the pleasure faded as she thought of Frank.
The invitation did not extend to him. If she showed him
this letter, this would be the first thing he would notice.
How could he not? She of all people knew how incredibly

sensitive he was about such things. He knew that neither Jackman nor Morgan, nor anyone else, would put an actor in front of an audience with such a disfigurement.

So how could she tell Frank that she would be spending time playing at Stratford with the new Jackman company? It would just be another thing to knock him further down. And even if she did, he would probably not allow her to go, she painfully admitted to herself. As her husband, he was entitled to stop her doing anything that he did not approve of, and she felt that he would not approve of this.

As she read the rest of the letter, she read between the lines that they had already invited Joe first, and had perhaps waited for his answer before they had invited her. What was the meaning of this? And why had they so pointedly told her that Joe had turned them down? Did they think that her being in the same place as Joe was a bad idea? What nonsense! She and Joe were good friends. She regularly went to see him at the Canterbury, and shared a drink with him afterwards, when she could afford it. It was good to get out of the house when she was not working herself, and she liked the fact that people sometimes recognised her there.

There was also another underlying feeling she had as she read Henry's letter, and it was one of discomfort. The Hartleys' marriage was such a good one, full of little touches of playfulness and mock teasing, but with deep affection. It was the kind of marriage that she had envisaged for herself with Frank. In her mind's eye, she saw Caroline leaning over Henry to read the letter, playfully swatting him with the back of her hand and laughing at the same time, following with some term of endearment. As she thought of this, the letter suddenly became blurry, and she wiped her eyes quickly, and folded the letter up.

After thinking about it for a couple of days, Isobel decided not to tell Frank that she had even received

Henry's letter, and she quietly wrote back to Henry, and the young Henry Jackman, saying that, with regret, she herself was committed to the Eagle, and was unable to get the time off for any period. As she sealed and stamped her letters, she was unable to shrug off a feeling that her world was closing in on her.

Christmas came and went without much to mark it, apart from some time with Kathleen and the Duncans, exchanging gifts, and the arrival of a beautiful green woollen shawl from Caroline, as Henry had promised. It was certainly timely, as the winter continued to bring some of the worst storms in living memory, and the newspapers were full of stories of shipwrecks and overturned coaches. Every time Isobel stepped out, she could not help but think of unstable chimneys, and kept a wary eye above her for signs of falling masonry.

Isobel continued to spend a lot of time at Cassie's house, where her daughter was living almost permanently. Sometimes she would spend several nights at the Duncan's, enjoying the company of her sister and brother-in-law, and their children. They were a happy family, and Isobel began to feel more at home with them than she did in her own home. Of course, the Duncans' house was a comfortable one, whereas Isobel's and Frank's small set of rooms was less so, and suffered from damp, and noise from adjoining apartments. It was all they could afford at present, and they could barely afford that.

Frank showed no signs of wanting to work, and Isobel broached the subject less and less, knowing that whenever she did so, it was likely to throw him into a bad mood, and create a difficult atmosphere. She noticed that whenever she stayed away with Cassie, Frank's mood seemed lighter when she returned, and often filled her with hope. Did he miss her so much that her return brightened him? Sometimes she brought Kathleen home for a day or two, in the hopes that it would help to bring Frank out of his torpor, and for a while it did. But he would soon sink back into apathy and moodiness, and Isobel took Kathleen back to the place that the little girl now thought of as home. It was certainly a brighter, happier place for the child to grow up in, and Isobel recognised this with a sharp pang of guilt and pain. She was a failure as a mother. She should be able to provide a proper home for her child, but no matter how hard she worked, there never seemed to be enough money, and she could see a time coming when they may not even be able to pay the rent. What would become of them? Pride prevented her from asking her brother-in-law for help. That would be failure indeed. Had she not always been able to pay her own way? Even now, with Frank dragging her further and further into poverty, she still felt she must find a way of managing on her own. So, she never discussed her problems with her sister. Cassie had made such a successful marriage. How could she begin to admit to her that her marriage and career were failing? So, she kept up the pretence that Frank was temporarily indisposed, and would soon be able to take on work again. But how long could she keep this up?

Inside that atmosphere of Frank's brooding darkness, and the shabby interior of their household, Isobel found it more and more difficult to remain hopeful and motivated. She continued to write to theatre managers, but no-one seemed to be looking for classical actors, or if they were, they were looking for young actors and actresses, or those who were already currently working and in the public eye. A creeping desperation began to fill Isobel's heart. Was this her life now? A steady decline from stardom to poverty? It had happened to other actors; why not her?

She went to the Canterbury less and less. It was a luxury she could no longer afford. But just now and then, to cheer herself up, she saved a few pennies to go and see Joe and spend an hour or two with him after the show, so that she could at least smile and laugh for a while. Joe was earning a good wage now, and she was aware of the irony that it was now he who paid for her cabs home, when once it had been her that did the same for him.

It was on such a night in February that she returned home late to find Frank sitting in front of their small fire, a bottle of whisky on the table and a glass half full in his hand.

As she walked into the room he drained his glass and immediately poured another one.

Isobel had long realised that Frank drank when he was alone, but she had never seen him sitting here drinking so openly. He was usually in bed by the time she returned home. All the gaiety and lightness of the evening fell away from her as she walked into the heavy, dark atmosphere.

Without looking up, he said,

'Where have you been?'

Isobel was taken aback. Frank never showed any interest in her movements, or even her work. She assumed that every time she went out, whether it was to the Eagle, or to the Canterbury, Frank did not really care, as long as she was bringing money into the household. It was true that she never told him about her nights at the Canterbury, but she never felt that she was deceiving him in any way. If he showed so little interest, what did it matter if he assumed she was out working?

But now he was asking her a direct question, she felt a pang of guilt that she had not been more open about her nights off. He would not like the fact that she was visiting a music hall unaccompanied. She paused, not knowing how to answer.

'Where have you been?' he asked again, his voice only slightly louder, 'and don't lie to me, Isobel.'

Although he was not shouting, Isobel could sense by a slight tremor in his voice that he was holding something back. His hand held the glass of whisky tightly; his whole body seemed tense, as if fighting an inner rage.

'I...'

'Don't tell me that you were at the Eagle tonight. I was there earlier, and you were not on the programme.' He continued to stare into the fire, but his voice was louder.

'No,' she said, trying to sound calm, and matter-of-fact, 'I wasn't. It was my night off. I went to see a friend.'

Frank laughed, but it was a slow, bitter laugh.

'Friend,' he muttered, 'is that what you call him?'

Isobel stood completely still, not knowing how to respond, or what she should say.

'What... what do you mean, Frank? What are you saying...?'

In the next instant Frank had leapt from his seat and threw the glass, with its remaining dregs of whisky, into the fire; the glass smashed into the coals, and the flames roared suddenly, dangerously, spitting sparks out onto the floor. Frank turned to her.

'Don't play the innocent with me, woman!'

He grabbed her arm, pulling her towards him and speaking into her face, so she could smell the sour smell of whisky on his breath.

'I know you,' he said, 'I know your kind. You're just like all the rest, for all your clever little wiles. You don't fool me!'

'Frank, stop it, you're hurting me! What is this about?'

He threw her back onto the other chair and stood over her, so she was unable to go anywhere.

'You really think you can flaunt yourself all over London, and I would not find out, eh? You think you can go and prostitute yourself with your so called "friend" – or perhaps, it is even more than one - in public places, and no-one would see you, no-one would recognise you? You think you can make a cuckold and a fool out of me? Am I so disgusting to you that you seek company elsewhere?'

'Frank! Of course not! What… why are you saying these things?'

'Because I have proof Isobel! You have been seen with that goddam Irishman; that ballad singer, who thinks himself oh so grand, and they all think is so "sweet", and sings so eloquently of love and honour. Ha! He is no better than any other singer on the circuit, after whatever he can get; and at the moment, what he can get seems to be the wife of Frank Douglas!'

Isobel found she was trembling, not with fear, but with a rage that she was trying to contain. She sat up straight in the chair and looked Frank in the eyes.

'Joe Denny is my friend. No more. He is a good man.'

Frank threw back his head and laughed, and staggering slightly on his feet.

'My dear girl, you must know, in all your great experience in this so-called business of ours, that there is no such thing as a "good man". Ha! Nor a good woman for that matter. I knew the kind of woman you were from the start. Why, when I took you into that pub all those years ago, and you thought I was going to propose to you, I knew I could get you into that bedroom even after you realised your mistake. If it hadn't been for that interfering old fool, Hartley, coming in and spoiling everything…'

Isobel stood up, taking advantage of Frank being unsteady on his feet. She felt sick to her stomach.

'I am not going to listen to any more of this, Frank. You are drunk, and you don't know what you are saying. I am going to bed, and we will continue this conversation when you are sober…'

He pushed her back into the chair.

'We will continue this conversation NOW!'

Isobel's mind raced. She had no idea how to deal with Frank like this. The quietness and the dark moods of the last two years were one thing, and horrible to live with, but this was something new, and for the first time since she had ever known Frank she felt threatened. She said nothing, realising that arguing with Frank would be useless while he was drunk, and would probably just make him even more angry. She sat in her chair, looking at him from the corner of her eye, wondering what was coming next.

Instead of speaking again, Frank threw himself back into his chair, picked up the bottle and drank from it. Almost under his breath, he said,

'I should get myself a pistol and have it out with him.'

Isobel's eyes widened in alarm.

'He's done nothing wrong!'

'So you say.'

'I do say, and it's the truth!'

'Ha!' he laughed, scornfully, 'Truth! I find my wife has been lying to me, telling me she's working when she has been putting herself about in the nightlife of London, and you talk to me of truth! How can I possibly trust you?'

'I've never lied to you, Frank. It is true that I probably should have told you that I was occasionally going to the Canterbury, but you have never seemed interested in anything I do, and...' she paused, wondering whether it was wise to say what she was about to say, but it came out of her mouth before she could make that decision, '...you haven't exactly been the best company recently. You must see that.'

She sat still, wondering whether he would explode again, but he remained sitting, again, staring at the fire.

'But...' she went on, 'I would never be unfaithful to you, Frank, I swear it.'

In the silence that followed, a small thought began nagging at Isobel. His words came back to her: 'You've been seen...'

There was something that didn't add up. As far as she

256

was aware, Frank never went out, and he had few friends, if any. But his words suggested that somebody had told him something. When could this have happened, and who was it?

Then, a memory entered her head. She remembered the day that Charles Dickens had met her at the Eagle, and he had said that he had seen someone who looked like Frank… where was it? Yes, that was it; one of those dark and dingy taverns that cater to "the criminals, the women of the night, the crippled and the disfigured…"

She had seen them at the Canterbury. Despite the efforts of the management to keep the establishment respectable, they still managed to get in. Isobel had seen them, discreetly plying their trade there, moving round the tables, hoping for a trick who would perhaps pay a little more than the usual clientele. Women of the night, coming further afield than their usual haunts, perhaps, where competition was high and wages low; the taverns of East London.

'Who was it?' she asked, quietly.

'What?'

'Who told you about me being at the Canterbury? Who recognised me? Who knew I was your wife?'

'That's of no concern of yours.'

Isobel stared at him, wondering if he had any recognition of the irony of him expecting her to be truthful, when he was obviously withholding things about his own life from her; of suspecting her to be unfaithful, while…

She slowly got to her feet.

'Of course, it is my concern. I am your wife. If you wish me to be honest with you, is it not only fair that you should be honest with me? Am I to be kept in the dark about where you go and what you do? My God, Frank, if you are not going to go out to work, if I am the only person in this marriage who earns a living, then at least have the decency to tell me where you go, and how you

257

spend our money. My money.'

She stopped, wondering if she had gone too far, but for a moment, Frank continued to sit there, staring into the fire, and she wondered whether he was considering the justice of her words. She relaxed.

But in the next moment, without any warning, Frank leapt from his chair and hit her so hard on the side of her face that she was thrown across the room, hitting the floor with such force that she felt the breath had been knocked out of her.

'How dare you question me!' he shouted, 'How dare you say such things, when you know I cannot work! You are not to question me, or what I do. It is your job to be a faithful wife, to look after me. What I choose to do in my own time is my right. You need to know your place! Don't you ever dare speak to me like that again, Isobel, or I swear you'll fare much worse than a mere slap!'

She heard him go to the door and put on his jacket, and then the sound of the door slamming as he went out into the night.

CHAPTER 23

Isobel did not know how long she lay on the floor. She made no move to get up for a long time. Numbly, she felt her life was over, and there was no point in moving.

But after a while she noticed that her left cheek was burning, yet the rest of her was beginning to feel chilled, as the fire in the grate died down.

Slowly, painfully, she got herself into a sitting position, and touched her cheek, recoiling in pain. Her fingers felt sticky. She realised that she had hit her head on the hard, wooden floor and she must have badly grazed it. On the other side of her face, where Frank had hit her, she felt a swelling around her eye.

The full memory and realisation of what had happened came rushing back to her and she began to sob; long, drawn out, racking sobs that seemed to tear her body apart.

It was not so much the way Frank had treated her that hurt her so much, though that was a large part of it. It was the realisation of what her life had come to since she had married him. Two years ago, she had been at the top of her profession, an independent woman; well-paid and living in comfort. Now, here she was lying on the bare floor of a shabby apartment, a tavern singer barely scraping a living, while her daughter lived elsewhere, and her drunkard husband no longer trusted or cared for her.

Slowly, her sobs got weaker, and she sat for a while in silence, feeling a heavy numbness descend on her. She felt exhausted, but she did not want to go to her bed. She had no idea what time it was, and Frank could return at any time; and what if he was in the same mood? What more might he say or do?

Her face was hurting, and she needed to do something. She slowly got to her feet, and went into the next room where she poured some water from the ewer into a bowl and sponged her face with a cloth. Peering into her mirror, she could see her face was already swollen and coloured with blue-black bruises.

Painfully, she admitted the truth to herself, the thing that she had been trying to avoid for the last two years, the thing that she had hoped would just go away. Frank was no longer himself. That accident in the fire had affected his mind as well as his body. He had, to all intents and purposes, lost his mind, and she did not know what could be done about it.

Oh, she knew he had never been perfect. Of course not. He was a rake when she first knew him, but she was sure he had changed for the better since then. She was sure he would never have treated her so cruelly if it had not been for him losing his looks and his career. Perhaps the accident had somehow brought out all the worse side of his nature and exaggerated it, obliterating the tender and fun side of him.

She leaned against the wooden table and found herself sobbing again, even though she had thought she had done all the crying she could do. But she cried now, not for the hurt of the events of the evening, but for loss, for grief. She had lost the man she thought she had married, and she could see no way of getting him back. Frank, as she had known him, was dead to her. The man she lived with was not her husband, not the Frank that she had once loved.

She stood up straight and hastily dried her eyes. She could not waste any more time. He might come back at any moment, and she was now fearful of him, this monster he had become.

She opened a tin in the corner of the room where they kept their spare change. It was empty. Frank must have taken the last few pennies and pocketed them before she had returned this evening.

She fumbled for her own purse which she kept hanging from her waist. Luckily, she still had the wages from her singing at the Eagle last night. It was not much, but it would be sufficient.

She went to her room and gathered a few things into a bag, including the portrait of Kathleen, and then put on her cloak and hood. She stopped for a moment, thinking of her daughter. How dearly she wished she could take her, but if she turned up on the doorstep of Cassie and John now, they would only be alarmed at her face, and it might frighten the child. Questions would be asked, and a fuss made, and she did not think she could bear that right now. Besides, if Frank tried to find her, it would probably be the first place he would go to.

No, she needed to get away from London. She would have to walk to the station if she stood any chance of affording a ticket. Walking through the streets of London in the dead of night was a daunting thought, but she felt safer doing that than waiting for Frank to come home.

As she took one last look round this dark and dingy place that had been her home for nearly two years, and shut the door behind her, she realised that all she had left of her life was what she stood up in, and the few meagre things she had packed into her bag. Frank would lay claim to all those bits and pieces of furniture or furnishings that she had held onto from her past life, that had not yet been sold. In the eyes of the law, she was deserting her husband, and would have no rights, and everything she had ever owned was his anyway. She faltered a little, as she also realised that Frank would have the rights to Kathleen, that he could shut her out as a mother, and she very nearly turned back.

But, Frank had shown very little interest in his daughter in the last few months. Would he really make any effort to get Kathleen back, even if it was just to spite her? *Well,* she thought, finding a little bit of her old spirit returning to her as she got further away from her home, *if he just tries that, he will have to fight me first. I would see him committed to a lunatic asylum before he would take my daughter away from me.*

And what about Joe? Would he be in any danger? She thought of Frank's threat earlier.

She would write to him. She would write to both him and Cassie and explain the situation. It would be humiliating to tell everyone how her marriage had turned out, but if that was what it would take to keep her daughter and her friend safe, then that is what she would have to do. It was no time for pride now.

The following morning, a post-boy arrived at the Golden Lion Inn in Stratford with a telegram for Mr Hartley.

ARRIVING ON 10:25AM TRAIN. SEND CAB. ISOBEL

Henry paid the boy and went to find Caroline to show her. She read it and looked at Henry in alarm.

'Something has happened!' she said.

'Should we be surprised?' he said, with a raised eyebrow.

When Henry and Caroline saw Isobel's face, they were both truly shocked. Her eye had swelled further so she was barely able to open it, and there was an ugly, purple bruise across that side of her face. She was also exhausted and hungry, having traipsed across North London in the dead of night to Paddington Station, terrified of pickpockets, or worse, and her bag that she thought she had packed so lightly getting heavier and heavier with each step. Several times she had been approached by men, thinking her to be a prostitute, but she gave them a sharp word and hurried on, terrified of them following her; a knife in the ribs, dragged into an alley, her bag taken and being left for dead. But thankfully, the worse she received was coarse insult and a curse. She could live with that. She had heard worse.

With only just enough money for her fare and the

telegram to the Hartleys, she had had no money left for food, and then had to wait for the next train, getting hungrier by the minute. She had then spent an uncomfortable and what seemed interminable train journey, terrified of falling asleep and being robbed or missing her stop, weak and dizzy with hunger. As she had watched the sun rise over the countryside from her train carriage, she could not think of what this new dawn would bring. What would become of her now? What would be the consequences of her actions?

Henry had elected to take the time to meet her at the station, while Caroline prepared a bed for her. Henry had had to catch her as she nearly fainted getting off the train. He had immediately taken her to the station coffee room and fed her on rolls, bacon and hot coffee. All the while she had kept her hood over her face, and Henry thought it best not to ask any questions until she was back at the hotel.

When they arrived at the hotel and Isobel took off her cloak, they both saw the state of her face and looked at each other in horror.

'Please,' she said, seeing their reactions, and realising that after a sleepless night she must look so much worse than she had done last night, 'please don't ask me anything now. All I need right now is to sleep.'

'Of course, my dear,' said Caroline, 'but we must do something about that bruise first. I will see if we have any arnica lotion, or at the least, some vinegar. I've made up a room and bed for you, and I will keep the children away until you've rested.' She got up, and then before leaving the room to see to these things, she threw her arms around Isobel.

'Oh, my poor, dear girl!'

Isobel shed a few tears on Caroline's shoulder through sheer relief at being with her dear friends at last.

When Caroline left the room, Henry said quietly,

'Is there anything we can do while you are sleeping? I have friends in London…'

Isobel understood him.

'No,' she said, 'please, do not do anything on my behalf. I will explain everything later, but until then…'

'Of course,' said Henry.

Isobel slept right through until the following morning, and was not disturbed once by the general sounds and hubbub of the hotel life. She woke feeling slightly disorientated but ravenous, and for several moments could not understand where she was until the throbbing around her eye brought the events of the last day and night flooding back to her.

There was a knock on the door, and when she said, 'Come in', Caroline was there with a tray of food.

'I've been knocking nearly every hour,' she said, 'but you were sleeping so soundly you did not hear me, and I thought it best to let you sleep. I thought you would prefer to have breakfast in your room, so I have brought you a tray.'

She laid the tray down, and sat at the end of Isobel's bed.

'Thank you so much,' said Isobel, feeling rather tearful again.

'Henry has business at the theatre later on,' said Caroline, 'but if you are up to it after you've eaten, we will see you in our private rooms before he goes, and you can talk, if you wish.'

'Thank you,' said Isobel again, 'I am feeling so much better. I will come down in an hour.'

Henry paced up and down the room like a caged tiger.

'The man should be thrown in gaol and the key thrown away!' he fumed.

Isobel was more calm.

'I don't claim to know much about the law, but I do

know that a man has a right to beat his own wife, if he believes she has done something wrong. While he is wrong in that belief in this case, I do not think that the police would give any credence to my side of the story. After all, in their eyes I am no more than a low entertainer, visiting a music hall on my own at night, and spending time with a man who is not my husband. What do you think they would make of that? What would the newspapers make of that? My name would be mud. My reputation, if I still have one, in ruins. I may never be able to work again.'

'An actress with a bad reputation is not always at a disadvantage when it comes to work,' said Caroline wryly, 'but it makes me so angry that so many assumptions are made about people in our profession, especially us females. And of course, you do not want said what is not true, but how many times do we actresses have to grin and bear it while people say unfair things about us?'

Henry laid a hand on her shoulder.

'The trouble with people like Frank,' he said, remembering a conversation a long time ago in a pub in Daventry, 'and others both in and out of the profession, is that they judge others by their own low standards. Frank does not trust you because he is himself untrustworthy.'

Isobel thought about this. Perhaps Henry was right. Perhaps, even without the accident, Frank would still have seen other women. Did a leopard really change his spots? The disfigurement had brought him to a low, and brought out the worst of his character, but if it had never happened, would she really ever have trusted him, knowing the kind of man he had been? But then, she thought, with a wry laugh, if it had not have been for the fire, she probably would not have married Frank at all. It was then that she fully realised what a fool she had been to marry this man out of pity, and for a past feeling that she had thought she would get back again, but had really belonged to the past, when she was a naïve young girl with no experience of men.

She leaned back on her chair, shutting her eyes for a minute.

'Oh, my friends, what am I to do now?'

Caroline took her hand.

'You will stay here with us until you are better, and then we will see what is to be done. For now, just rest.'

'I must write to my sister, and to Joe!'

'I will get you some writing paper. Feel free to use our private rooms until you are ready to face the rest of the world.'

Isobel looked at Caroline, and then up at Henry.

'Whatever would I have done without you two? I really don't know…'

Tears began again; they were all too much at the surface at present. Caroline squeezed her hand, and they left her to do whatever she needed to do.

That afternoon she wrote three letters. The first was to the Eagle Tavern to apologise for not turning up to sing, and to release herself from her contract, explaining that she was suddenly ill and unable to perform for the next few weeks at least. She knew the manager would be angry and unlikely to have her back again, but there was little she could do about that. She was burning her bridges, and she could not really see herself working there again. It was part of her life that she felt now she had to leave behind. She felt a sense of relief in writing that letter; although she had no idea what lay ahead for her now, there was a sense of starting afresh. She now had no income, no possessions and no home. It was a frightening, but strangely liberating feeling. Looking in the mirror, her face bruised, swollen and grazed, she thought again of the confident, independent and happy woman she had been just three years ago. It was frightening how quickly things could change, but, oh, how important it was to have good friends. If it was not for the Hartleys, things at many stages in her life could have been so much worse.

The second letter she wrote was to her sister.

My dear Cassie
I am writing to let you know that I am staying with my friends the Hartleys in Stratford, and will probably be here for the next few weeks at least.

I do not wish to go into too many details, and I do not wish to alarm you my dear sister, suffice to say that something has happened between myself and Frank, and I am separating myself from him for the time being.

If Frank contacts you, or appears in person, please do not divulge my whereabouts; and please could you let me know by the most urgent of correspondence, if he does so. My fear is that he will take Kathleen, and for that reason I will be sending for her as soon as I can, but I cannot do so immediately. Please give her many kisses and cuddles from me, and tell her that Mama will be with her soon. I miss her more than words can say.

I know my sister well enough to understand that you WILL find this letter alarming. But please rest assured that I am with the dearest people that I possibly could be, apart from you, my beloved sister. All will be explained in due course, and I hope it will not be long before I see you again.

Yours with affection and love
Izzie

The letter to Joe was more difficult.

Dear Joe
You will see from the postal address above, that I am presently in Stratford with our mutual friends.
Since I last saw you, some events have occurred of an

alarming nature, and my purpose in writing to you is as one in friendship, to warn you to be on your guard concerning a certain person.

It is of immense sorrow and difficulty that I have to set down in writing the next piece of information, but unfortunately, I feel it is necessary to do so.

Two nights ago, Frank made it clear to me that he was aware of my visits to the Canterbury, but has got the erroneous idea into his head that my relationship with you is not entirely of an honourable nature. I am afraid that since his accident in the fire two years ago, his character has changed for the worst, and this has made him distrustful and I fear he may even become violent. I am afraid that he even suggested at one point that he would do you some harm, but I am hoping very much that it was said in the heat of the moment. However, I do feel that I should warn you of this, all the same.

I feel so terrible, Joe, that I am responsible for bringing this possible danger upon you. I am mostly to blame, and I should have been more honest with Frank about my visits to the Canterbury – though if I had done, it is likely that I would not have been able to come. I have so enjoyed our evenings together, but for now it seems that they are at an end. It would be unwise for me to see you at all in the near future, for no matter what happens next, I am married to Frank for better or for worse, and I see no possible good coming from our meeting again, at least for the foreseeable future.

Please do let me know if you hear from Frank.
I remain
Your friend
Isobel

After writing this, Isobel felt exhausted, but she made sure that all three letters went out by the next post. There was possible danger in delaying any further, and she had already lost a day in sleep.

Once she had sent the letters, there was nothing for her to do except to rest. Her only immediate plan was to send for Kathleen as soon as her face looked a little more normal. Beyond that, she had no idea what she would, or could, do next.

CHAPTER 24

Despite being with the Hartleys, Isobel's next few days were lonely and dull. She did not want to see anyone except her friends, and Bridget had gone to stay with her brother in London to keep house for him. She spent her time between her room and the Hartleys' private rooms, seeing no-one except for Caroline and Henry. To keep her occupied, Caroline brought her some back copies of *Household Words*, and she spent much of her time catching up on the instalments of Dickens' *Bleak House,* a long and complex story which suited her mood. As she read about some of the more shady characters in the novel, she could not help remembering Charles explaining how he visited the lowest places in London to find his characters, and it made her shiver, thinking how true to life they were. She cried at the death of little Joe, the crossing sweeper, remembering the crossing sweeper of Covent Garden, whom she occasionally threw pennies to, and wondered whether he was still alive. She became totally immersed in the story, and for a while, as she read, she forgot about the problems of her own life.

Joe Denny came out of the Canterbury stage door, and pulled his cap down over his face. He felt tired. He was doing what he loved most in the world, singing for an audience, but lately he had not felt happy. He was happy only when he sang, but much of his life felt dark and lonely. He was glad that Bridget was staying with him, and she was a great comfort to him; but he knew there was something missing in his life. He missed his family, and the noise and hubbub of his old life in Ireland; he missed his friends in Stratford; but most of all, he realised, he missed Isobel.

When he had received her letter, his first thought was to rush up to Stratford, without a care for his contract in

London, and make sure that she was all right. But then, she had suggested in her letter that their meeting would not be a good idea. If there was distrust in her marriage with Frank, it would only make things worse if he were to be seen in her company. He must do as she requested, and make no plans to see her, at least for the present.

Pulling his scarf around him against the cold night air, he looked for a cab, and as he did so he thought he saw a figure behind him, who quickly lurched back into the shadows as he turned.

He had been alarmed by what Isobel had relayed in her letter, that Frank had threatened to come after him, but he thought, as she had said herself, that it was probably something said in the heat of the moment. Yet, it had made him a little nervous all the same, and he was wary of spending too much time on the dark streets at night. Most nights he left the Canterbury when the streets were still busy with people coming and going, but tonight he had been delayed by some young fans, a couple of young ladies and their male escorts, who wanted to talk to him about singing, and how they could make their way in the music halls. He never had the heart to turn such people away, and had spent some time talking about the need to learn your craft and make sure you were thick-skinned enough to survive such a precarious business. Listening to his own words, Joe sometimes wondered whether he had enough thick skin of his own; it was a strange world, that of entertainment. Your audience might love you, and cheer and applaud you, but they mostly did not respect you. He found an uncomfortable hypocrisy in the attitudes towards actors and singers, but he could no more give up singing than he could give up breathing, so it was something he would have to live with.

He got a cab at last near the embankment, where there were always a few ready to go over the bridge, and he arrived home within ten minutes, where Bridget was there waiting with a hot bowl of soup.

'You're a little later than usual tonight, Joe,' she said, as she helped him take off his jacket, 'I was getting worried.'

'Well, here I am safe and sound,' he said, pecking her on the cheek, 'I was just talking to some people who wanted some advice about singing.'

'Your admirers, you mean, Joe – don't be so modest! Here come and get your soup before it goes cold!'

Joe was just sitting down at the table when there was a loud knocking at the door.

'Lord have mercy, what is that!' cried Bridget.

Joe went to the window and looked out. There was a cab waiting outside and a man standing at the door. He was alone.

'Wait here, I'll go and see who it is,' he said.

'Oh, be careful, Joe. Who should be calling at this hour? I don't like it!'

Joe opened the door a crack, asking 'who is it?'

But the door was pushed open, flattening him back against the wall, and the man strode into the house.

'Where is she?' he demanded, 'I know she's here. I saw you through the window!'

'Who?' said Joe.

'My wife sir! That's who…!'

But before Joe could protest the man had thrown open the door into the parlour, and grabbed Bridget by the wrist, who shrieked in alarm.

'Take your hands off my sister!' shouted Joe, and threw himself at the man's back, his arm around his neck. The man, though of large stature, was unsteady on his feet, and they both lurched towards the table, which tipped, and the bowl of soup flew onto the floor, breaking the bowl and splashing hot soup over their legs.

Bridget screamed again, and breaking free, went to the fireplace to pick up a fire iron intending to hit the man over the head.

'Wait!' cried Joe, and she stopped, holding the weapon in mid-air.

Joe righted himself, while the man still leaned against the table, unable to get himself upright.

'Allow me to introduce my sister, *Miss* Bridget Denny,' said Joe in mock civility, 'She is a single woman and not married to anyone.'

The man turned towards Bridget, and then grabbed a candle from the wall, holding it up to her face while she stared back, recoiling as she saw that one half of his face appeared to be horribly scarred.

There was a long pause, and then Frank shakily put the candle back, turned again to Bridget, took his hat off and bowed, 'my mistake,' he said, 'Mr. Douglas at your service,' but in bowing he lost his balance, and fell to the floor where he started to laugh hysterically.

Joe stood over him, holding his hand out to help him up.

'You are drunk, sir, and I would be very grateful if you would leave my house immediately, otherwise I will be forced to call a policeman.'

Frank stopped laughing and stared back up at him, eventually holding out his hand to be helped up. He did not immediately leave but continued to stare at Joe through narrowed eyes.

'Then, where is my wife?'

'I do not know. She is not here. You can search all the rooms if you wish, but you will not find her here.'

Frank swayed a little from side to side, then picked up his hat where it had fallen on the floor. He then pointed his finger at Joe.

'If I find… that you have… been intimate… with my wife… Sir… then expect to hear from me… or my seconds…'

He turned to Bridget and bowed again, this time only enough so he did not lose balance.

'Good evening to you,' he said, as if they had just spent

a pleasant evening together, and left the house.

'Oh Joe!' cried Bridget, running to him and throwing her arms around him, 'who was that horrible man? And why did he think I was his wife?'

'That,' said Joe, 'was a very sad shadow of a man who was once a good actor. His name is Frank Douglas, the husband of our very good friend, Isobel. I am very much afraid that things are far worse than I thought.'

'Isobel's husband? Surely not! Oh, Joe, how could our dearest friend have married such a man. And where is Isobel? What will he do if he finds her?'

Joe went to the bureau and took out a letter.

'I should have shown you this before,' he said, 'but I did not want to worry you. It is from Isobel. She is quite safe, and in good company as you will see, but I think we should let her know that we have had a visitor.'

'To be sure, Joe,' said Bridget, as she ran her eyes through the letter, and then sat down, suddenly feeling exhausted.

'Why,' she asked, hesitantly, 'why could she not have married you Joe? I know you could both have been so happy…'

'Shhh…!' said Joe, 'it is best not to speak of things that cannot be.'

But he went to the window and looked out for a very long time before he said another word. Bridget quietly mopped up the spilled soup.

She sat down again.

'What will you do, Joe? Will you write to her?'

Joe came and sat down at the table, his head in his hands.

'I feel responsible. If I had not allowed her to visit me at the Canterbury… I always felt it was not right, but it was obvious she was lonely, and she was so happy when we were together. And so was I. To a degree, Mr Douglas has every right to be angry.'

'Oh, what nonsense! For sure, it was a little foolish for Isobel to go alone to such places, but you know what she is like! That is not your fault. You mustn't blame yourself Joe.'

Joe sat in silence for a long time.

At last he said, 'A letter is not enough. I will go to Stratford.'

'But what about…'

'The Canterbury will have to do without me. I will write to say I am not well. I know Isobel told me not to come, but perhaps she does not realise the danger she is in. Did you hear him? He all but challenged me to a duel! The man is deranged and there is no knowing what he might do. He may well realise where she is and…' Joe banged his fist on the table, '…well, if anything happened and I was not there I would never forgive myself!'

'Then, I will come too, Joe. May I?'

He took her hand. 'Of course, my sweet sister. I would not dream of leaving you behind, not now that man knows where we live. We must leave by the next train, though. I do not want to delay. If you will pack a few things now, I will write to Morton and tell him I have been taken ill. By Jesus, I hate to lie, but surely God will forgive us when it's in the best interests of a person?'

Bridget squeezed his hand.

'I will pray for us Joe.'

The following morning, Isobel was sitting in the Hartleys' private rooms at the back of the inn by the window, reading in the light of the cold, pale February sun. She was engrossed in the story, and although there was a commotion outside as a carriage came and went in the yard, she paid no heed. She was used to carriages arriving at the inn, dropping off customers, and taking them away.

She was vaguely aware of excited voices in the hallway,

and a hurried conversation, but in the last few days she had retreated from the world, engrossed only in the story she was reading that allowed her to escape from a world that she could only view with disappointment and sadness. Reading of others' sorrows and difficulties was somehow soothing, even if they were only fictional, and allowed her heart to grieve and weep, whilst remaining detached from her own troubles.

But a sudden knock at the door startled her out of her absorption, and Caroline walked in with a strange look on her face, shutting the door behind her.

'My dear,' she said, sitting in the chair opposite her, 'we have visitors. Some very good friends of yours have arrived and would dearly love to see you. Would you be happy to receive them?'

Isobel frowned, puzzled.

'But who could that possibly be?' she asked.

Caroline leaned forward, putting her hand on her arm.

'It's Joe and Bridget,' she said.

Isobel's eyes widened with delight, but then with alarm. She put aside the magazine and stood up, and then sat down again. Her heart was suddenly beating too loudly.

'But what are they doing here? I expressly told Joe not to come here!'

Caroline, who had been watching Isobel's reaction with interest, smiled.

'Something has happened, and they thought it best that they told you personally, rather than by letter. Will you see them? They are tired, and have come up on the early train without sleep, but they wish to see you first before resting.'

Isobel's hand went to her face.

'I have told them you had an… accident, so they are prepared for you to be… not quite at your best.'

'Thank you, Caroline. Please, let them come in.'

In the short interval that followed, Isobel smoothed her

hair and brushed out imaginary creases in her dress, wondering why her stomach was fluttering so.

Then the door opened, and in walked Joe, and all anxiety left her when she saw his gentle face, and she went to him, her hands out to grasp his in welcome.

'Oh, Joe! How good it is to see you!' And she knew in her heart that it was so, because suddenly all seemed right in the world.

'My dear friend!' said Joe.

Behind him. Bridget stood shyly in the doorway, and Isobel went to her and they hugged each other warmly.

Isobel ordered some tea, and they all sat down.

'But Joe, what brings you here? Caroline told me something had happened?'

Joe and Bridget looked at each other, and then Joe told Isobel about their visit from Frank, his drunken state, and all the things he had said.

'I did not want to relay all this in a letter,' said Joe, 'I very much felt it was best to tell you in person, and to help if we can. This man, your husband, is not in his right mind, and I do not like to think that you may be in any kind of danger.'

'I feel safe here, Joe. I doubt that Frank would come all this way, even if he did realise where I am. He – I just cannot imagine him walking out, getting on a train…, oh, I don't know. He has not been himself for a long time, he rarely goes out; he has not recovered from the emotional suffering of losing his looks and his career. No matter how I've tried, nothing helps, and he just got worse…'

All the troubles of the last two years crowded in on her, and she was unable to speak for a while.

'He is not a bad man…' she began again, 'but all that was ever good in him seems to have been buried. I do not know… I do not know how to save him…'

There was a silence. Bridget handed Isobel a clean handkerchief.

'Perhaps…' said Joe, not quite knowing how to say what he wanted to say, 'he should have some sort of care…'

'You mean a lunatic asylum,' said Isobel.

There was another silence.

Isobel shook her head. 'They are terrible places. I could not bear to think of him there. Anyway, how would it be arranged? No. Please, you are so good to me, and I cannot tell you how sorry I am that you have become so involved, but I am perfectly safe here. You must not trouble yourselves for me.'

Later, after Joe and Bridget had had a rest, they met with Henry and Caroline.

'Bridget and I have no plans to return to London,' said Joe. 'I cannot explain it, but I have a feeling in my bones I am needed here. Will you find room for us? We will pay full board. I will not leave her, no matter what she says.'

Henry and Caroline exchanged glances.

'Of course,' said Henry, 'feel free to stay here as long as you wish. And as for payment, Joe we would love you to sing again, and if you would entertain our guests, there is no need to pay for your rooms.'

Joe smiled.

'Nothing would make me happier,' he said.

The sound of Joe's voice again was healing to Isobel's spirit, and in the evenings that followed, whilst she still did not want to meet people, she sat in her rooms with the door slightly ajar so that she could hear him singing in the bar downstairs. It brought her happiness, yet at the same time, she could not help remembering the first time she had heard his voice in that slum building of Seven Dials, and thinking back to that time, when she was her own person with wealth and freedom, it also brought tears to her eyes.

A few weeks after she had arrived in Stratford, she

started to appear in the bar, sitting in a dark snug with a beer, sometimes with Bridget or Caroline for company until Joe finished his set and would come and join them. By now, the Jackman company had arrived to start their season, and the bar was loud and rowdy with her old colleagues and stage fellows, but she kept to herself, not wanting to be seen, or have to explain her presence there. On the nights when they were here and not at the theatre, she kept to her room again.

As her bruises healed and the weather became a little warmer, she began to go for long walks by the river with Joe and Bridget, feeding the swans, and visiting the church and the resting place of her beloved Shakespeare.

One spring-like day in March, Henry and Caroline joined them for a stroll along the Avon.

'Oh!' said Isobel, as a thought struck her, 'would it not be a lovely thing for there one day to be a permanent theatre here upon the river dedicated to the works of Shakespeare?'

Henry smiled as he came to walk beside her.

'You are not the first person to think so,' he said, 'but it would need so much money to begin such a project. It is my fervent hope that one day some wealthy patron of the arts will invest in such a glorious plan. In the meantime, we have our little theatre on Chapel Street, and, speaking of which, may I have a private word with you?'

He took her by the elbow and led her a little apart from the others.

'Do you remember the letter I sent you at Christmas, and the little business proposal I put forward?'

'Oh yes,' she said, thinking how long ago that seemed, though it was barely three months, 'the company are doing well I hope?'

'Houses are fair to middling,' he said in his old professional way of speaking that she knew so well, making her grin to herself, 'but, Isobel, the offer still stands. I spoke to young Henry yesterday, and he said he would be delighted to have you in the company if you wished it. Perhaps you might start with a little song – perhaps a duet with Joe, who has also been asked to appear as a guest – but Henry has suggested that a suitable play be got up within a few weeks where you could star in the lead, and so make something of a return? What do you think, my dear?' he looked at her with concern, 'of course, you are under no obligation. It would be entirely up to you. If you do not feel you are ready…'

'Oh!' said Isobel, and stopped, leaning against a tree.

The others came quickly towards them.

'Isobel?' said Caroline, 'are you ill, my dear?'

'No,' she said, 'no. I am just suddenly a little breathless. I was not expecting…'

'Henry, what did you say?'

'Nothing more than what we have already discussed, my dear…'

'Oh, but perhaps it is too soon…'

Isobel started to laugh.

'No, no! Really! I am perfectly well. It was just so… unexpected. I am so…' tears welled up in her eyes, '…so grateful. I thought my career was over. I did not think, would not have dared to think that such an offer would ever come again…'

She was half laughing and half crying, and Joe hovered at her side, almost weeping himself from her joy.

'Oh Joe,' she said, 'is it not wonderful? And we can sing together again, like we did before. We could do "I Dreamed I Dwelt" again, and perhaps some Irish ballads!'

'That would be delightful!' said Joe.

Henry looked a little worried.

'It is, of course, just a little theatre. Not what you have been used to in London…'

'Oh, but it does not matter! Just to be on stage again! With an audience. I did not know how much I had missed it until you said those words just now. Please, please tell Henry I would be honoured to join the company again. Oh, it will be just like old times!'

Feeling more like her old self again, Isobel wrote to her sister to arrange for her to bring Kathleen to Stratford. She also asked Cassie to stay with her for a while, so that the little girl would not be too alarmed at such a change. She was so used to living with the Duncans that Isobel worried that she thought of Cassie as her mother, but rather than make a sudden change, she thought it best if the transition to her was a gradual one.

There would be no problems with looking after the child. The company, being made up of married couples, were used to having children to look after, and while most of the children of the company were now much older than Kathleen, those of the company who were mothers, particularly Caroline and her sister, Frances, were happy at the thought of such a young one around again. A nurse would be appointed for times when all the women were rehearsing or on stage.

Isobel was nervous about meeting the company again. While she had loved those early days, she had not always felt as though she fitted in, with it being such a family-based company, and there had been difficult relationships in those days, the worst of which had been with Sophia. As Sophia had worked for her sister and brother-in-law for several years now, Isobel had got to know her a little better, and the relationship had eased into a mutual acceptance of each other's closeness with the Hartleys, though Isobel was never quite sure what Sophia now thought of her, and the fact that she had married Frank. Sophia was a resigned spinster, happy to work behind the bar at the inn, and with no ambition to return to the stage, though she did occasionally sing.

Isobel's nerves about joining the company were soon

dissipated. Her status had changed, and she found that the company treated her with the respect due to a star of the London stage. And while she was never going to be part of the 'Jackman' family clique, there was a comforting familiarity working with her old colleagues again.

Cassie arrived with Kathleen and a nurse appointed in London who had travelled with them by first class carriage on the train. Isobel met them at the station, full of worry and anxiety that her own child would not remember her, but as the little party alighted onto the platform, Kathleen broke free of the nurse's hand, and ran to Isobel, shouting 'Mama!', and then did not stop talking about the ride on the train and all the things she had seen from the window, that she had never seen before: cows and sheep, and fields and woods, and how fast the train was, all the way in the carriage back to the inn.

'This child has not stopped talking since she learned to talk,' said Cassie, with a grin.

'She has such spirit,' said Isobel, fondly.

'Yes,' replied Cassie, looking at Isobel with a twinkle in her eye, 'she reminds me of somebody. I cannot imagine who it is…'

Isobel grinned, seeing, as Cassie did, her own self in her daughter. But she also had a twinge of fear for her, recognising how close her own spirit had been to being broken.

'I hope she always has such friends and family as I have,' she said.

Cassie squeezed her hand.

In London, Frank woke, groaning, to a loud banging at the door. His head ached, and his stomach lurched as he sat up, and he realised he was still fully dressed and had been lying there unconscious since he had fallen onto the bed just a few hours earlier.

'What the hell!' he cried, as the beating on the door grew

louder.

He splashed some water onto his face, and moved unsteadily towards the door, cursing as he tripped over empty bottles, sending them spinning across the floor.

Opening the door, he found his landlord, Mr. Brumby, standing on the doorstep with two official looking gentlemen behind him. Recoiling slightly when he saw Frank's face, Mr Brumby recovered himself and announced that he was here for the rent, which was in arrears of two months, and if it was not forthcoming, he would be forced to gain entry and take furniture and effects to the value of the arrears, or give notice for eviction.

Frank peered at him hazily, his words sinking in to his brain slowly.

'It is my wife who deals with such things,' he said eventually, finding that it took a huge effort to speak.

Mr. Brumby looked strangely at him, and peered into the rooms behind Frank. 'Then,' he said, 'may I speak to Mrs. Douglas?'

Frank looked behind him, as if expecting Isobel to appear. There were just the empty, filthy rooms, devoid of much furniture, which had been mostly sold in previous months to pay for the rent and food. No-one had cleaned for some time.

Frank then remembered that he had not seen Isobel for several weeks. He, himself, had hardly been home, spending what little money was left on ale, gambling and whores. To fund these activities, he had sold some of Isobel's ornaments and paintings that she had bought for herself over the years.

He turned back to Mr. Brumby, being careful not to move his head too quickly.

'No,' he said, 'my wife is not here.'

'When will she return?'

'That,' said Frank, laughing sardonically, 'appears to be

the question of the day. I do not know!'

Mr. Brumby drew himself up to look his most official and commanding (he was not a large man), and took a piece of paper from his colleague.

'Then it is incumbent upon me, Sir, to give you official notice that unless I have the rent arrears in full, along with the next month due, by the date written here upon this paper, then an order will be made to enter into these premises and seize any goods to the value owed, and if this is not possible, then you will have notice to quit this place by force or otherwise. Good day to you, Sir.'

And looking very much as if he did not mean the final salutation, he tipped his hat and left.

Frank stared at the piece of paper in his hand.

He closed the door, and sat down, tossing the paper onto the bare table next to him. He sat with his head in his hands for a few moments, trying to get his head clear.

'I have to sober up,' he said to himself.

Then, 'Where in God's name is Isobel?'

Then he stood up, looked around him at the bleak, dark, smelly and cold place that his home had become, as if noticing it for the first time, and said,

'I have to find Isobel. Goddamit! I have to get my wife back!'

CHAPTER 25

After some deliberation and discussions with young
Henry Jackman and his co-manager, Frederick Morgan,
the husband of Caroline's sister Harriet, it was decided
that a Shakespearian comedy would be got up. Isobel had
no stomach for tragedy at present, and looked forward to
something light and fun to play. She could not decide
between *As You Like It* or *A Midsummer Night's Dream*.
She like the part of Rosalind, and had played it before, but
she wanted to try something new, and finally it was
decided that she would play Titania, Queen of the Fairies,
in the *Dream.* Henry Hartley, ever respected as one of the
funniest comedians of the company, was elected to play
Bottom, whom Titania falls in love with when he is in the
guise of an ass, both of them under a spell. Her old
colleague, George Partleton, was to play opposite her as
Oberon, while the younger members of the company, who
had been children when Isobel was there before, would
play the younger lovers, muddled over who exactly they
were in love with.

While rehearsals got under way for the play, Isobel and
Joe produced a repertory of songs and duets that they
performed in the theatre intervals, where the company was
currently putting on *Hamlet.* How strange it seemed to
Isobel, as she watched from the wings, that this was the
first play she had ever seen, and it was the one in which
she had first seen Frank. So many mixed feelings ran
through her as she heard all those lines that she had heard
Frank say all those years ago: the unweeded garden grown
to seed, and 'Frailty, thy name is woman…' that seemed
now so much more poignant to her. How long ago, and
yet like yesterday it seemed. How like a child her old self
seemed to her now, hearing those words that were so
tragic and electrifying, but not really understanding their
meaning. Now at thirty-four, she felt her maturity and

experience gave her a little more gravitas, and as she stood in the wings she felt little sparks of excitement as she contemplated her future. Perhaps now she was ready for some of the greater tragic roles: Lady Macbeth, perhaps, or Cleopatra again? She had not really had the maturity that role deserved, when she had played it opposite Frank some years ago. Slowly, she began again to contemplate what the future might hold for her, but still she did not know how it should come about. This time at Stratford may be a passing phase. How should she ever become the star she had once been again?

Her days had become busy again, as she was either rehearsing the play, or rehearsing with Joe. Both work was full of joy and laughter. How good it was to share the stage with Henry again, and as in the old days, he constantly brought her to tears of laughter, and she often wondered how she would ever get through the play when he was at his comic best.

Rehearsals with Joe were also full of laughter, and while Isobel preferred acting to singing, she looked forward just as much to working with Joe as she did working with the company. They understood each other's thoughts and feelings about the music and words and, well, she just liked being in his company. Despite their different backgrounds, they thought in the same way, they laughed at the same things and were always able to find something to talk about. The times with Joe flew by, and were never long enough.

In April, Cassie came to her room with a letter from her husband, John.

'Izzie, dear,' she said, a little frown on her face, 'John has had a visitor.'

'Oh,' said Isobel, 'it was Frank, wasn't it? Oh dear! Thank goodness Kathleen is here with us. Was he drunk? Did he make a scene? I'm so sorry…!'

'Actually, no;' said Cassie, 'apparently, he was quite sober and polite. He said he had turned over a new leaf and wanted very much to see you, and Kathleen of course. John said he seemed quite contrite and admitted that he had not been quite kind to you, and was willing to overlook the fact that you had all but deserted him, if you would just come home.'

'Oh,' said Isobel, sitting down, 'Oh dear. Oh Cassie, what should I do?'

Cassie frowned again.

'Oh Izzie, I… I do not know what to think. He is your husband…' she turned the letter over and over in her hands, unable to know what to say.

'We must talk it over with Caroline and Henry,' said Isobel, standing up again, 'Come, Cassie, bring the letter with you.'

'I do not trust him,' said Henry, 'the man, for all his faults, is a good actor. If he wished to play the remorseful husband, it is not outside his capabilities to do so for his own ends. The way he throws in this word "desertion" is a veiled warning. I do not like it one bit. And anyway, you are committed to the company here for several weeks. You cannot just go back to London; the playbills have been printed and tickets have already been sold…'

Caroline digged him in the ribs.

'Oh, but he is right, Caroline,' said Isobel, 'I have a commitment here. But, I also have a commitment to Frank, and whether it was a warning or not, Frank would have every right to take Kathleen from me if I stayed away. Oh, my,' she said, sighing and putting her hand on her head, 'I have put myself into a terrible dilemma. Perhaps I should never have left London. After all, I married Frank, for better or for worse; I should never have left. I am a terrible wife!'

'Oh nonsense!' said Caroline, 'you have tried your

hardest to do your duty as a wife, but a marriage has two people in it. I do not think you have anything to reproach yourself with; you tried your hardest to make your marriage work…'

'But still, in the eyes of the law…'

'"The law is an ass!"' said Henry.

Despite her dilemma, Isobel grinned, hearing the words of her friend, Dickens.

'So, what should I do?' she asked.'

'Perhaps, if you wrote to him,' said Caroline, 'and told him that you are committed to a play, and that you will talk to him when you are able…'

'But then, he will know where I am, with the post mark…'

'I doubt very much he has not worked out where you are already,' said Henry,' he did not find you at Joe's house, or Cassie's. There's really only one other place you could be. I hate to say it, but he is not a stupid man. He will know where you are.'

Isobel looked up in some consternation.

'Then, do you think he will come here?'

'If I were a gambling man, I would put money on it.'

Over the next few days, Isobel felt apprehensive, wondering whether Frank would appear. Several times she sat down to write a letter to him, but being unsure of his state of mind, could not compose anything that she was happy with. She tried to open the letter with an apology for her disappearance, trying to explain that she had not been well, and needed some time away. But when she started to write that Kathleen was with her, and she was in a play, she began to worry that Frank would see this as a way of taking the child away from her. She could find no way of explaining things without feeling that she was playing into his hands. And a part of her felt it to be so unfair that she should even be writing such a letter. Why should she be the one to apologise when he, as her husband, had given her no support for two years? It did not seem fair that he had all the legal rights on his side, and before she was half way through writing her letter, she would tear it up. It seemed that she would just have to wait and see what would happen. Perhaps he would not be able to take Kathleen. Surely, the law would not allow a child to be taken back into squalor and poverty? Surely, they would be able to see that she would be better off with her mother? Even if her mother was an actress? Isobel could not see how things would work out, and could only watch and wait.

She did not have to wait long.

She and Joe had the theatre to themselves for an hour on a heavy, cloudy day in May, in order to go over a new song they were trying.

The pianist was not free that morning, so Isobel sat at the piano to play the few chords necessary to keep them on track. She was not a great piano player, but over the years she had learned enough to keep a simple melody underneath a song.

She started now, and Joe started the first lines of the song in his clear, steady voice, until Isobel hit a wrong note, crying 'Oh bother!', and making Joe wobble comically on the note he was singing, and they both stopped, falling into peals of laughter.

'How very charming,' came a voice from the shadowy auditorium.

Isobel swung round. She knew that voice. Neither she nor Joe had heard anyone come in, but he must have let himself in quietly and unseen, and have been watching them for the last few minutes.

Isobel stood up slowly, while Joe peered towards the voice, trying to work out who had spoken.

'Frank?'

He came out of the shadows, and bowed a greeting.

'My dear wife, how very nice to see you,' he said, and she could hear the slight mocking tone of his voice.

She looked at him to see any signs that he had been drinking, but she could tell that he was perfectly sober. That did not bode well. In many ways, a drunken Frank was easier to handle. A sober Frank would be able to argue with acute sense and logic.

Isobel's mind flew to where her daughter was right now. Caroline was looking after her at the inn. She would be in their private rooms and, thank goodness, Frank would not be able to gain access without being invited, which she knew he would not be.

'What are you doing here Frank?' she asked, more to play for time than because she did not know.

Frank turned his palms up, as if to implicate that the question was an odd one.

'What am I doing here? Why, I have come to take my wife and daughter home to where they belong, of course.' His eyes flickered towards Joe and back. 'Come, my dear, there is a train leaving this afternoon. Let us go and find my daughter, and we will be on our way.'

Isobel stayed where she was. She felt Joe edge closer towards her.

'I am contracted to play here, Frank. I may not leave.' She wanted to end the sentence with, 'even if I wanted to,' but she decided against it.

Frank moved closer to them, his hands behind his back, still talking in a casual manner, as if they were doing no more than passing the time of day.

'I do believe,' he said slowly, 'that you also have a contract with me. Do you not think that a marriage contract is more binding than a theatrical one?'

Isobel swallowed. He had a point.

Then Joe spoke.

'Why should Mrs Douglas return to a place where she is

not respected or supported? Do you not think, sir, that marriage should have two people in it? Should it not be mutually supportive, otherwise the contract has no worth?'

Frank turned to Joe, and bowed, lifting his hat slightly.

'Mr. Denny, we meet again. I suppose I should not be surprised to see you here too. Your association with my wife has been well known to me for some time, and really, I would be quite within my rights to challenge you… However, we are both gentlemen, are we not? Let us settle this amicably. I will take my wife home, and we will say no more about it. However, if you wish to continue your association with my wife, then you should expect to be named as a co-respondent, and expect never to work again.'

Isobel felt Joe tense at her side, and her own face felt flushed.

'Frank, you are mistaken in your assumptions. My association with Mr. Denny is purely professional. He often has worked for the Hartleys as a singer, you know that, and it just so happens that he is working here now, while I was offered a good part, and the play opens next week. Surely, you realise that this is a good thing for me. For us! I am sorry that I have not written, but if I do well here, it might help me to break back in to the London theatres, and that would help us both would it not? Can you not wait until the play is finished here, and then I will return, and we will continue as before?'

Standing beside her, Joe said nothing, but she saw out of the corner of her eye the slight incline of his head as he wondered if she meant what she said.

Frank too, seemed to be pondering her words.

'How sweet,' he said, 'the way you both rush to defend the other. That was a very sincere sounding little speech, my dear wife, but I am afraid that unless you return with me now, we have no future together at all. And if that were to be the case, I think that both of you might find it difficult to find work in the future. I will drag you both through the courts, and you will never see your daughter again.'

Joe bristled by her side, but Isobel saw through his words. She knew Frank, and she knew when he was bluffing.

She softened her voice.

'Would you Frank? Would you really? Ruin the lives of two people, and take Kathleen away from her mother, to live with a father whom she barely knows? For the sake of what? Your pride, your honour? There is nothing to be defended or revenged, for you have not been insulted or cuckolded. I left our home because you were making it impossible for me to live with any happiness or any feeling of security.' She moved a little closer to him. 'Can you blame me for that? You may have the law on your side, but surely you still have some sense of humanity? If… if only you would promise to treat me better, I would return. We could be a family again.'

She saw the shift in Frank. She had seen it once before, when he had dropped the outer shell of cynicism and sardonic wit, and revealed to her his true feelings for her that day, a long time ago in Aylesbury, when he had returned her dropped glove. She knew that it was rare for Frank to let his guard down and let his true nature be seen, but she knew it was there, and it was the part of him that she still loved.

He remained silent, looking down at the floor.

'I know you are an honourable man. Why,' she said, attempting a smile, 'did you not once leave me to do the honourable thing for another woman? It broke my heart, but looking back, I knew that you had done the right thing, and it made me love you more, to think you would not have left someone in such circumstances. You are a better man than even you know yourself, Frank. I wish I could see that man again.'

Frank replied, his voice gruff and low.

'Isobel… come home. I need you. I cannot live without you.'

Tears sprang to Isobel's eyes and ran down her face.

'I will, Frank. But, please, give me a little time here. You know how I love my work. I must complete my contract here…'

Frank drew himself up. He glanced at Joe.

'And give you time to develop your "friendship" with your dear Mr. Denny here?'

He laughed to himself, and shook his head.

'No. No… It is too late…'

Isobel took another step closer.

'Frank… you have not been well. Your spirits have been so low, and, and it is not easy to think properly when everything seems dark. Why do not you stay here, in Stratford, and we could meet then, and talk, and I could continue with the play, and you could get well again…'

'To do what?' said Frank, 'what would be the point? How could I stay here, with that Jackman company, and be the subject of all their pity?'

'Mr Douglas,' said Joe, softly, coming forwards and standing next to Isobel, 'your wife is trying to help you. I understand you have had terrible troubles, and perhaps no-one is capable of understanding what you have been through, but you must see…'

'I do not need a lecture from you, Sir,' said Frank, 'you of all people. You! With your black hair and, your, your Irish charm, and your beautiful voice – and your perfect face! You should not be allowed to speak! You took my wife away from me!'

'But that is not true Frank!' cried Isobel.

But in that same moment, Frank had reached inside his coat and brought something out which he now held in front of him, pointing at Joe. It was a pistol.

'Frank, No!' shouted Isobel, 'Please! Do not do this! I

293

will come home with you. We will take Kathleen. I will do anything you say, just please don't…!'

Frank took a few steps back, looking from Isobel to Joe, and back again, and then laughed.

'Just look at the two of you. Looking after each other.'

He looked to the ground, and Isobel saw the gentleness in his face, that only she ever saw. For a moment, she thought he was going to drop the gun.

But then he looked up again, and said, 'It ends here.'

He raised the pistol.

Isobel screamed.

A shot rang out, and at the same time, Joe fell against Isobel, and they both tumbled to the ground, his weight falling across her.

'Joe! Joe!' screamed Isobel. She opened her eyes, and saw rivulets of blood in front of her. She shut her eyes again.

'You've killed Joe!' she sobbed.

But then she felt a breath against her ear.

'No,' said Joe, 'I am not killed. But…' she felt him shift to move himself and sit beside her, and a huge relief came over her, '…but do not look.'

She sat up, and looked.

Frank's body lay in front of them. He had turned the pistol on himself. There was little left of his head.

She turned quickly away, her head against Joe's chest, and retched.

They sat like that for a few moments, unable to speak, until they heard the sound of voices and running feet, as people, alerted to the sound of the gun shot, came to see what had happened.

CHAPTER 26

The inquest, held at the Golden Lion, returned a verdict of 'Suicide, whilst temporarily insane', and Isobel returned to her rooms exhausted and numb, but relieved. There would be no repercussions, and no further enquiries. The Hartleys had given her excellent character references and clearly explained the reasons for Isobel's flight to Stratford, and Joe, as a main witness, had been honest, clear and thoughtful about his own interpretation of the event.

'He was obviously not in his right mind,' he had said. 'He had followed Mrs Douglas, hoping to take her back to London with him, and, to be sure, he would have had every right to do so, but he was rambling, and did not seem to have a grasp of reality. It was clear that he was under the impression that his wife was not faithful to him, and I can assure you that nothing could be further from the truth. Mrs Douglas loved her husband very much. It is true that he had made life difficult for her, so much so that she had come away, but she would never be unfaithful to him, never. Despite her protests, he decided to take his own life.'

As Joe sat with Henry and Caroline later that night, Joe told a slightly more detailed version of the events.

'He was going to kill me. He was pointing the pistol at me. I think that may have been his intention all along, for why else did he bring a pistol with him? Despite everything that was said, he still seemed to think that… well, you know. But I knew, in that moment, that he saw his life ahead of him. Isobel would despise him; he would be a murderer. Even if he was on the run, there could be no life for him. I saw it in his eyes. There was a man with nothing left to live for. I saw him move the pistol towards himself, and that was when I rushed at Isobel. I did not want her to see… that.'

'Why did you not say that at the inquest, Joe?' asked Caroline, gently.

'Well, the way I see it is, it is bad enough for Isobel that her husband took his own life. Add to that, that he could have been a murderer, could have contemplated killing another man; it could have been devastating for her, let alone what that fact might have done to her reputation – for are we not tainted by the actions of our loved ones? No, it is enough that Mr Douglas destroyed himself. And, you know, I believe in the end, he did it to release her. Out of love for her. That will be a comfort in times to come, I hope.'

Caroline smiled at him, her eyes moist. 'I believe she will take much comfort in times to come,' she said.

After several days of needing peace and quiet, and to be alone, Isobel wanted to be in company again. She grieved for Frank deeply, but she knew that in many ways, she had already been grieving for him before his death. A large part of him had died on that day of the fire. The theatre, and his fame, had been too important to him; it was his life, and he had not the inner resources to deal with a life without them. She was saddened and overwhelmed by the fact that neither she nor anyone else could have helped him. She also saw that in taking his own life he had released her from a life where she could only have been dragged down again into his dark world. It comforted her to know that he loved her enough to do that.

She thought about what Joe had said at the inquest. When he had said 'Mrs Douglas loved her husband very much', she wondered how much that was really true. She had been very fond of Frank after they had met again, but she was not sure whether she had really loved him. When she had agreed to marry him, she had been thinking about the practicalities of such a marriage, not seeing how much his disfigurement would affect him. If she had really loved him, would she not have taken more effort and time to try and help him out of his melancholy?

There was one wonderful thing that had come out of her marriage, and that was Kathleen.

Sitting now by the river, with her friends, and Cassie, who was still staying with them, she watched Joe, who had taken Kathleen to show her a mother duck with her ducklings making their way in single file along the riverbank. She smiled as Joe pointed to them and Kathleen, innocent of the huge thing that had just happened in her life, laughed with joy to see the little fluffy birds peeping and swimming furiously to keep up with their Mama.

'Mr Denny is very good with little Kathleen, is he not?' remarked Cassie.

Isobel noticed Caroline and Henry exchanging grins at this remark, and she looked again at the two by the riverbank, both engrossed in the family of ducklings.

She could never imagine Frank being such a father, sharing this little moment of joy with his own daughter. What a sad thought that was, but, how lovely it was to see Joe and Kathleen together, Joe crouching down to her level and talking to her like an equal. As she watched, she saw Kathleen's hand touch his so naturally and trustingly, as she exclaimed something, and Isobel immediately thought how much more like a father and daughter they were, than Frank had been with her. The thought both made her want to weep and to laugh at the same time.

The theatre company had been quite prepared for Isobel to wish to cancel the first performances of *A Midsummer Night's Dream*, but Isobel would not have it. People had already paid for their tickets, and she did not wish to disappoint anyone. Besides, she needed the work to keep her mind away from what had happened. Rehearsals resumed after a few days, but for the sake of Isobel's feelings, they did not use the theatre where that last dramatic scene of Frank's had played out. Instead, they used spare rooms at the inn, and only went into the theatre for the final dress rehearsals. Going back into that space was not easy for Isobel; she could not help but look at that part of the floor where a dark stain still remained, despite several attempts at cleaning. She could not help but feel a little queasy and dizzy at first, but she spoke to no-one about it (except Caroline and Joe later), and was determined that no-one could call her unprofessional.

The opening night went well, with the scenes between her and Henry as Titania and Bottom making the audience roar with laughter, so they had to pause several times to let the audience quieten before they could continue. At the end, as the players took their bows, Isobel received a standing ovation, which brought the tears to her eyes, and brought back memories of her very first night with the Jackman company when she had felt such joy, and knew she had found her calling. Now, fifteen years later, she felt she had returned home.

Isobel and Joe remained in Stratford until the end of June, when the play came to the end of its run, and the Jackman company prepared to pack up and travel to their next venue, where they would again stay for several months. The days of travelling week by week were over.

Isobel was asked if she wished to stay with them, but she declined. She had very much enjoyed her return to her old company, but she knew she had to move on. There were matters to see to in London. If her rooms she had shared with Frank had not already been repossessed, she would have to pay the unpaid rent, find work and find somewhere else to live. She could not lean on the hospitality of the Hartleys for ever.

On her last night in Stratford, Joe asked her if she would accompany him for a walk by the river. It was a warm evening and a walk was a very pleasant idea, so she wrapped a shawl round her shoulders, and they walked down to the waterside and strolled under the trees.

'What will you do now, Joe?' asked Isobel, 'will you return to London, or stay on here for a while?'

'Oh, I will be returning to London,' he said, 'I will have to see if Morton will have me back, which is doubtful after my rather sudden departure!' He smiled wryly. 'But I hear there are more music halls to open soon. It seems to be the big thing now, so perhaps it won't be too difficult to find work.'

'I am glad, Joe. I would miss you. We must do our best to meet if we are both to be in London.'

Joe stopped, and turned to her, emboldened by her words.

'Well, I was thinking, and I hope you do not think I am speaking out of turn, with it being so soon after… after all your troubles, but I was wondering if, when you return to London, whether… well, as long as I can find work of course, whether you would consider… at all…'

Isobel smiled and took his hand.

'Joe, you had better say it this time, if you are about to say what I think you are about to say. For it would be unfortunate indeed if we missed each other again, and someone else asked me before you were able…'

Joe looked at her in alarm.

'Oh! Is there someone…?'

Isobel laughed.

'Oh Joe, you are always so easy to tease. Of course, there is not! But please say what you were going to say. You know very well I am not the most patient of people.'

'Well then,' he said, 'would you… consider… doing me the honour of becoming my wife?'

'I will not consider it, Joe…'

His face fell.

'…for I do not have to. It matters not to me whether you

have work or not. We will both manage very well together, I think, whatever life chooses to put in our path. Oh, Joe, of course I will be your wife!'

So, after a short time in London, tying matters up that needed to be tied up, and making enquiries for work and a place to live, and where Bridget could stay with them as housekeeper and help to look after little Kathleen, Isobel and Joe returned to Stratford. They were married at the Holy Trinity Church, in front of the burial place of Isobel's beloved Shakespeare, and with their friends the Hartleys, the Duncans, Bridget, and several members of the Jackman and Morgan Theatre Company.

'Well,' said Henry Hartley to his wife, as they sat in the inn after seeing the happy couple off to London, 'at last, a happy end. "Jack shall have Jill, and all shall be well…"'.

'Yes,' said Caroline, 'but I do hope that they both will find work again.'

'Oh,' said Henry, winking slyly at his wife, 'I think they will. I took the, er, liberty, of writing to a few people during the run of the *Dream*, and I do know that our friend Maddox was in the house one night.'

'Henry!' said Caroline, 'you never said anything!'

'No, but, well, I did not want to raise false hopes, but I have had rather a nice letter from him since, saying that he was thinking of offering Isobel a place at the Princess. Charles Kean is to direct and star, I believe. It will be a marvellous opportunity. I hope it will come as a pleasant surprise for our Isobel.'

Caroline stared at him, her mouth open.

'Why, Henry Hartley, you sly old fox!'

Henry chuckled.

'Well, we all have to look after each other in this business.'

Caroline laid her head on his shoulder.

'Not just in this fickle old business we call the theatre, my dear, but in life in general.'

'That, my dear Mrs Hartley, is very, very true.'

HISTORICAL NOTE

With the exception of Isobel and her family, Frank Douglas and Joe Denny, the characters in this novel are mostly based on real people.

During some research I was carrying out for my degree, many years ago, I came across a bundle of letters at the Northamptonshire Record Office from members of the Jackman Theatre Company, mostly to the company's solicitor, Thomas Gery. The company, headed by Henry Jackman, travelled the Midland Circuit up until around the time of Henry's death in 1852. Most of the company were his children and their various spouses, with the occasional guest star from London or elsewhere.

Because of my own interest in the theatre, having grown up with an actor father and having worked in the theatre both as actress and stage manager myself, I was fascinated by these actors from another age, their lives and ambitions. I remained intrigued by them long after my degree had finished, and so it was inevitable that they would become part of a novel.

The most prolific of the letter writers was the actor called Henry Hartley, married to Jackman's daughter, Caroline, and as I read his letters, I grew particularly fond of Hartley and his wife. He was intelligent and witty, and did not suffer fools gladly. He certainly had ambitions to reach the London stage, and described his attempts to find a place, often expressing his frustration when his dreams were constantly dashed. Further reading (I am indebted here to the late Lou Warwick, who wrote several books on the Northamptonshire theatres) led me to learn more about Henry. He and Caroline did leave the company to run the Golden Lion Inn in Stratford-upon-Avon (now unrecognisable, and formed part of what is now Marks & Spencers, and the shop next to it on the right). He became a Town Councillor, and had shares in a small theatre on

Chapel Street.

The characters I have given Henry Hartley and Caroline are based entirely on his letters.

The London managers were all real managers, and the characters I have given them are based on the research I have carried out. I have, however, taken a few liberties with the historical facts by placing Isobel as an actress at the Theatre Royal, Drury Lane. At the time of the novel, Drury Lane was suffering from low audiences, and had bankrupted its managers several times. As I have stated in the novel, its manager at the time, Alfred Bunn, was striving to attract audiences by putting on big operas and spectacles. It was for a time the 'home of the opera', and it is unlikely that a dramatic actress like Isobel would have played there. However, with so little information to be found about actual productions during those years, I have used poetic licence to have Bunn putting on a mixture of opera and high drama, allowing Isobel herself to be the main attraction for a short time.

Charles Dickens was a great lover of the theatre, and a close friend of the actor, William Macready. It was therefore not too much a stretch of the imagination to have him befriend my fictional heroine! He also spent much time walking the streets of London at night, visiting its seediest and poorest neighbourhoods in order to get ideas for his characters.

BIBLIOGRAPHY

I have used many books and websites for my research, but I have listed below those books that I have found most useful in the writing of this novel:

Dickens by Peter Ackroyd (2002)
Drama That Smelled by Lou Warwick (1975)
The Night Has Been Unruly by J. C. Trewin (1957)
The Terrific Kemble by Eleanor Ransome (1978)
Theatre in the Victorian Age by Michael R. Booth (1991)
Theatre Royal, Drury Lane by W. J. Macqueen Pope (1945)
Theatre Un-Royal by Lou Warwick (1974)
Theatrical London by Richard Tames (2006)
Victorian Theatre by Russell Jackson (1989)
Women and Victorian Theatre by Kerry Powell (1997)

For more information about my work and other books, please go to:

http://www.rosamundebott.com

Lightning Source UK Ltd.
Milton Keynes UK
UKHW02f1844050618
323781UK00029B/438/P

9 781979 984850